# The Chaos Code

Justin Richards is the author of *The Death Collector*. He has written over twenty novels as well as non-fiction books. He has also written audio scripts, a television and stage play, edited anthologies of short stories, been a technical writer, and founded and edited a media journal.

He is best known for his series of children's books *The Invisible Detective*, and as Creative Director of the BBC's highly successful range of *Doctor Who* books.

Justin lives in Warwick with his wife and two children, and a lovely view of the castle.


Praise for *The Death Collector* by Justin Richards:

'This is a real page turner. The book starts with a dead man walking back into his kitchen and then dragging his terrified dog out for a walk! . . . Once you've finished it, you'll want to find another book just as exciting.' *CBBC Newsround*

'A very exciting novel, reminiscent in some ways of Philip Pullman's Victorian novels. Well-written and nicely paced, a real page-turner – and the ending is quite spectacular.' *Books for Keeps*

'This thoroughly absorbing page-turner is a terrific blend of horror and mystery with three teen protagonists. It is a quick read packed with twists, turns, and just enough gore to keep things interesting. A great choice for horror fans.' *School Library Journal*

'Like a steam-punk X-files . . . a fine work of speculative fiction. *The Death Collector* joins *Mortal Engines*, *Varjak Paw* and *Tithe* in the books that should make the jump into an adult market.' Ottakar's *Outland* magazine

'A brilliant, brilliant book full of twists and turns . . . A real great, fun read.' Amazon five-star customer review

# THE CHAOS CODE

## Justin Richards

**ff**

*faber and faber*

First published in 2007
by Faber and Faber Limited
3 Queen Square London WC1N 3AU

Typeset by Faber and Faber Limited
Printed in England by Mackays of Chatham plc,
Chatham, Kent

The right of Justin Richards to be identified as author
of this work has been asserted in accordance with Section 77
of the Copyright, Designs and Patents Act 1988

A CIP record for this book
is available from the British Library

ISBN 978–0–571–23394–6
ISBN 0–571–23394–5

2 4 6 8 10 9 7 5 3 1

*For my Father, who enjoyed treasure hunts
and all things historical*

1

As Matt watched the rain through the window, the rain watched him back.

He wasn't looking for a face, but it was there. If he had run his finger over the grimy window of the train, tracing the paths of the drips and rivulets and pausing where the water hung in bubbles, then he might have made out the rough features. Mouth, nose, eyes . . .

But he was more interested in watching the way that the tiny drops joined into streams that became unpredictable rivers that ran down the other side of the glass. The steady rhythm of the train had soothed Matt into a state somewhere between waking and sleeping. Just watching the rain.

By the time the train got to London he was fully awake. Matt was the first at the door, clutching a plastic bag with the packed lunch he hadn't eaten and the book he hadn't enjoyed, with his rucksack over one shoulder and his suitcase tilted back on its little wheels. A fifteen-year-old boy eager to get home from boarding school, dark hair in need of a wash, a cut and a brush. Coat grubby and creased where he'd been sitting on it.

As the train passed under a final bridge, Matt's reflection stared back at him, broken by the spattering rain. Then into the grey cloudy daylight again and the reflection was gone. The train shuddered to a halt, jolting Matt sideways. The doors slid open and he joined the stream of passengers hurrying to the exit barriers, tickets clutched, jostling and pushing.

Mum was waiting the other side of the barrier, checking her watch. 'Nine minutes late,' she announced. 'Not bad, I suppose. These days.' Then she smiled, as if suddenly remembering this was pleasure rather than business. She pulled an immaculate small white handkerchief from the pocket of her immaculate jacket, licked the corner of it and dabbed at Matt's face. 'Chocolate,' she accused as he brushed her hand away, embarrassed. 'And have you been using that spot cream I got for you?'

'Yes, Mum. I can't wait to get home,' Matt said.

'Thanks for meeting me.' Usually she was working and he got a taxi.

'Let's just grab a coffee while we're here, Matthew,' Mrs Stribling said.

From the fact she said it, and the way she called him 'Matthew', Matt knew he wasn't going home.

There was a Starbucks in the station, and Matt had orange juice. His mouth was dry after the long journey from his school in Havensham. He was quiet, sulking – he'd been looking forward to spending the holidays at Mum's flat in London. It didn't look like that was going to happen now, and he could guess what the alternative was. He wanted to tell her that it was knowing he'd come home for the summer that had made boarding school bearable.

Mum had a latte, and Matt thought she'd probably only got that because she thought it wouldn't be so hot and she could drink it quicker. Sure enough, as soon as they were seated: 'I have to go in thirteen minutes,' Mum told him.

That was typical of her. So precise. Matt liked to be precise too. He preferred his digital watch that told the exact right time to the second rather than one with a face and hands that you had to look at and work out where everything was to tell the time.

But Mum took it to extremes. Thirteen minutes – why not 'quarter of an hour', or 'soon'? She had to be so exact. Probably because of her job.

She used to work for a large computer company, but left when it was bought out by an even larger rival. Now she had her own company, though the only employee was herself. She did 'computer consultancy', which as far as Matt could tell meant she got other companies to pay her to do what she had always done. She was into network balancing, and requirements prioritization, and systems analysis. Matt didn't really understand the business terms or that side of it. But he had picked up enough about computers from spending time with Mum and messing about with the equipment she kept. Matt knew all about computers and how they worked.

That was one of the attractions of coming home. Mum's flat was full of computer hardware and the latest digital kit. Cameras and digital recorders and webcams and DVD-rippers and PCs and Macs and mainframes and even games machines.

'Why the rush?' he asked. 'Where are we going?' He stressed the 'we' to let her know he wasn't just accepting it.

Mum sighed and put down her coffee. There was

a faint pale line along her top lip from the milk, but Matt didn't tell her. She reached across the table to take his hand. He let her.

'I'm not going to Dad's,' he said.

She took her hand away. 'It won't be for long,' she promised.

'That's what you said at Christmas.'

'It wasn't for long then.'

'Two weeks. That's long enough. I'm staying with you.'

'You can't,' she said flatly. 'I'm sorry. I shan't be here. I've got a job.'

'I can look after myself during the day. I've done it before.'

'The job isn't in London, Matt. It's not even in this country. It's a marvellous opportunity and the money's good.'

'Great.' At least he was 'Matt' again. He tried to sound interested: 'So who's it for?'

'I . . . I can't tell you,' she said, looking round as if she expected someone she knew to be sitting nearby. 'Client confidentiality.' She turned back and laughed to show it was all so silly. 'I'm sorry but he – er, they – insist.'

'Mum – you're my mum. What if I need to talk to

you?'

'My mobile will work.' She frowned as she said it. 'At least, I think it will. Anyway, I know where you will be.'

'So do I,' Matt muttered. 'Either in the spare bedroom or up to my knees in mud. It's just awful, Mum. I mean, Dad's all right, when you can make him listen to anything you say. But at Christmas my bed was covered in books and papers, there was no food. I mean, at *Christmas*. The village shop was shut for a week and the freezer was full of ice samples from some Antarctic survey.'

Mum smiled. 'That sounds about right,' she admitted. She checked her watch. 'I do know what it's like to live with your father,' she said gently.

'Yeah,' Matt told her. 'And you gave up doing it.'

She ignored this. 'I've got you a ticket. You'll have to get a taxi from Branscombe, I'm afraid. But your father can pay for that.'

'Give me some money anyway,' Matt said. 'He won't have been to the bank.'

'He knows you're coming,' she said. But she sorted out a couple of notes from her purse anyway. More than enough.

Matt took the money and the ticket, realizing that

at some point he had just accepted that he was going. 'He doesn't know I'm coming,' he corrected her. 'You've told him I'm coming, that's different. He won't remember. He'll be planning some dig, or going through some ancient papers, or writing some lecture about pre-whatever pottery fragments found in an old cellar in Nottingham. Or something.'

Mum drained the last of her coffee and Matt realized he had hardly touched his juice. He made one last appeal: 'Can't I at least stay with you till you have to leave? Even if it's only a day, I can get some shopping done, go to the museums . . .'

'You hate museums,' she told him. 'And shops. Look, if I'm to make my flight I really need to leave now. And your train goes in seventeen minutes.'

'Can't you even stay and see me off?'

'I have to pack and then catch a plane.' She stood up, expecting him to do the same. Matt stood awkwardly in front of her, knowing what was coming next. Mum gave him a quick hug and pecked him on the cheek. 'You'll manage. You're a big boy now.'

He watched her hurry out of the station, checking her watch on the way. 'So treat me like one,' he said.

Struggling with his luggage, Matt went to look for a book in the newsagent's. But he could barely get along the aisle between the bookshelves, and people glared at him as if having a suitcase and bags in a railway station was completely thoughtless and unnecessary. One woman tutted audibly as she was forced to move slightly to let Matt past. So he made sure he drove the case over her foot.

'Oh, I'm sorry.' He smiled apologetically, hoping she realized he didn't mean it.

But when she mumbled, 'Yes, well, that's all right, young man,' Matt felt instantly bad about it and turned quickly away.

There was nothing really that he fancied reading. But he chose a book anyway – something about a kid who turned into a werewolf and fell in love with a werewolf girl. He paid for it out of the money Mum had given him. There was still more than enough for a taxi.

As it was, he dozed off almost as soon as the train pulled out of the station. He was jolted awake an hour later, surprised to see how far they had already got as the train pulled out of yet another tiny village station. Better not fall asleep again, he thought, or he'd miss his stop.

Another hour and the train finally drew into the little station at Branscombe Underhill. Sure enough, just as Matt had expected, there was no sign of Dad. It was an hour's brisk walk from here to the even smaller village where Dad lived. But with his luggage there was no way that Matt was going to attempt it, even though the rain had stopped.

In the waiting room there was a phone that connected directly to a local taxi firm. Matt knew from experience that he'd probably have to wait half an hour for them to bother to send a car.

'Oh, what bad timing,' a cheerful lady at the taxi company said when Matt told her where he was. 'Charlie's just left there.'

'Then tell him to turn round and come back,' Matt thought. 'Never mind,' he actually said. 'I guess I'll have to wait, then.'

'Be about ten minutes,' the lady told him.

Matt hung up the phone. 'No, it won't,' he said. And sure enough, it wasn't.

Half an hour later, the summer afternoon was clouding over into an autumnal twilight. The taxi driver insisted on talking non-stop about nothing in particular. Matt sat in the back and made the occasional half-hearted comment or reply. It seemed to suffice.

'Don't know why anyone wants to live out here,' the driver said as he turned into the narrow lane that was the only road through Woldham. 'Not even a pub.'

'There's a shop,' Matt said. But he had no real enthusiasm for defending the place. The driver was right – it was tiny, it was in the middle of nowhere, there wasn't a pub and the library came to call once a month in a van. If it remembered.

'So dark, too.' The driver wiped at his misty windscreen with the back of his hand.

'No street lights,' Matt pointed out.

'And the wind's kicking up something rotten.'

Matt wasn't sure you could really blame the village for that, but he said nothing.

'So where shall I drop you?' He made it sound as if right here would be best for him.

'Just up on the left, before the war memorial. There's a turning.'

The turning was into an even narrower lane that ran past just four houses. They were all the same, though built at slightly different angles. Modern, boxy and boring. Not the sort of house where Matt would ever have expected his dad to live. There were fields behind, leading down to a river. Maybe he'd chosen the place for the view rather than its character.

Matt paid the driver, and tipped him just enough to avoid being glared at. The driver didn't get out to open the boot, but pressed a button on the dashboard and let Matt unload his own luggage. You get what you pay for, Matt decided. He watched the headlights cutting through the gloomy evening as the taxi turned in the little close and then drove back down the lane. They were somehow too bright and clear and clean for the village. The whole place seemed happier once the taxi was gone and the gathering darkness began to close in once more.

The driver had been right, it was windy. Leaves were swirling like water going down a plughole. Skeletal trees dripped and swung. Clouds skidded across the darkening grey sky and somewhere an owl hooted forlornly. But there was a light on in the house, shining softly through and around the drawn curtains of a side window. Dad's study. Dad was working – probably hadn't noticed the time.

But at least he was here. Matt gathered up his

bags and, for the first time since he met Mum, he felt as if things were not so bad after all.

✝

The feeling did not last. He rang the bell and waited. And then he waited some more, before sighing heavily and putting down his suitcase. Dad was probably too engrossed in some old, dusty text to hear the bell. Fortunately, Matt had a key. Somewhere.

He fumbled in his pocket and finally managed to extricate his set of keys – school locker, suitcase, Mum's flat and Dad's house. It was difficult to see where the hole in the lock was, so Matt pushed the key at the rough area and moved it round, waiting for it to slide into the keyhole.

But instead the door moved. It wasn't locked. It wasn't even shut properly – the latch hadn't quite caught. The hall was in darkness. Matt pushed the door fully open and hefted his suitcase and rucksack inside.

'Dad – it's me!' he called.

No answer. He found the light switch and the hall was bathed in sudden white light. It was a mess. Muddy footprints criss-crossed the bare wooden floor. Unopened post lay beneath the letter box. What looked like a shroud was lying at the bottom of the stairs, and there was a pile of papers by the study door. It had toppled over, leaving pages scattered across the doorway.

Matt dragged his case into the living room and dumped it by the sofa. Not that you could see much of the sofa under the books and papers that were strewn across it.

'He's getting worse,' Matt muttered. 'Dad!' he shouted again. 'I'll put the kettle on. If I can find it.' Dad lived on coffee, and Matt held out little hope that he'd find Coke or lemonade in the fridge. There was a door from the living room through a tiny dining room to the kitchen. The dining table, and most of the chairs round it, were also piled with papers and journals. So, no surprise there.

The kitchen looked like the scene of a major disaster. Matt switched on the light to be greeted by the sight of dirty dishes and cooking utensils. Pots and pans were everywhere – even on the floor. There were dirty mugs on every available surface. Bits of broken plates lay scattered across the worktops and on the floor, and the fridge door was open. Matt didn't dare look inside, just pushed the door shut. The fridge was humming loudly in protest as it tried to keep cool.

'Keep cool,' Matt said out loud. 'What's happened here?' This was worse than usual – worse than it should be. Even without the broken plates, he was beginning to sense that something was wrong. 'Dad?' he called again, but he wasn't calling so loudly now – a plea rather than a shout for attention.

More anxious with every passing moment, Matt went back to the hall. He hesitated outside the study. Should he knock on the door? But what if there was a problem. What if Dad was ill, or . . . Or what? Only one way to find out.

He pushed open the door.

It was difficult to tell if the study was in more of a mess than usual. The light was on and the curtains over the side window were drawn. But the French windows behind Dad's desk were standing open. The wind was blowing papers off the desk and across the floor. The desk light was on, but angled upwards, towards the ceiling, where shadows danced and fought frantically.

The floor was a mess – as if someone had emptied the desk drawers and every filing cabinet across it. Books had been pulled from the shelves and lay bent and twisted. Matt looked round in open-mouthed amazement.

And a hand clamped over his open mouth, cutting off his cry of surprise. Rough, sharp, like sandpaper, he felt the palm of the hand biting into his face as he was dragged backwards. Someone had been standing behind the door, waiting for him. Matt struggled to break free, his only view of his attacker a huge shapeless shadow entwined with his own across the floor. But now the hand was over his nose as well – cutting off the air. He was gasping and wheezing, trying desperately to breathe.

The room turned and swam. Papers blew off the desk and spiralled down. The shadows darkened and the carpet seemed to be hurtling towards Matt's face.

Then everything was dark.

✠

The wind had dropped, though the French windows were still open. It was completely dark outside now. Matt's head was throbbing and he had to blink to get rid of the spots of light in front of his eyes.

He picked himself up from the floor and stumbled over to close the French windows. What had happened? It all seemed hazy now, like a bad dream. Matt leapt to his feet, turning quickly – suddenly afraid there was someone behind him, ready to attack again. But the room was empty. There was no one there. Had they gone? He walked quickly and cautiously to the windows and pulled them shut. Then he locked them. A burglary? But then where was Dad?

Maybe, Matt thought, Dad had gone to the station and missed him. Maybe he was there, waiting for Matt to arrive on the next train. Still wary and disorientated, he wandered back to the living room, his heart racing with every shadow he passed. He almost expected them to solidify and reach out at him with grey, shapeless hands. He took a deep breath and told himself not to be so stupid. Whoever had been there was gone now. Probably. The only sound was Matt's own anxious breathing.

Clearing a space on the sofa, Matt flopped down. He rubbed his eyes with the heels of his hands and began to feel a bit better. Someone had been here, he was sure of it. OK, the place was always a mess. But it seemed worse than ever – the stuff strewn across the study floor; the broken crockery in the kitchen. A rough hand across Matt's mouth . . . Looking up, he saw the telly and DVD player were still sitting in the corner of the room. In fact, there didn't seem to be anything missing – just untidy. So maybe not a burglary. But why break in and take nothing?

In the kitchen there was an old brown teapot on a shelf above the worktop. The spout was chipped on the side facing away, so you couldn't see. Inside, Dad kept spare cash – odd notes to pay the milkman and provide funds when he'd forgotten to go to the bank. If the teapot was empty . . .

Well, actually that wouldn't prove anything, Matt realized, as he went back to the kitchen. Except maybe Dad had not been to the bank for a while and the milk and papers needed paying for.

But the teapot was lying broken on the counter top. The spout had been knocked off and the handle was cracked. The lid was lying close by and several ten-pound notes were sticking out of the debris. So, not a robbery. Not for money, at any rate. Had he really been attacked – grabbed and thrown to the floor? Or had he fallen somehow? The more he thought about it now, the less certain he was of what he really remembered. It had all happened so quickly. Could he have fallen, or fainted? It had been a long day. Long, and stressful, and he was hot and bothered, and probably dehydrated, after the journey. But he had been so sure. He could almost feel the sandpaper texture of the rough hand on his face. He could remember the pressure, the blackness closing in, and he shuddered at the memory.

Matt got himself a drink of water, rinsing the mug well first. His hand was shaking, and the more he tried to control it, the more it shook. He had been putting it off, he realized, but he should really check the rest of the house. Maybe Dad was asleep in bed. Maybe he'd taken a sleeping pill or been up all the previous night working, or . . . Matt wanted to believe it, wanted to open the bedroom door and see his father staring blearily back at him and asking what time it was. What *day* it was, even. But he was terribly afraid that if he found Dad at all, it would be lying on the floor – attacked by the same person who had attacked Matt.

The house was empty. Every room was a mess, almost every floor covered with papers and books and journals. Even the bathroom. But there was no one – no Dad and no intruder. Matt was sure of that. He was alone in the house now.

Without really thinking about it, he went back to Dad's study. He rubbed at his face where it was sore – from the rough hand that had grabbed him? Or from where he had hit the floor?

He checked his watch and was astonished to see

that several hours had passed since he had arrived at the house. It must have been some bump on the head. He should check the answerphone, he decided. Look to see if there was a scrawled note by the phone, telling him Dad was out and not to worry and he'd be back soon. And if not . . . What? Should he call the police? It seemed sensible, except – what would they say? What would *he* say?

He mentally went through the conversation he might have. Was there any sign of a break-in? Well, no, not really. Had Matt's father ever just gone off before without leaving any message or any indication of where he might be? Actually yes, all the time. Did Matt see who attacked him? No. Was he sure he had actually been attacked. Any signs of the intruder? No, Matt thought. They'd say it was all in his imagination. He was sure it wasn't, but there was no way he could convince anyone else of that. No real evidence at all. Except . . .

There were *footprints*. Matt saw them as he turned to go. A trail of pale, sandy marks led past the desk to the French windows. He had not noticed them before. But then he had not been looking, and his vision had still been blurred and speckled from the blow. Curious, Matt followed them, opened the windows and stepped out on to the patio outside.

The moon had struggled through the clouds and, combined with the light from inside the study, Matt could see that the footprints continued across the paving slabs and to the lawn.

He stood at the edge of the patio, trying to make out if there were marks on the grass – indented foot marks, or more sand . . . Where had the sand come from? Where did it lead? He shuddered as he wondered why anyone would walk out across the back garden, where there were just fields and the river, rather than round to the front of the house and the lane. Unless it was Dad . . .

Matt stared into the night, out over the garden. For a moment, he thought he saw a dark shadowy figure standing at the fence, in front of the field. A cloud covered the moon for an instant and the wind picked up, whipping the trees into a frenzy of thrashing branches. Matt stepped back, out of the light, afraid he might be seen – that someone might be watching him.

When the moon returned, a moment later, the figure was gone. The sandy footprints had also disappeared, blown away by the breeze and scattered across the garden. Matt stepped back inside. He shivered, and not just from the cold of the night.

2

It was late and his head was throbbing again. There was no message on the phone or scribbled near it. Matt walked once more round the house.

Everywhere was a mess, but nothing seemed to be missing. Except his dad. He thought again about calling the police, but having to explain why he was alone in the house and then that he had no idea if there had even been a break-in still didn't really appeal. There was no sign of anyone forcing their way in. He couldn't be sure anyone would believe that the mess in the kitchen – and everywhere else – wasn't business as usual for Dad. And whether he convinced them there was something wrong or not, it would be hours before he would get to bed. Assuming they let him stay in the house alone. Would they put him in a hotel? Or a police cell?

Could they do that? He didn't want to find out.

So he rang Mum instead. The flat number connected at once to an answering machine that told him she was away and to try her mobile. Her mobile was switched off and offered to take a message. He hung up while he thought about what to tell her. But he really couldn't think of anything. Maybe she was on her plane. There was nothing she could do and no point in bothering her. She'd just tell him Dad had wandered off somewhere and would be back soon and not to worry.

The only room that seemed reasonably tidy was the spare room where Matt stayed when he was visiting. Even Dad's bedroom had several large chunks of stone piled up by the bed – they were carved, ornate, like bits from ancient columns or salvaged from an old cathedral. So, with some relief, he dragged his bags into the spare room and slumped on the bed.

Still feeling dazed and woozy, Matt got undressed. He climbed into bed with a mouth tasting of toothpaste and wearing his pyjamas. Just as he pulled the covers back up, he suddenly realized there was an easy way to tell if Dad was away or had disappeared – whatever that meant. He all but ran downstairs.

There was a door from the kitchen into the garage. It was locked, but the key was in the door. Matt opened the door and felt for the light. He breathed a sigh of relief as the fluorescent tube flickered to life. The garage was empty. Dad's car was gone.

Feeling much better, Matt went back inside. Dad had driven off somewhere – that was all there was to it. He'd forgotten that Matt was coming, or mistaken the date, or never got Mum's message. Everything was fine. A mess, but fine. Apart from the bump on the back of Matt's head, but he ignored that. The pain was almost gone now anyway, just a dull ache. He'd fallen. Got scared and fainted. Whatever.

Matt hesitated in the hallway, sure that something had changed – something was different from when he had arrived. His luggage was gone, but that wasn't it . . . The crumpled sheet in the corner, the pile of papers . . . Must be his imagination, he decided, as he went back upstairs.

Matt finished the book he'd bought for the train journey – annoyed to find it was the first in a trilogy and didn't really end. Then he slipped off to sleep, sure that by the time he woke in the morning Dad would be back and the events and worry of the evening would seem like a bad dream.

✛

The sound of whistling and the slam of a car door woke Matt. It was the early morning of another grey day. He recognized the whistling – it wasn't Dad. It was the postman.

The post.

That was what was different in the hall. There had been a pile of post under the letter box – he'd assumed that Dad simply hadn't bothered to pick it up. And then, when he checked the garage, the post was gone. He remembered the muddy footprints across the hall floor and the similar, sandy marks in the study. Had someone broken in just to steal the letters? What was the point of that?

He checked Dad's room – empty. He stumbled downstairs, almost tripping on one of the books at the side of the stairs. He kicked it away in annoyance and it tumbled down into the hall. A bunch of letters was appearing through the letter box and fell to the floor. The book skidded into them.

Matt ran to the door and yanked it open. The postman was already on his way to the next house. He'd left the van's engine running and it was puffing white exhaust into the morning as it stuttered and chugged.

'Hi there,' Matt shouted.

The postman turned. 'Morning. You staying again?'

'Just for a bit. You haven't seen my dad, have you?'

'Not for a day or two,' the postman admitted. 'Probably off on one of his expeditions.'

'Yeah, probably. Thanks.'

'Does he know you're here?' the postman wondered. 'Not on your own, are you?'

'He knows,' Matt said. 'And Mum's . . .' He shrugged, not wanting to lie.

The postman pushed a bundle of post through next door's letter box. 'You get your letter?' he asked Matt as he went back to the van.

'My letter?'

'The one at number three. Bit odd, that.'

Matt checked the latch wasn't down and hurried over to the postman, conscious that he was still in his pyjamas. 'Sorry, what do you mean? What letter?'

'Old Mrs Dorridge has it if you've not picked it up.' He pointed to the house opposite – number three. 'It was addressed to you but care of her. Came yesterday. I nearly stuck it in with your dad's post, but it said on the envelope "care of Mrs Dorridge at number three" and it was underlined. So I thought . . .' He shrugged. 'Well, I dunno. Not my business to think, is it? But that's where it is if you've not got it.' He climbed into the van and banged the door shut. 'Cheerio, then.' He waved out of the open window and the van pulled away.

There was no sign of life at number three and Matt didn't really know what the time was. He went back inside and got dressed. It was just before eight o'clock and Dad's car still wasn't in the garage. There were a few dry slices of bread on the side in the kitchen, so Matt made himself some toast. He put the telly on, but didn't really pay attention. He checked the letters that had come today – two were from charities that he guessed were after money, one was obviously a bill and the rest was junk mail of various kinds.

He'd decided to give it till nine o'clock. But by ten to nine Matt could wait no longer and hurried across to number three. He didn't really know Mrs Dorridge. She was old with a face so weathered and lined that it looked like the side of a cliff. Her eyes were pale and watery and she peered round the door at Matt suspiciously.

'Er, I think you have a letter for me,' he said.

There was a hint of a smile. 'Oh yes. Matthew, isn't it? I told the postman he'd made a mistake.' She disappeared back into the house, her frail voice barely reaching Matt as he waited outside. 'But he said no, look what it says. And I said, well, be that as it may . . .' She reappeared, pushing the letter at Matt. 'Very peculiar, I thought. I wonder who it's from.'

Matt took the letter, but Mrs Dorridge was reluctant to let it go until he answered. She raised her thin grey eyebrows, encouraging him to reply.

'I think perhaps they knew Dad might be away and wanted to make sure I got it,' he said. He managed to tug the letter free of the old lady's shaking fingers. 'I don't recognize the handwriting,' he lied.

In fact, he knew the handwriting only too well. He forced himself to get back into the house before he tore open the envelope. Despite the toast, he felt empty inside – like he'd not eaten for days. Inside the envelope was a single sheet of paper, and again he recognized the handwriting. It was his dad's. Why was Dad writing to him and sending the letter to Mrs Dorridge? Why not just leave him a note, or give him a call?

'Dear Matt,' the letter said. 'You might find this interesting. Before she married me, your mother would have been able to help you with it.'

He read it three times. Just two lines of hand-written text, followed by another line, printed in capitals. It started HTTP:// and Matt recognized at once what it was. Things were not getting any clearer, but for some reason Dad wanted him to look at a website.

☩

Dad had a laptop and Matt remembered seeing it on the desk in the study with papers blowing round it. Another thing that suggested Dad was expecting to come home soon – he wouldn't leave his laptop behind.

Typically, the laptop was half-buried, its silver-metal casing gleaming through the detritus – papers, an old book, a dark stone disc . . . Digging down to find Dad's desk was like the archaeology that Dad did, Matt thought. All sorts of junk needed shifting before you reached the important stuff. He swept the bits and pieces aside and opened the lap-top. While it was powering up, Matt tidied the papers that had not actually been blown off the desk into a pile and looked for somewhere to deposit the things off the laptop.

The stone disc, he found, wasn't stone at all. It was clay. A copy of some relic or other which Matt could feel squashing slightly in his grip as he picked it up. He had thought it was a plain circle, about ten centimetres in diameter. As it caught the light, though, he could see that there were markings on it.

The symbols looked a bit like Egyptian hieroglyphs – tiny pictures of a man's head in profile, a flower, a jug or vase. There were what might be tools of some sort, perhaps a shield, and more abstract shapes that were little more than lines and squiggles. One looked like the > maths sign, while another was a small triangle filled with dots. The symbols were arranged between thin lines spiralling inwards. On one side they covered the surface, while on the other the symbols framed the main picture in the middle of the disc.

The central picture was a strange, irregular shape – or rather two shapes, one about three times as big as the other. Matt turned the disc slowly as he looked at them, hoping to make out what they represented. But they were just shapes, he decided – like a child had drawn round something rather badly. Maybe it was a picture of something that had been broken apart in the middle?

The computer loaded the welcome screen and Matt put down the clay disc at the side of the desk and clicked on the little picture of an archaeologist's trowel that represented Dad's user ID. It prompted him for a password, but Matt knew what it was from when he'd borrowed the computer before to do his homework: parchment. Dad had talked about setting up Matt an ID of his own, but he hadn't done it yet.

While the computer loaded the desktop and connected to all the things it had to connect to, Matt picked up the book that had been lying with the disc across the laptop. It was called *Maps of the Ancient Sea Kings* and was written by someone called Charles Hapgood. Just the sort of book that Dad would be reading. Just the sort of book that Matt found really boring. He flicked through it – the dense-looking text, diagrams and old maps confirming his opinion.

As he did so, a sheet of paper fell out. Matt picked it up, feeling a bit guilty at having lost Dad's place in the book. It was a printout from a travel agent company, some sort of itinerary. He glanced at it, and saw that it must be a trip Dad was planning – flying to Copenhagen, then by train and boat to some-where called Valdeholm. Digging up boring bits of pottery, most likely.

Matt was about to push the paper back between the pages of the book when he saw that the other side had writing on it – notes scrawled by Dad, probably as he read through. They looked just about as boring as the book and itinerary did, but Matt skimmed through them as the computer continued the click and whirr and showed him its hourglass.

Piri Reis & Oronteus Finaeus cf. Mercator and Buache. Show America and Antarctica clearly
Ant. 'discovered' 1818 but mapped by Russians b4 – and Mercator = 1569!!
Buache (1737) shows Antarctica landmass pre-glaciation (as in 13,000 BC??) – seismic survey didn't confirm shape till 1958
M & B both based on older maps – from Alexandria (or Constantinople & taken by Venetians 1204?)
Conclusions – obv

'b4' was Dad's way of writing 'before' and 'obv' was his abbreviation for 'obvious', though Matt knew from experience that what was obvious to Dad wasn't always apparent to anyone else. He tucked the paper back into the book.

The top drawer of the desk seemed to be where Dad kept his pens and stationery – stapler, sticky tape, Post-it notes. Matt helped himself to a pen and found a blank piece of paper. Then, on an impulse, he stuffed the book of ancient maps and the clay disc into the drawer. Maybe Dad wanted them kept safe and together.

The web page that came up was blank apart from an entry field headed: 'Password'. Matt stared at it for a moment, then typed 'parchment'. But there was only room for eight letters, which appeared as blobs in the box. So he actually typed 'parchmen'. The screen changed – but only to display a single line of red text beneath the now empty entry field:

Password incorrect

Maybe he'd mistyped the address and gone to the wrong page. He checked it against Dad's letter, but found it was the correct website. So what was the password? It would be something Dad would expect him to guess. Matt had no idea what the secrecy was about, but obviously Dad wanted Matt to be the only one able to see whatever was on the page behind the password screen. Otherwise he'd have simply written whatever message he wanted to get to Matt in the letter. He'd need to work out the password to find out why Dad was being so cautious. Or maybe it was a game – Dad had arranged treasure hunts with cryptic clues when Matt was younger. But he was too old for that now, surely.

But someone had taken the letters, Matt realised. He sat rigid, staring at the screen as he thought about that. Had Dad sent this letter to Mrs Dorridge because he *knew* that his mail was going to be stolen? Was it Matt's letter that the intruder had been looking for? Matt's mouth was dry, and swallowing did no good.

He picked up the letter and read it again. Maybe there was a clue to the password in there, but it didn't seem to be any use. Or was it? That last sentence had seemed weird to Matt when he first read it, but now he wondered if it was the clue he needed: *Before she married me, your mother would have been able to help you with it.*

Well, he needed help. But why Mum? She was certainly good with computers. She'd been working for the company that serviced the university computers when she met Dad. He was head of the Archaeology Department, and had told Matt that he'd found her in his office one day under the table.

'She was connecting up the new computer systems,' Matt remembered Dad saying. 'I wouldn't let her out from under my desk until she agreed to go for a drink with me.'

Matt had laughed, but Mum didn't. 'Your father was younger then,' she said. 'We both were.' And that seemed to close the topic.

Which didn't really help. There were no cables to connect. Matt got down and looked under the desk. There was nothing hidden so far as he could see – no envelope with secret codes taped to the bottom of any of the drawers. But there was a metal plate with a manufacturer's name stamped on it: Timberly. He counted the letters – eight.

He bumped his head in his haste to get out from under the desk, catching the bruise he'd got the previous night. He scarcely noticed as he typed in the name.

But it wasn't right. He got the same error message and almost thumped the screen in frustration. Why wasn't it 'Timberly'? It made sense. It fitted the clue. But was it the only answer that fitted the clue?

And then he got it. Really got it, he was sure – even more sure this time. Mum's name. Before she was married and became Sarah Stribling she'd been Sarah Milligan. He typed 'milligan'. It didn't work. He stared at the red error message. The error had to be wrong, he thought, smiling despite himself at the notion of an error being itself a mistake.

A mistake. That might just be it. He typed 'Milligan' again, but this time with a capital 'M'. There was an agonizingly long moment when nothing happened. Progress blobs crawled along the bottom of the web browser as it contacted the server computer, wherever that was. Then the screen changed.

It showed a plain window of text – black on white. A letter, addressed to Matt.

'Yes!' he said out loud, his hands bunched into triumphant fists.

Dear Matt
Sorry about the cloak and dagger stuff, but you can't be too careful these days! Actually I thought you'd enjoy the challenge and I'm glad, though not at all surprised, to see that you're up to it. Well done.

I'm sorry I'm not at home now. Your mother

did warn me you were coming, but I've had to go away. It was sudden, though not unexpected. I really don't know when I'll be back, and so I thought I'd better give you some clue what to do and where to go while I'm away. Like learning Latin, it could be quite an adVenture. And you might need some help with it. Remember those games we used to play when you were younger? Notes and cryptic clues? Let's Find Treasure, I used to say, and you were always so good at it. But maybe you're too old for that now. I'm sure you'll think of something to do.

Great, capital, so the real question is where you can *go*. Obviously you're welcome to squat at The Old house for As long as you like. Unless maybe you think you should find a school friend like Ned or Tim or someone to Join for the Annual holidays. No more Encouragement needed.

I'll be in contact just as soon as I can, but don't worry if you don't hear from me. (Too many negatives in that last sentence, I fear!)

Remember – LFT (doesn't work on the computer, sorry!)

Love

Dad

Matt read it through several times. He couldn't believe it was as innocuous and unassuming as it seemed. Why go to all the trouble – the 'cloak and dagger stuff', as Dad described it – just to say he was away for a few days and Matt would have to look after himself. No, Matt decided, there had to be more to it than that.

He read the letter again, thinking carefully about every word and phrase. First of all, he was sure it *was* from Dad. The mention of 'Let's Find Treasure' brought back more memories of the treasure hunts Dad had set up when Matt was about eight years old. Dad used to plant clues for him round the house and garden – simple coded messages, like lists of numbers where 1 represented 'A' and 2 stood for 'B' and so on through the alphabet. Then Dad would pretend it was a mystery to him as well and help Matt work them out . . . All the messages were marked with a symbol – like a capital letter E with an extra line across the top. It was, Dad helped Matt work out, an amalgam of the letters L F and T all drawn over the top of each other. They decided between them it must stand for 'Let's Find Treasure'. And like Dad said at the end of the letter, the symbol wouldn't work on the screen – you'd need to create a graphic for it, and Dad probably wasn't up to that.

All of which meant, surely, that the text on the screen was itself a clue. There was a message hidden in it. Maybe several messages. 'You might need some help with it' told Matt he needed help from someone else. He wasn't sure about the mention of Latin. He learned Latin at school, though he wasn't any good at it. Dad had insisted he do the option and of course Dad knew Latin as well as the ancient Romans did. But he wouldn't expect Matt to decipher a clue in Latin, would he?

So, what else? What else in the message on the screen was odd or strange, pointing to a hidden meaning? Matt's attention focused on the mention of his friends Ned and Tim. He didn't know anyone called Ned, and he didn't know a Tim that he'd call a friend. Dad knew some of Matt's friends – he'd met Nick Blows several times, and Alex Moon had been to stay . . . So why make up names? Ned was an anagram of 'end', was that important? What about Tim though – short for 'time' perhaps?

He started again from the beginning. And stopped when he got to: 'Great, capital'. That didn't seem to fit. Neither was the sort of word Dad would use. 'Great' – well, maybe. 'Capital' – certainly not. And why was 'go' in italics?

Actually, now he read it again, that whole paragraph was rather odd. Why was Dad calling it 'The Old house'? Why not capitalize 'house' if he was using capitals on 'The' and 'Old'? And then he got it.

Of course, that was why Ned and Tim were there – Dad needed two names that Matt would realize were made up, were there for some specific reason. And they had to be names that started with N and T. Capital – capital letters. And 'go' was italicized because the first two capitals in that paragraph were G and O from 'Great' and 'Obviously'. Spelling 'GO'.

He grabbed the biro he'd found in the desk drawer and the nearest piece of paper to write down the capitals from the whole message. The biro scratched 'D' but no ink came out. So he stuck it back in the drawer and took out a pencil – broken.

Third time lucky and the gel pen he tried worked. It was green, but that didn't matter. Matt traced his finger along the lines on the screen and copied down the capital letters:

DMSAᴉᴉWᴉᴉYᴉ

He stopped – it was just gibberish. Matt stared at the message on the screen. Perhaps the italicized 'go' was where he should start. Perhaps he just needed the capital letters from that paragraph. He tried again – and almost at once could see that he was right.

GO TO AUNT JANE

Matt stared at what he'd written. Well, he thought, that's clear enough. He read back through the last few lines on the screen in case there was more.

I I T I

Didn't look like it. More gibberish. But the comment about 'Too many negatives' made sense now. Take out a negative from the sentence and what Dad was telling him was: '*Do* worry if you don't hear from me.'

'Thanks,' Matt said out loud. 'Like I couldn't have guessed that by now.' He was feeling queasy as he wondered what had happened to Dad. This was more than a game – what had happened that made Dad feel he had to send Matt a coded message?

He printed out a copy of the web page, folded it up and put it in his pocket. Then he shut down the computer and went up to his room. He hadn't bothered to unpack yet, which was a good thing, because it looked like he was off again.

Taking the money from the broken teapot in the kitchen to pay for a taxi, Matt then went to the phone. There was an address book beside it, and Matt found the number of a local taxi company and called for a lift to the station. He knew there were trains to Cheltenham every half-hour. Then he hunted through for Aunt Jane's number. She was Dad's older sister, so he looked under S – Jane Stribling wasn't listed. Matt sighed. What if Dad knew the number off by heart and hadn't bothered to write it down? He tried in the J section – and the first entry was 'Jane'.

He lifted the handset again and was about to dial. 'You can't be too careful', Dad's letter had said. He tapped the handset against his chin as he thought about that, the dial tone buzzing. Was the house being watched? The phones tapped? He remembered the figure he thought he had seen across the fields the night before. And he put down the phone. He scribbled Aunt Jane's number on the back of the printout of Dad's letter, and let himself out of the house.

✛

Miss Dorridge was wary, but finally allowed Matt to borrow her phone for a quick call. He managed to catch Aunt Jane just as she was leaving for work. She still lived in the same village where she and Matt's dad had grown up.

'Nothing about your father surprises me,' she said in response to Matt's hurried explanations. 'Hasn't done for years. It's just typical he's run off on some archaeological beanfeast and left you all on your own. Of course you must come to stay with me here. I've plenty of room and I'll be glad of the company, though you'll have to fend for yourself during the day, or you can help out on the estate. I'm sure Mr Venture won't mind.'

He'd not been to Aunt Jane's for years. Usually she came to visit Dad. Matt could remember her little cottage, on the edge of a wooded area just off the main drive that led through the estate to the enormous manor house where Aunt Jane worked. Matt wasn't really sure what she did – she was some sort of personal assistant to a reclusive multi-millionaire. Or something.

'I'll call you when I get to Cheltenham station. I've got a taxi coming.'

She laughed at that, sounding suddenly much younger. 'If you're getting a taxi as far as Branscombe station, you might as well come all the way here. It'll take you for ever otherwise, because you need to change at Gloucester. Don't worry, I'll pay.'

'Thanks,' Matt said. He was aware of Miss Dorridge watching him carefully from her living-room door and hurriedly said goodbye.

'I hope you get your phone fixed soon,' Miss Dorridge said sternly as she saw him out.

'I hope so too. Thanks ever so much.'

'Works all right to call taxis then,' she observed through narrowed eyes.

'Er, yeah,' Matt admitted. 'It's a bit weird. Intermittent fault, they said.'

The old lady nodded, evidently far from con-vinced.

✝

The trees in the fields were hardly moving, but the wind had whipped the leaves in the close into a whirlwind. Matt sat on his suitcase outside Dad's house waiting for the taxi. He watched the shapes the leaves made as they whirled and spun around him. It was odd the way the wind seemed to be trapped within this area. He hadn't noticed it before. It made him uneasy, and he had the strange feeling he was being watched. Had someone been watching the house – been in the house last night? Had they attacked him? Were they still watching? Would they come back? Matt's stomach felt empty and he shivered despite the morning sunlight.

He didn't have to wait long for the taxi – and was both relieved and irritated to see that it was the same driver as the previous evening.

This time the man did help Matt with his luggage. 'You off again?' he said. 'Don't blame you. Couldn't stick it here myself. Back to the station, then?'

'No,' Matt told him as he got in the back of the big car. 'I decided there's no point bothering with the train. You might as well take me the whole way, if that's OK.'

The taxi man reversed the car on to the driveway and turned round. 'So, where to?'

Matt told him, and the driver nodded. 'Take about an hour. That OK?'

He really meant, could Matt afford it? 'That's fine,' Matt assured him. 'My aunt's expecting me. She'll pay when we get there.'

The driver glanced round, grinning. 'No problem, then. Quite an adventure, eh?'

The man spoke most of the way, but Matt hardly listened. There was something niggling at the back of his mind. Something the taxi driver had said or done. It echoed something Aunt Jane had said on the phone that had made him think again of Dad's message. Matt took the printed copy from his pocket and read it through once more. He couldn't read much in cars or he'd feel sick, so he skimmed through quickly, then looked out of the window while he tried to work out what had bothered him.

He replayed Aunt Jane's words in his head, trying to remember what she'd said which had made an impact. A word or phrase, no more. He'd half made a connection, just for a second. Then it was gone. It was when she'd been saying he could help out on the estate . . . He glanced at the printed page again, and suddenly it seemed obvious.

There at the end of a sentence – a word broken across two lines and hyphenated. On the screen, it had seemed quite normal, but on the printout, with different margins, it seemed as if the word had been deliberately split:

> I'm sorry I'm not at home now. Your mother did warn me you were coming, but I've had to go away. It was sudden, though not unexpected. I really don't know when I'll be back, and so I thought I'd better give you some clue what to do and where to go while I'm away. Like learning Latin, it could be quite an ad-
>
> Venture. And you might need some help with it.

The bigger space before the next line and the capital letter at the start clinched it for Matt. Venture – that was the name of the man that Aunt Jane worked for. Julius Venture – he remembered Aunt Jane and Dad talking about him. And as for learning Latin, Matt knew enough to understand that 'ad' was Latin for 'to'. So, in Latin, 'adventure' – or rather 'ad Venture' – meant to go to Venture.

Was Dad telling him again that he should go to Aunt Jane's, he wondered? Or was there more to it than that? Was it really the reclusive Julius Venture that Dad was sending him to for help? And what sort of help did he need? Matt watched the countryside going past outside without really seeing it. He was pleased with himself for having worked out Dad's clues. But at the same time, he was anxious and worried – wondering what had happened to Dad, and what he could do about it . . .

✝

As the car sped along the narrow Cotswold lanes, a flurry of leaves and a spattering of rain followed it on its way.

3

The taxi driver was impressed by the wide gateway into the estate. Huge wrought-iron gates swung silently open as the car approached, and closed just as silently behind it.

'Quite a place,' the driver said as they caught sight of the manor house through the trees. It was an imposing seventeenth-century mansion built of Cotswold stone.

'Yes,' Matt agreed. 'But that's not where we're going.'

The driver was less impressed with Aunt Jane's cottage as they drew up outside. 'Oh,' he said. 'How quaint.'

The cottage had been built at the same time as the main house, providing accommodation for the gardener or groundsman, Matt assumed. It was like the manor house in miniature – same grey stone, same style of windows and door, same slate tiles on the roof. It had its own little forecourt, paved with irregular slabs of stone, just off the driveway. Nestling as it did in the shadow of a small wooded area of the grounds, it looked like the setting for a fairy tale. A rather bleak fairy tale, though, Matt decided – dull and grey and square and shadowy.

He stood with his luggage on the forecourt as Aunt Jane emerged and hurried to pay the taxi driver.

'Oh, let me give you a hand with that,' she said, taking his suitcase from him. But she didn't take it inside; instead she set it down again, took a step back and inspected Matt.

'You are *so* like your father,' she said. 'Goodness, how you've grown. It's been too long since I last saw you. How old are you now?' She shook her head. 'No, don't tell me. I don't think I want to know.'

She was much as Matt remembered her, thin and willowy and serious. Only she seemed smaller. Which made Matt realize how long it must have been since he last saw her, and how much he must have grown. He'd changed far more than she had. She was noticeably older – older than Matt's mum, he knew. Her shoulder-length hair was streaked with grey where it had been uniformly dark brown, and her face was beginning to gain a texture like the stone of her house.

Matt smiled. 'I'm fifteen. You sent me a card, remember?'

'Oh, that just happens automatically. If your birthday is in my diary, you get a card. I don't keep count. Come on inside. I won't ask how your father is,' she said as she led the way, carrying his case, 'because I'm sure you won't know. But how's your mother?'

Matt almost said she'd run off too – both his parents had upped and left. If that was really what Dad had done. He tried to tell Aunt Jane he was worried, but her expression told him she was not at all concerned about her brother. He wondered about mentioning the intruder, the missing letters, Dad's weird website message. But now he was here and safe, Matt decided to wait until he had his own thoughts in order and Aunt Jane was more responsive.

Still muttering about her brother's selfish absent-mindedness, Aunt Jane showed Matt to the spare room. It was tiny and square, with bare stone walls and a small window that faced the main house. He could just see it through the trees, the morning sunlight reflecting off the windows. The only furniture was the bed and a small chest of drawers beside it. There was a lamp on the top of the chest.

'I hope it will do,' Aunt Jane said. 'Julius – Mr Venture – said that you can stay up at the manor house if you want. There's plenty of room there, of course. But I thought this was more cosy and I'd rather you were with me. If that's all right?'

Matt nodded. 'I'll be fine. Thanks.'

'Of course, you're welcome to use Mr Venture's library and do your homework or whatever you have to do up there. I'll show you round this afternoon if I have time. I'm sorry I'm going to be rather busy, but of course I didn't know you were coming until . . .'

'That's OK,' Matt assured her. 'I'll be all right. It's lovely here. And thank you for letting me stay.'

'Oh, my pleasure. Now, you must be hungry – I know it's early for lunch, but I also know what growing boys are like with food.' She led the way back down the narrow staircase and into the kitchen – which seemed to be the biggest room in the house. 'I need to organize lunch up at the manor, and I have a lot to do this afternoon. So I'll get you a sandwich or something and then leave you to unpack and explore. Help yourself to anything you need. My home is your home.' She smiled, and it made Matt feel welcome and wanted, and it made Aunt Jane look suddenly younger.

'So what do you do, Aunt Jane? For Mr Venture? And who is he anyway?' Matt asked between bites of his ham sandwich. Aunt Jane had given him a bowl of salad too – lettuce and slices of cucumber and small tomatoes. He left that.

'I suppose I'm a sort of estate manager and personal assistant,' she told him. 'Mr Venture is a businessman and an academic. He'll be off to meetings and visiting archives at a moment's notice. He leaves it to me to keep the day-to-day things going while he's away and to organize his time and run the place when he's actually here.'

'So, he's a bit like Dad?' Matt said. 'Researching and stuff.'

'A bit.' She busied herself at the sink. 'Their interests stem from rather different sources, but I suppose so.'

'And you and Dad grew up here. In the village, I mean?'

'Yes. The village is further down the road, on the west side of the estate, so I don't imagine you drove through it. The church is actually on estate land, though.' She turned back to face him. 'So many questions.' The light was behind her, so she was just a dark silhouette, but Matt thought she sounded sad and he wondered why.

'Why did you stay?' he asked.

'Here? In the village?'

He nodded. 'Dad left, but you stayed.'

'I had to look after our mother. Your father got interested in archaeology and was off studying. Then he got the job at the university, met your mother . . . I just never felt the need to move on, I suppose. Everything I wanted was here.' She sat down at the table beside him. 'Still is.'

'So you're happy here?'

She smiled thinly. 'Oh yes. Not a lot to do for young people like you. Your father and I used to play in the woods behind this cottage. We had the run of the estate, made friends . . . They were good times,' she said quietly. 'But things move on, change, come to an end. It's different now, and yet it's the same. Perhaps the world has moved on and I haven't really accepted the change. But I keep busy and I enjoy my work, and Julius is . . .' She shrugged. 'Well, he's Julius.'

'He's a good man to work for?'

She stood up, the chair scraping back across the stone floor. 'The best. I couldn't work for anyone else, not now.' She laughed, but Matt got the impression it was for his benefit. 'Must be getting set in my ways in my old age.'

'You're not old,' Matt told her. 'Well, not really.'

'No,' she replied. 'No, I'm not. But we're none of us as young as we were, are we?'

✝

It was a clear, crisp day – cold, despite being July – and Matt's misty breath hung for a moment in the air. Aunt Jane had shown him a map of the estate and he set off through the woods towards the village. Before long, he saw the shape of the church tower through the trees and he headed towards that.

The church looked older than the manor house. The graveyard surrounding it was well kept, the grass cut and the borders edged. Matt wondered if the church people maintained it, or whether it was something else that Aunt Jane was responsible for. He walked all round the church, then he stood at the main gate, looking out into the village. The church, despite being on the edge of the community, seemed to be a focal point. Next to it was a village green, with houses round the edge. Beyond that he could see the main road and a modern housing development stretching further into the distance.

Dad and Aunt Jane must have lived on or near the green, he guessed, for them to play in the grounds of the manor house. Probably the village was tiny then – maybe no bigger than where Dad lived now. It seemed strange that his father had swapped one tiny village for a different one. Did he resent the new developments here? Had he decided he needed to get away? Or was it just the luck of things – his academic work, marrying Mum and then getting divorced? Was it a deliberate decision or just how things had worked out?

Thoughts of his father were making Matt sullen and anxious again. Where was Dad? Had he sent Matt to Aunt Jane just so he was with an adult, or was he actually supposed to be doing something to help? Did Dad *need* help – after all, he'd managed to send Matt the letter and the message. What, if anything, should he tell Aunt Jane of his worries? She seemed to think Dad had just wandered off, absent-minded, the way he did. Letting her continue to think that helped Matt to convince himself it might even be true.

Rather than explore the village, Matt decided to return to the cottage. Perhaps Aunt Jane would be back and he could talk to her, share his worries. There was a hint of rain in the air and the breeze was getting up. He watched the leaves spiralling round the gravestones, whipped up and spun round in patterns. Matt retraced his path through the churchyard and out of the gate that led back into the Venture estate. There were the remains of a path outside the gate, winding up past the woodland and round to the manor house. It was overgrown and all but reclaimed by the grass, but the line of it was just about visible. Matt followed the path round.

After a few minutes, the rain started and he decided he'd rather be in the shelter of the trees. So he left the narrow path and set off back through the woods. He wasn't sure he was aiming for the cottage, but he knew if he kept going in a straight line he'd eventually reach the main driveway. Then he could follow that back down to Aunt Jane's.

It was eerie in the woods. The wind sounded like someone moaning or crying. Leaves drifted and curled and branches dipped and swayed. The sky had clouded over and was a uniform grey, so it was like twilight among the trees. Rain was blowing in his face now. It was a fine rain that was almost a mist, as if he was walking through his own breath. He blinked and peered into the gloom ahead.

There was a clearing, an open area near the edge of the wood. You could stand here, Matt realized, hidden in the trees but with a good view across the driveway and the lawns up to the manor house. It was obviously a deliberate feature, as there was a large stone bench positioned to give the best view. It was old, cracked and weathered, with moss growing over the stone supports. The bench was curved gently, so sitting on it must be like being in the front row of an amphitheatre, watching over the estate as if it was a play being acted out in front of you. The best place to sit would be in the middle of the bench.

Exactly where the girl was sitting.

She was so still that Matt didn't see her at first. And when he did he wondered if she was a statue. But while everything round her was dull grey and brown, she was wearing a bright red coat. Her long black hair was glistening with the moisture of the fine rain. When she turned to look at Matt, he saw that her eyes were a startling, unexpected blue.

'You must be Matt,' she said. 'Jane said you were coming. Why don't you join me?'

She talked like a grown-up, but she didn't look any older than Matt. 'Nice to be famous,' he said, sitting down further along the bench. It was cold and damp and clammy through his trousers.

'Jane asked father for a couple of hours off to meet you. I overheard.'

'Father?'

She had a strange half-smile. In anyone else, Matt might have found it mocking, but somehow he got the impression it was just how she was – amused and yet cynical; optimistic but not naïve.

'Jane works for my father.'

'Julius Venture. I didn't know he had a family.'

'Just me.' She tilted her head to one side as if appraising him, then held out her hand.

It was a strange gesture, not quite the offer of a handshake and more as if she expected him to kiss the back of her hand like in olden times. But Matt took her hand and made an effort at shaking it. She held his hand tight.

'You're cold,' she said.

He tugged his hand free, unsettled. 'I didn't catch your name.'

'I didn't tell you my name.'

Matt waited, but she didn't add anything, so he said slightly nervously, 'So, will you? Tell me your name, I mean?'

She was still half-smiling and her blue eyes seemed to deepen with amusement. 'Robin,' she said. 'Robin Venture. It's a pleasure to meet you, Matt Stribling.'

'Thanks.' Now they'd introduced themselves he felt even more awkward. But Robin did not seem the least bit unsettled. Well, Matt thought, she lives here. I'm just a visitor. A joke, probably.

'I'm sorry,' Robin said. 'I'm not laughing at you, you know.'

'I didn't think you were,' he said quickly.

She turned back to the view. 'Yes, you did. You still do. And I'm not, I promise.'

'All right.'

'It's nice to have some company. Someone young about the place.' She turned back to face him. 'How old are you anyway? Sixteen?'

'Fifteen,' he said automatically. 'Not that –'

'Not that it's any of my business. I know. Just curious, that's all.'

'So, how old are you? Fifteen?'

She laughed. It was a musical, light sound in the gloom of the wood. Her hair glistened as she threw her head back. 'Ladies don't tell their age,' she said. 'But you're welcome to guess.'

He said nothing for a while. Then he admitted, 'I am cold, actually.'

'It's a cold day,' she pointed out.

'It's the wind, I think. It sort of cuts through you, doesn't it? Especially the ears. And it's weird.'

'Weird? What is?'

'The wind.'

She was frowning now, forehead creased and eyes flint-hard. 'What do you mean?' she asked, sounding surprisingly stern.

'Nothing. Just the way it blows the leaves round and everything. Like little pockets of air, mini-cyclones. I noticed it in the churchyard. It was the same back at Dad's – before I came here.'

She watched him intently for a long time, saying nothing. Then she stood up abruptly. 'It's time I went. I'm late for luncheon.'

'Luncheon?' The archaic word amused him.

'Lunch,' she corrected herself. The half-smile was back. 'We're a bit old-fashioned here, I'm afraid.

Jane will tell you. Here she comes.'

As soon as the girl said her name, Aunt Jane appeared at the edge of the wood. Matt had not seen her coming down the drive, but he supposed that Robin must have a better view from where she was standing in front of the bench.

The girl turned to meet Aunt Jane as Matt stood up and pulled at his damp trousers to separate them from his skin.

'Hello, Jane. Is it lunch time?'

'Yes,' Jane said levelly. 'I see you two have met.'

'We were just chatting,' Matt said cautiously. Aunt Jane's tone made him feel that he'd done something wrong.

'Matt's a nice boy,' Robin said. 'Arnold must be so proud of him.'

'I'm sure he is, Robin,' Aunt Jane said.

It took Matt a moment to realize that by Arnold she meant his dad. 'Do you call everyone by their first name?' he asked.

'Just my friends,' Robin replied. 'Matt.' Her mouth quivered as if she was about to burst into laughter again. But she nodded, and waved, and started through the trees towards the driveway. 'I'll see you later,' she called as she went, without looking back.

'What a strange girl,' Matt said to Aunt Jane when Robin was out of earshot.

'Yes,' Jane replied.

'Still, she seems nice enough.'

Aunt Jane looked at him sadly. 'Oh, Matt,' she said quietly, and sighed.

'What?'

'Nothing. Just . . . It's just that I'd rather you didn't spend too much time with Robin.'

She avoided his eyes as she said it. Matt almost laughed, it seemed so out of character for her to be warning him off like this. 'Afraid if I hang around with Robin then people will call me Batman?' he joked.

Aunt Jane forced a laugh. 'It's for your own good,' she said. 'How many times have you heard that? And yes, Robin's a lovely girl. But trust me, she'll bring you nothing but trouble.'

Without further explanation, she turned and walked back to the driveway, leaving Matt standing in the damp woods with the breeze tugging at his coat.

4

Matt spent some time looking round the little cottage. Aunt Jane had given him a quick guided tour and there was not much more to discover. He had hoped to find a computer. No chance Aunt Jane would have any decent games for it, but a broadband internet connection seemed a good bet. He could check his email and surf the web.

But he was out of luck. Aunt Jane had a small study in what was supposed to be the third bedroom. It was tiny, with barely room for the desk and a chair. From the cables and wires, Matt guessed Aunt Jane had a laptop, and she'd taken it with her up to the manor house. Which made sense – she was working, after all.

It left Matt with little to do. He'd finished the book he'd bought for the train journey, so he inspected

Aunt Jane's shelves for something to read. Agatha Christie seemed the least worst choice. He wasn't desperately interested in the other titles – books on gardening, accounting, how to manage your personal space, a few 'ancient mysteries' books that purported to reveal the secret of the pyramids or the truth of a lost ancient civilization. And a lot of romantic historical novels with painted covers showing women in big dresses swooning in the arms of men in tight suits.

The television did at least get satellite and Matt flicked lazily through the channels. He watched a Bugs Bunny cartoon, but after that was some rubbish series about insects with big eyes who flew round saving the world from improbable menaces. So he turned it off again.

He looked along the shelves once more, in case he'd missed something interesting. But he hadn't. It didn't seem likely the village would run to a bookshop or a library, and anyway it was raining more heavily now. Then he remembered that Aunt Jane had mentioned Julius Venture had a library he could use for homework. It wasn't likely to be the sort of library Matt was interested in, but he might at least have a computer Matt could use. And maybe Robin had some decent books.

Matt thought again about the way Aunt Jane had been with Robin. Polite, but a bit distant – not like her at all. And then her words to Matt: 'She'll bring you nothing but trouble.' Well, he thought, maybe she'll bring me something to read or a DVD first. She was a bit weird, but at least she was his age.

☩

The main door was set within a stone porch jutting out from the middle of the house. Matt welcomed the fact that it sheltered him from the rain. There was an old-fashioned bell-pull – a metal rod down the wall with a handle at the end. But before he could try it, the heavy, dark wooden door swung open.

'I saw you coming up the drive,' Aunt Jane said. 'Come on in. I'm sorry, you must be bored silly.'

'Well, a bit,' Matt admitted.

The door opened into a large hallway. In fact it was more like a big room. A wide staircase swept up from the back of the hall, with doors either side of it leading deeper into the house. There were other doors at intervals round the hall. Between two of the doors stood a suit of armour. Further along was a low table with a modern cordless telephone on it. It looked out of place among the oak panelling and the dark oil paintings hanging on the walls.

'So when do I get to meet Mr Venture?' Matt asked. He'd almost referred to him as 'Robin's dad' but didn't think Aunt Jane would be impressed by that.

'Soon,' she promised. 'He's a busy man, but I'm sure he'll want to meet you too.'

'Great,' Matt said. Maybe when he met Julius Venture, he'd have some idea why Dad thought he could help – if that was what Dad had really meant.

'I'm rather busy this afternoon,' Aunt Jane told him. 'But I'm sure Julius won't mind if you look round. There's lots to see. He has quite a collection.'

'A collection of what?' Matt wondered.

Aunt Jane shrugged as if the answer was obvious. 'Everything.'

'I was hoping to look in the library,' Matt told her. 'Or maybe use a computer.'

'There are computers in the library.' She smiled. 'It isn't all stuffy and old-fashioned like this.' She tapped the suit of armour as she led him past the staircase and to one of the doors. It was standing open, revealing a panelled corridor beyond.

'Down here?'

'The library is at the end of the corridor. You

won't miss it. I have an office on the first floor. Up the stairs, turn right and it's the second door on the left.'

'And you're busy.'

'Very.'

'I'll be fine,' he assured her. 'Down here?'

She nodded, still smiling. Maybe she was anticipating his reaction to the library when he finally got there. Or maybe she was making up for being so short with him earlier.

'Is Robin around?' Matt asked, as much to see her reaction as anything.

Aunt Jane's smile flickered, but she kept it pretty much in place. 'I think Robin's busy,' she said. Then more quietly: 'I meant what I told you. But I know you won't listen. Boys your age never do, do they?' She sighed. 'Anyway, I shouldn't interfere, I know. Oh, and the password for the computer is secret.'

He was puzzled. 'Passwords usually are.'

She smiled – properly this time. 'You'll work it out, if I know you. Your mother always said you'd follow in her footsteps not your father's. Goodness me, I hope she's right.'

There were little spotlights set into the ornate plaster ceiling of the corridor – another strange juxtaposition of the new and the old. And there were doors set into the panelled walls. They were so similar in design to the panels that Matt only knew they were there because of the handles and keyholes. They were all closed, and he didn't try to open any. He made his way slowly along, pausing to look at the pictures. Some were framed documents, including several old maps, and an engraving of the opening of the Great Exhibition in the Crystal Palace in 1851. There were a couple of small portraits and, like the ones in the entrance hall, they showed people with striking dark hair and blue eyes. A family trait, Matt decided, remembering Robin's distinctive looks.

One was different, though. Standing on a narrow table midway along the corridor was a small framed portrait. The delicate brushwork depicted a woman with fair hair and green eyes. Her hair was arranged in curls on top of her head and the picture had faded with age. There was a name at the bottom of the picture in a little white plate painted into the foreground: *Elizabeth Venture*. Another ancestor, but without the same family looks. Maybe she'd married into the family.

Further along was a faded, sepia-toned photograph hanging under a wall light. Matt had to stand at an angle to see it through the glass, as the light reflected back at him. It showed two women standing outside the manor house porch where Matt had just come in. But they had been there a hundred years ago or more. One of them was young – maybe only Matt's age. Her hair was arranged in curls and was jet black. Matt could only imagine her blue eyes. The other woman had white hair and was very old. Grandmother and granddaughter perhaps.

It looked like the same girl in the last painting in the corridor. But the date in the corner beside the painter's signature was 1833, which Matt reckoned must be before photography. The grandmother as a girl maybe. And with her was another girl of about the same age, but with fair hair and pale green eyes. There was a similarity between her and the woman in the little picture on the table, Matt realized. Not as close as the dark-haired girls, but a resemblance nonetheless.

'I bet the holiday snaps are just as interesting,' Matt muttered to himself, and stepped out of the corridor into the enormous room beyond.

Matt had once spent an especially boring afternoon with his father at the Bodleian Library in Oxford. He had been expected to amuse himself quietly while Dad examined books that were so old they looked as if they'd fall apart if he turned the pages too quickly. The only thing that had come close to impressing Matt had been the size of the library.

Venture's library seemed even bigger.

Matt was shocked to find such an enormous place at the back of an old country house. Part of the effect was because it was all pretty much one huge circular room. Though, in fact, when Matt looked more closely he realized the room wasn't round at all. It was made of so many flat sides meeting at shallow angles and lined with bookshelves that it just seemed circular.

The domed roof high above added to the effect. Matt felt giddy looking up and his feet tingled. There were several spiral staircases leading to higher galleries lined with yet more bookcases. He guessed that there was probably a way into the upper levels from the upstairs floors of the house as well.

Directly under the dome was a large circular table surrounded at intervals by high-backed chairs. The table was made of dark wood, so highly polished that, looking down at the surface, Matt could see the dome and the galleries above reflected. As if he was looking into a deep, dark pit. He pulled out one of the chairs and sat down, angling it so he could look all round the room. Books and papers, so far as he could see. No sign of a computer, though. But there had to be one somewhere, because Aunt Jane had said so.

'You look lost, young man,' a voice called to him.

Startled, Matt looked round. There was no one there – the room was empty.

A laugh. 'Lost and confused.'

Matt looked round again. Still no one. But there was movement, a flicker of light deep in the 'pit' of the table. He looked up and found that there was a man looking down at him from the gallery above. The light had been his reflection as he moved, walking towards the nearest of the spiral staircases and coming down to join Matt.

He was a tall man with short dark hair, wearing a suit but with no tie. His shirt collar was folded back outside the suit jacket so that he looked both smart and comfortable. His eyes, Matt was not surprised to see, were a startling blue.

'Julius Venture,' the man said, holding out his hand as he approached.

Matt stood up and shook hands. Venture's grip was firm and confident without being tight or intimidating. 'I'm Matt Stribling. And I like your library.'

'It's good, isn't it?' Julius Venture agreed, looking round as if he'd not really noticed before. 'Though I do wonder if it's going to be big enough. I seem to acquire so many books. As well as other things.' He fixed Matt with his blue eyes. 'Do you read much?'

'A bit. But actually I was looking for the computer. I wanted to check my email.'

Venture nodded. 'There's no substitute for reading, you know. Well, actually reading is a means to an end – to several ends. Knowledge, enjoyment, understanding.'

'You can get that off the internet now.'

Venture laughed. 'I can see that you still have a lot to learn.' He shook his head. 'I'm sorry. I'm not mocking you. I think maybe we have different perspectives, different ways of looking at the world, but that's hardly surprising.'

He was walking across the library and Matt followed. Venture led him towards an opening which Matt had not noticed before between two of the bookcases.

'Robin said that you were pleasant enough but a bit weird.'

'Thanks,' Matt said. It was a description he'd have applied more readily to Robin than himself, he thought. Different perspectives again.

The gap between the bookcases was actually a doorway, and Venture led Matt through into another room that seemed to be formed out of bookcases. It contained a desk on which were a flat panel screen and a keyboard and mouse. The computer system unit must be inside the desk, Matt thought, hidden behind a door or fake drawer fronts.

Venture gestured for Matt to sit down. He leaned over and moved the mouse gently, bringing the screen to life. There was a prompt for the password and a box to type it into.

'Aunt Jane said there was a password,' he murmured.

'Did she tell you what the password is?'

He hadn't thought Venture would hear him, so Matt was surprised. 'Er, no. She said it was a secret.'

He seemed amused. 'Did she? Are you sure that's what she said?'

'Yes,' Matt protested. The man's amusement annoyed him. 'That's what she said.'

'*Exactly* what she said? Think back, carefully. Hear her voice in your head.'

'Why?'

'As I said, you have a lot still to learn. It's time you made a start. What is the time, by the way?'

Matt could see that Venture was wearing a watch, so it seemed an odd question. But he checked his own watch anyway. 'Three seventeen.'

'Thank you. So precise,' Venture said. 'And so wrong.'

'Sorry?'

Venture leaned forward and said quietly, as if he was revealing a secret, 'Digital watches don't really work, you know.'

Matt checked his watch again. Sure enough, the seconds had progressed. As he looked at it, the 17 became 18. 'It's working fine.'

'That's not what I meant. You see everything as numbers, just like a computer. It deals in ones and zeros. You see digits, flicking from second to second. As if time is granular, as if nature is made up of bits and pieces – bits and bytes.'

'But it's accurate.'

'Is it? What happens between the seconds? I know, I know – you could have a watch that showed the tenths, the hundredths, even the thousandths of a second. But still it's click click click as the numbers change.'

He sat down beside Matt and showed him his own watch. 'I don't pretend it's entirely accurate,' he admitted. It was an expensive, heavy watch with a segmented metal strap. It had a traditional analogue dial with numbers round the edge.

'So?' Matt said, not seeing the point.

'So the second hand moves smoothly between the numbers. On some clocks the second hand jumps between the seconds, but even so it has to pass through the space between. In your digital computer world you'd try to break down the intervals into smaller and smaller pieces, and time – the world isn't like that. In your model, if I can use that word, the next second will never come. The world –' he stood up again and shrugged – 'stops.'

'What do you mean?'

'I mean that before you can get to the next second you have to get to the next tenth of a second, right?'

'Yes, I suppose.'

'And before you get to that next tenth of a second you have to get to the next hundredth, yes?'

'OK.' He was beginning to see where this was leading.

'And before that you need to get to the next thousandth. And before *that*, the next ten-thousandth . . .'

'And the next millionth and ten-millionth.'

'Exactly. You see the problem? You can go on breaking down the second into smaller and smaller pieces for ever. So, mathematically, you never get anywhere.'

'I see,' Matt said, though he wasn't sure he'd got exactly the point that Venture was trying to make.

As if knowing what Matt was thinking, Venture said, 'Just don't rely on the numbers. Look around you, see it all properly. There are more things in heaven and earth than are digitized in your computer.'

'But computers are useful,' Matt protested.

'Of course. But you have to be aware of their limitations. They don't allow for ambiguity or misunderstanding. Imprecise input won't give you an approximate answer, and there's no sense of interpretation. You need to know the difference between data and information – between the numbers and what they are actually telling you. And don't expect them to be as accurate as your senses.'

Matt laughed at that. 'Computers can be faster and more accurate than you can,' he said.

Venture laughed as well. 'You think so? Does the computer know the value of pi?'

'To more decimal places than I do,' Matt told him. 'Henry in my maths set learned pi to a hundred decimal places. A computer can go further even than that.'

'Well, that's impressive,' Venture said levelly. 'Over a hundred decimal places, eh? You see, you're thinking in numbers again. Granular, and imprecise.'

'What do you mean?'

'I mean that the computer can rattle off pi to as many *million* decimal places as it likes. Yet I only have to look at the table you were sitting at in the library and I see pi exactly. More exactly than the computer can ever know. A computer, relying on pixels on the screen and digits in its brain, doesn't really *know* what a circle is. It can only ever approximate.'

Matt stared back at him, disconcerted at the thoughts that were beginning to form at the back of his mind. 'I see.'

'You're beginning to,' Venture agreed. 'Which is good. A good start. Now, I have work to do, so I'll leave you to it. Help yourself to anything you want.' He hesitated, then added, 'You're very welcome here, did I tell you that?'

'Thank you.'

'As I said, you're welcome.' He turned to go.

'Excuse me,' Matt called quickly. 'The password?'

Venture paused in the doorway. 'Password? Oh, a computer would never work it out. But you will. Remember what Jane told you.'

Then he was gone, leaving Matt looking at the empty password field on the screen, and the realization that he had not mentioned his dad. Though he didn't know what he should have said, or what Venture might have been able to tell him. Matt did his best to push his irritation from his mind and concentrated on solving the more immediate puzzle. Aunt Jane had told him the password was a secret, he knew she had. So how could he ever work it out. He looked round the room for clues – a book title perhaps. But which one? There had to be a thousand books just in this one small room.

Venture had told him to hear Aunt Jane's words in his head. Was it something to do with the way she'd said it – her inflection? But Venture wasn't there, so how could he even know?

'The password for the computer is a secret,' he heard her say in his memory. But there was something wrong with it. It didn't sound quite right. Because, he realized, that wasn't what she had said.

What she had actually said was, 'The password for the computer is "secret".'

Matt typed 'secret' into the entry field and the computer came to life.

✝

There was an email from Alex saying he'd tried ringing Matt and just got his mum's answerphone saying she was away. Matt didn't have a mobile, since they weren't allowed them at school, and he couldn't remember Aunt Jane's number. So he emailed Alex his address as best he knew it and told him the number would follow and that he'd check his email.

After surfing the web a bit and playing an online game called *Udder Worlds* – where you had to herd cows into a milking shed before aliens kidnapped them and sent them on missions to other planets – Matt was getting bored. He logged off the computer and went back through to the main library, surprised to find how overcast it had got. Where pale light had streamed through the windows round the top of the dome despite the rain, there was now the gun-metal grey of gathering storm clouds.

Incongruously, Matt saw, the library was lit by candles. A large candelabrum with half a dozen candles stood in the middle of the round table, casting flickering light that was reflected back off the table top. The light reached barely further than the table itself, so that the edges of the room were lost in shadows – the table could have been in the middle of a black void or stuck in a field, for all you could see.

Matt made his way carefully and slowly to the table, straining to see where the door out of the room and back to the corridor might be. In the worst case, he thought, he'd simply walk round the edge of the enormous room until he found a way out. Or a light switch. Or take a candle from the table to light his way.

But then a door opened opposite him, across the other side of the table. An elongated rectangle of light fell across the wooden floor. Framed in the doorway, light shining round her so that she was barely more than a silhouette, was Robin.

'You've finished, then?' she said.

'I'm done,' he agreed. 'I was just looking for the door.'

'You were busy earlier.' She waited in the doorway for him.

'You were checking up on me?'

He could see her face now as she stepped back into the light to let him through. 'If you like.'

Matt wasn't sure what to say to that. So he just nodded. 'Hang on. Where are we?'

The door didn't lead back to the corridor he'd come along earlier. It gave directly into another room. This one looked more like a museum than a library. There were glass-topped display tables and glass-fronted display cabinets on the wall. A statue of a woman dressed in a toga stood on a low plinth in one corner of the room, an ancient grandfather clock ticked away the moments in another. The second hand clicked from second to second, and Matt wondered if it was this clock that Robin's father had in mind earlier.

There were other items displayed on tables and shelves, but too many for Matt to take in as Robin led him across the room to another door. 'Jane left a while ago. I said I'd tell her when you were done with the computer. I didn't want her disturbing you if you were busy.'

'Well, you know,' Matt said. 'What is all this stuff?' he asked.

She shrugged. 'It's just stuff. Dad can't resist collecting things. He tries not to these days, but it sort of accumulates over the years. It's the same with the books.'

'Imagine what the place'll be like when he's sixty,' Matt said.

She smiled. 'Yes,' she said. 'Imagine.'

'But what are they all for?' He pointed to the nearest display table. Inside, protected beneath a glass lid, was a pile of gold coins. 'I mean, where did these come from?'

'They're Russian,' Robin said, as if that was obvious. 'All that remains of the five tons of gold and silver that Admiral Kolchak took from the imperial treasury to fund the Tsar's cause in 1917.'

'What happened to the rest of it?' Matt wondered.

Robin opened the door and Matt could see that it led into the corridor. Opposite was the little table with the picture of the fair-haired woman standing on it.

'He had it tipped into Lake Baikal. It must have been so sad, standing on the narrow roadway that ran along the cliffs at the side of the lake, watching all their hopes and aspirations, their only chance of victory, sinking out of sight in the deepest lake in the world. Perhaps Kolchak wept, or perhaps it was just the cold wind stinging his eyes and making them water. But they knew by then it was all over and they wanted to deny the Communists anything they could. A small victory perhaps.' Her voice was quiet, almost a whisper. 'Kolchak was captured soon after,' she said as she led him back to the hallway. 'They executed him, poor man.'

Matt said goodbye and stepped out into the dark, windy evening. He stood in the protection of the porch for a few moments before setting off down the drive. 'Pleasant enough, but a bit weird,' he said out loud.

✝

The lights were on downstairs in the cottage. As he approached, Matt could see through the front window into the living room. Aunt Jane was sitting in an armchair beside the fire. He watched her for a few seconds. She was facing away from him, but he could see that she was looking at a book.

It was a big book, and she turned the pages slowly and carefully as she examined them. There were pictures and news clippings glued to the pages. A scrapbook, containing memories and keepsakes. Matt couldn't make out any details.

The front door was locked, so he pressed the bell. He could hear Aunt Jane moving about inside – a door banging and hurried footsteps.

'Hello, Matt. I hope you've had a nice time.' She stood aside to let him come in. 'Goodness, it's got cold, hasn't it?'

He hadn't noticed. He didn't notice now. He was more concerned with Aunt Jane. 'Are you all right?'

'Fine, fine. I'm fine.' She sniffed. 'Just the beginnings of a cold, I think. Nothing to worry about.'

But it didn't look to Matt like the beginnings of a cold. Her eyes were moist and her cheeks stained. Her face was blotchy with embarrassment or emotion. It looked to Matt like she'd been crying.

He closed the door behind him and went and sat in the chair opposite Aunt Jane, close to the fire. There was no sign of the scrapbook.

5

Aunt Jane had tea keeping warm in the oven – lamb chops and vegetables with new potatoes. She asked Matt how he had spent his time in the library as they ate in the little dining room, but she seemed distracted, and Matt wondered if she was listening at all. He had to ask her twice for the salt.

There was no dishwasher, so Matt dried the plates and cutlery as Aunt Jane washed them.

'I think I'll have a mug of cocoa,' she said as she emptied the sink and dried her hands. 'Do you want one?'

'Thanks.'

'Then I'll get an early night, if you don't mind. My cold . . .'

'That's fine,' Matt assured her. 'I could do with some sleep too. It's been a long day.'

'I'm sure. You must be worn out, you poor thing. If you want to ring your mother, help yourself to the phone.' She busied herself with the cocoa.

'What'd be the point?' Matt muttered. He wished he knew where Dad was. He could leave a message for him on his answerphone, but after the strange warnings and the palaver with the website and password, he wasn't sure that was a good idea. And it wasn't like Dad would be there to get the message.

Matt helped himself to an Agatha Christie from the bookcase and took it up to bed. Tomorrow he'd see if Julius Venture's library had any decent novels. It seemed to have everything else. He put on his pyjamas and climbed under the duvet. The book was better than he'd expected and he was soon absorbed. When he reached for his cocoa what seemed like only a minute later, it was cold and a thick skin of congealed milk caught on his upper lip and trailed out of the mug.

Matt went to the bathroom to wash the milk off his hand and face. He was still thirsty and there was no beaker in the bathroom, so he went down-stairs. Aunt Jane's door was pushed almost shut and the light was out. He could hear the rhythmic sound of her breathing. Nevertheless he went as quietly as he could for fear of disturbing her.

After his slurp of cold cocoa, Matt fancied something different to drink. He couldn't be bothered with boiling water or milk, so he decided on a cold drink. There was a bottle of squash in a cupboard and half a carton of fruit juice in the fridge. He decided on the juice and poured himself a small glass. Rather than take it up to bed he sat by the remains of the fire in the living room. The embers were glowing faintly, wreathed in a powder of grey ash that seemed to stir in time to the sound of the wind from outside.

On the other side of the fireplace was a wooden cabinet. The top half was made up of shelves with glass doors. There were ornaments and glassware arranged neatly on the shelves. Beneath this was a cupboard and Matt could see that one of the doors was not quite closed. He finished his drink and stood up. As he passed the cabinet, he pushed the door gently shut with his foot.

It sprang open again. Something inside needed moving to allow the door to close. So Matt put down the empty glass and knelt beside the cupboard. He opened the door and saw immediately what the obstruction was.

A scrapbook. It had been replaced hurriedly in the cupboard on top of a pile of photo albums and cardboard boxes. It was angled so the corner was catching the inside of the door. Matt turned the scrapbook and pushed the door gently shut. It clicked as the latch caught and Matt stood up.

He put his glass in the sink. Then he picked it up again and rinsed it out, before putting it upside down on the drainer. He turned to go back to bed, then changed his mind and picked up a tea towel from the rack over the radiator. He dried the glass and put it away, his mind now made up.

The pages of the scrapbook were dry with age, seeming to draw the moisture from his fingers as he turned them. There were yellowed news clippings about Aunt Jane's family – Dad's family. A short birth notice for Dad from a local paper. An account of a village fête opened by some television actor that Matt had never heard of. A school photo – *Billy the Squirrel's Class of the Week* – from a county paper, with names under the picture. Matt found Aunt Jane and looked at the smiling little girl she had been when she was ten.

There were photos too. Some were in black and white, some faded colour pictures. They all had thin white borders round them, which made them look old-fashioned as well as old. He saw the same girl as in the class photo and realized that the younger boy playing with her must be his own father, aged about eight. He would never have guessed.

But he did recognize the setting for an increasing number of the pictures – the grounds of the manor house. In several he could see the house behind the children as they played. They were older now, teens. Posing carefully for shots, rather than relaxed and unaware. There were three of them – Dad, Aunt Jane and another girl. Matt stared at the pictures of the three children. There was no mistaking the third child. Aunt Jane looked about sixteen now and Dad was maybe fourteen. The same age as the other girl – the one who looked so like Robin. It had to be Robin's mother, and the daughter had obviously inherited the mother's looks and appearance. The two sets of parents must have been friends, he thought. All those years ago . . .

There were older people too in some of the later pictures. Matt knew his grandparents from other pictures he had seen in the past. He could dimly remember his grandmother – Dad's mum – as a frail, elderly lady. But here she was only in her forties, fifty at the most. She looked so happy with her husband. His hair was grey and thinning and in most of the pictures in which he appeared he had a pipe clamped in his mouth.

In one final picture, the last in the book, was another figure that Matt knew. Or rather, that he thought he did. Julius Venture, standing with Robin's mother and Matt's dad and Aunt Jane. Of course, the man in the picture couldn't be Venture himself, but must be his dad – Robin's grandfather. Again the family resemblance was obvious, and Matt recalled the pictures he had seen in the house. Matt wondered who had taken the picture – one of his grandparents, probably.

He closed the book and returned it to the cupboard. I wonder what happened to Robin's mother, he thought, as he made his way quietly back to bed. It seemed strange that there were no pictures of the young Julius Venture either, since he was the one who lived at the manor house. He must have been friendly with the girl; after all, he'd ended up marrying her. They must have all played together in those days – Matt's dad, Aunt Jane, Robin's mother and her future husband, the young Julius Venture. So why were there no pictures of Venture? A mystery, he thought, as he picked up the Agatha Christie novel again.

And almost at once he realized there was no mystery at all. Of course the young Julius Venture was there, in most if not all of the pictures. He must be the photographer. It was his camera, that was why he never appeared.

Pleased with himself for working it out, but also disappointed at the simplicity of the solution, Matt turned out the light. The wind rattled the window and whispered round the casement. But Matt didn't listen to what it said.

✠

The bedroom was bathed with warm summer sunlight when Matt woke. He saw from his watch that he'd slept in till mid-morning. He must have been more tired than he'd thought. Aunt Jane had left him a note on the kitchen table, saying she'd gone up to the manor house and hoped Matt could look after himself. She had obviously thought he needed his sleep. She was probably right, he decided, yawning at cereal packets.

There must be buses from the village to somewhere worth spending the day, Matt thought.

Gloucester or even Cheltenham wasn't that far away. In the other direction there was a castle at Berkeley, wasn't there? What he needed was a bus timetable. He couldn't see one lying around in the cottage, but he could probably print one out from the internet. Or he could walk into the village and look for a bus stop – there'd be a timetable there.

But all thoughts of buses were put out of Matt's mind by the arrival of the helicopter.

He had barely left the house when he heard the thwock-thwock-thwock of the rotors. Far off in the steel-grey sky, above the trees to the side of the manor house, Matt could see the tiny shape of the helicopter as it approached. He ran out on to the main drive for a better view as it got closer and larger.

The rotor blades were a blur in the air above the machine itself, which was dark and angular like a brutal insect. It tilted back slightly as it paused over the lawn beside the drive in front of the house, then started slowly to descend.

There were leaves on the drive and at the edge of the woods, blown down by the strong winds of the last few days. They were caught in the down-draught, spiralling upwards in a kaleidoscopic flurry

– all the shades of the trees mixed into a maelstrom. Just for a moment, as the helicopter settled on to the lawn, it looked as if the mass of leaves were taking on a shape – picked out in variations of green. Like seeing animals made out of clouds, Matt thought. A face – eyes, nose, mouth. Just for a second. Then the engine noise died down, the rotors spun slower and slower, the wind dropped and the leaves fell form-less to the ground.

Beyond the now motionless helicopter, Matt could see Julius Venture and Robin standing outside the porch, watching. Robin waved. Matt waved back. Then immediately he felt stupid – she was probably waving at the people in the helicopter, not at him. Embarrassed, he almost turned away.

He stopped at the sight of the man who jumped down from the helicopter and started walking purposefully towards the house. There was some-thing familiar about him, Matt thought. He watched the man all the way up to the house. He was big – tall and broad, wearing a long, expensive-looking coat. His hair was dark grey like a cloud-heavy sky. He shook hands with Venture, and together they went into the manor house.

Robin stayed where she was, outside on the drive.

She waved again, and this time Matt was sure she was waving to him. He started quickly up the drive towards her.

She waited outside the porch, watching him with that slightly mocking half-smile of hers. Matt smiled back. It was just her manner. He was pretty sure that she wasn't really mocking him. Almost pretty sure.

'Who was that?' he asked. 'I recognized him from somewhere.'

'Atticus Harper,' Robin told him.

'Really? Dad's mentioned him. The millionaire.'

'Billionaire, more like. He called my father late last night, asked if he could come and see him.'

'What about?'

She raised an eyebrow. 'Like it's any of your business!'

'Sorry. Just asking.'

'That's OK.' She opened the door and he followed her inside. 'I don't know anyway. He just said he wanted to discuss something.'

'You know much about him?' Matt asked.

'Do you?'

He shrugged. 'A bit. He's rich. He's an archaeologist – a "hobby archaeologist", Dad called him. Owns about a dozen businesses, from oil to computer systems to an ice hockey team . . .'

'It's a start.' Robin was leading him through the hall and down the corridor towards the library. 'Let's look him up on the internet.' She paused, turning to face Matt. 'Unless you have other plans?'

'No,' he said, all thoughts of bus timetables dismissed. 'No other plans.'

✝

There was an abundance of information about Atticus Harper on the web. The problem wasn't finding a site, it was deciding which of them would be most use from the search engine's list.

They started with one of his companies. It made computer components and silicon chips, and the site included a page about its founder and owner. It didn't tell them much they didn't already know between them. In fact, the more sites they looked at, the more detail they got but the less Matt felt he knew about the man.

Atticus Harper was in his fifties. He had been a young computer genius when Bill Gates rose to fame, founding a similar software company. But, being in Britain, his rise to fame and fortune was less spectacular or obtrusive. He seemed to be a private man. There was lots about what he owned or where he had been, very little about what he thought or did in his spare time.

'Probably doesn't have any,' Robin said. 'These people work all the hours God sends. And then some. Obsessive. That's why they're so successful, of course. That and intelligence and good business sense.'

'And luck,' Matt said.

'And arrogance,' Robin added. 'We've got a heli-copter pad behind the house, but he still landed on the lawn. He obviously likes to make an impression.'

'Like, in the grass you mean?' Matt joked.

Robin smiled.

Harper's interest in archaeology seemed always to have been there, beneath the surface of his corpo-rate work. They found a brief biography from a respected history journal which mentioned that Harper had insisted his companies donate funds to several research projects in the 1980s. Since then he had taken a more active – and financial – personal interest. He had funded archaeological digs and projects all over the world, as well as donating to libraries and institutes.

'Look at this,' Matt exclaimed in surprise at one web page, though he knew Robin was reading it with him.

She laughed. 'If it's true.'

Matt was still impressed. 'He tried to buy Stonehenge. Wow.'

'He owns loads of ancient sites,' Robin pointed out. 'Most of them not so high-profile, though. There's that Inca village, and the prehistoric caves in the south of France.'

'Yeah, I know. And he's saved loads of others by personal intervention in out of the way countries where they could have been destroyed. It's more than a hobby – it's an obsession. He collects old stuff, from coins and trinkets to castles and estates . . . Hey!' An idea had occurred to Matt.

'What?'

'I bet that's why he's here. He wants to buy you out.'

'No way.' Robin closed the browser and shut down the computer. 'Dad would never sell. We've been here for . . .' She stood up. 'The family's lived here for centuries. We'd never sell.'

Matt was teasing really. He didn't think that was why Harper had come, but he was amused to see how it unsettled Robin. 'He might offer your dad millions.'

'Dad's got millions,' she said.

She said it quietly, matter-of-fact. So probably, Matt thought, it was true.

'Maybe some particular relic, then,' he suggested. 'Plenty of those round the place, after all.'

She was still serious. 'They're not for sale.'

'Not even the pictures?'

The half-smile was back. 'Don't tease me.'

'Sorry. But I bet he wants something.'

'Everyone wants something,' she told him. 'I'm going for a walk. Coming?'

Matt paused in the corridor, beside the table with the photograph on it. 'I saw some old pictures yesterday,' he said.

'How interesting,' Robin said sarcastically.

'It was actually. Aunt Jane's got a scrapbook. There's pictures of her and my dad, when they were kids. About our age, I suppose.'

'Yes?' She sounded bored. Or wary.

'There are pictures of them playing in the grounds.'

'They grew up here. In the village.'

'I know that.'

They had reached the hall. The sound of Julius Venture's voice was a low murmur from the other side of a door that wasn't quite shut.

'They were playing with another girl,' Matt said. He felt the blood go to his cheeks as he said it, though he wasn't sure why he should be embarrassed. 'I think it must have been your mother.'

'Why do you think that?' There was no emotion at all in her voice.

'Because she looked just like you.'

Robin nodded. 'Yes. Yes, she would have done.'

'Sorry.' Matt turned away. 'I guess maybe you don't like to talk about her.'

'I can hardly remember my mother,' she said. 'It's not a problem.'

'She seemed very happy,' Matt said, turning back to face her. 'They all did. In the pictures. They were having fun.'

Robin nodded. Her reply was so quiet it was almost a whisper: 'The girl that broke your father's heart.'

As she said it, another voice cut across the low murmur of Venture's. The voice was louder, deep and resonant. It carried, the words reaching Matt clearly: 'Which still leaves us the problem of what to do about Arnold Stribling.'

Robin and Matt stared at each other.

'Dad?' Matt mouthed, feeling suddenly cold and empty inside. Why were they discussing his father? Again he wished he had spoken to Venture about Dad when they'd met the day before. The man knew something – perhaps Dad had tried to tell Matt that.

'No, Matt,' Robin said. 'Wait.'

But he was already turning, walking quickly to the half-open door without pausing to think about it. Pushing it open wide and stepping into Julius Venture's study. Finding Venture and Atticus Harper turning in surprise to look at him as he stood in the doorway.

'This is Dr Stribling's son, Matthew,' Venture said, standing up and gesturing to Matt to take a seat. 'Do join us, Matt. I think you'll find this . . . interesting.'

He was aware of Robin coming into the room behind him. 'What about my father? Do you know where he is?'

Venture and Harper exchanged a look. 'Not exactly,' Harper admitted. 'But in a sense it's because of your father that I'm here. Tell me, have you ever heard him mention the lost treasure of the Knights of St John of Jerusalem?'

Matt shook his head as he sat down. 'I don't think so. What's it got to do with my dad?'

'I employed your father to find it for me,' Harper said.

Venture sent Robin to find Aunt Jane. 'She should hear this too,' he explained to Harper. 'She is Dr Stribling's sister.'

Harper raised a grey eyebrow. 'Quite a family gathering.'

'Indeed.' Venture offered no further explanation. Instead he turned to Matt. 'Please forgive me. I knew nothing at all of all this when we spoke yesterday or I would have told you. I didn't realize you came here to your aunt because he is missing. You must be very worried about him – I'm sorry. Arnold has been a dear friend of mine for many years.'

Matt nodded, unsure what to say to this. While they waited, he looked round Venture's study, avoiding the man's deep, blue gaze. Venture himself was seated behind a large desk made of dark, polished wood. The top of the desk was clear apart from a computer screen and a large leather-bound notebook. Behind the desk, the wall was shelved from floor to ceiling and the shelves were packed with books. Two of the other walls were panelled with wood up to about chest height, then shelved. Matt could see DVDs, video tapes, CDs, computer disks . . . The fourth wall was dominated by a large window that gave out on to the front of the house. Matt could see the black shape of Harper's helicopter standing silhouetted on the lawn. Making an impression.

Harper himself was sitting in front of the desk, a metal briefcase standing close to his feet. He was a big man – tall and broad-shouldered, but not overweight. He seemed to be composed entirely of greys. His hair was steel grey, his suit was dark grey. His long face seemed somewhere between the two. Even his eyes were a blue-grey. His bloodless lips twitched faintly, but whether into the ghost of a smile or a sneer it was difficult to tell.

He angled his chair so he could speak to Matt as well as to Julius Venture. There were a couple of other upright chairs against the wall beside the door. One of them, Matt could see, was hinged at the back and he guessed it opened out to form a set of library steps. Robin sat on that when she returned with Aunt Jane, who took the slightly larger chair. For Aunt Jane's benefit, Venture introduced Atticus Harper, and they all waited expectantly for him to speak.

Sitting in front of the desk, Harper had looked almost like an animated corpse – devoid of colour or much expression. But as he spoke, he seemed to come to life, and Matt saw something of his own father's enthusiasm and excitement rise to the surface. He felt that he understood the man's passion, what drove him, and he found himself caught up in the story and the mystery and the emotion of it all.

'Forgive me if you know something of this,' Harper said, his voice rich and deep, 'but a story needs its background and beginning. And the start of our tale is in the build-up to the Fourth Crusade, when in 1198 Pope Innocent III called for the Christians to invade Egypt . . . But he had a problem, because the Crusaders couldn't afford to pay for transport, and so it was agreed that the ships for the enterprise would be provided by Venice. Which was all well and good, except that the Venetians traded with Egypt. So they weren't too keen on attacking their business partners. Given the choice, they'd far rather have attacked their biggest rivals – the Byzantine Empire.

'So, being pragmatic as well as more than a little devious, that's what they did. Since they couldn't pay for the ships, the Crusaders were forced to agree that instead of attacking Egypt they would take the city of Zara, and then move against the Byzantine capital – Constantinople.

'The story of the siege is long and bloody and complicated, and it needn't concern us. But in 1204, a year after it fell to the attackers, Constantinople was ransacked. The destruction and the looting were terrible, and much of what survived that was worth anything was taken back to Venice. But not the Treasure of St John, as it was commonly known by then.

'There was a knight known as Sir Robert of Lisle, who may have been Italian or French or even English, given his apparent title. Accounts vary. When Constantinople first fell, in 1203, he was charged with compiling a register of all that was precious in the city. No, not the gold and silver, not the artwork and precious stones. The *literature* – the scrolls and books and parchments and tablets. The idea was to create an inventory of all the learning that survived in the ancient city. And when the massacres and the looting started on 13 April 1204, it is said that Sir Robert and seven of his comrades in arms each took a page of the register and went through the city, locating and saving the items on their list.

'I imagine them, you know. Sometimes I see them in my dreams – going from door to door, from private house to public building, palace to library. Walking tall amid the chaos, silhouetted against the blood-red sky as the city burns around them and they struggle to save its very heart. Its learning. Its wisdom. Working ruthlessly and methodically through their list, putting to the sword anyone who gets in their way. Oh, the sword may not be as mighty as the pen, but there are times when the one comes to the service of the other.

'Because these men were all Knights Hospitallers – members of the Hospital, or Order, of St John of Jerusalem. Originally the order was a charitable one, set up to care for pilgrims who became sick in the Holy Land. But by the fall of Constantinople they were not just men of learning out to help others. The Hospitallers were a military as well as a religious order, and Sir Robert and his colleagues fought their way out, taking what they had recovered with them.

'Again, accounts vary. Some say that two of the knights were killed in Constantinople during those three days of bloodshed. Others say that three of them died. But all agree that Sir Robert and several of the others escaped, and took with them the literary treasures of Constantinople, as well as an unspecified amount of more traditional treasure.

'What happened to this treasure afterwards is surprisingly well documented, though still we have no inventory – which is ironic, given how Sir Robert came to acquire it in the first place. In 1291, when Acre was lost and the Knights Hospitallers were forced to move their headquarters to Limassol in Cyprus, the treasure went with them. It is listed in their records as "Numerous items of value and wisdom acquired by Robert de Lisle et al." It is noted that three carts were set aside for transporting the treasure.

'In 1309, when the Hospitallers again moved, this time to Rhodes, there is no explicit mention of the treasure. But there is a "collection of items" that again took three carts to transport, and is the only set of goods not otherwise accounted for from previous inventories or known acquisitions.

'However, there the trail ends. Or almost. There is one last tantalizing mention of Sir Robert's treasure. In 1523, the Hospitallers were expelled from Rhodes by the Turks. In the process of leaving, they were forced to abandon much – and there is mention in the journal written by one of the knights, a certain Edward Duboeuf, that another knight – Henri Sivel – had been forced to surrender "that which should never have been returned" to the Turks and which Henri subsequently vowed to retrieve.

'That was what intrigued your father, Matt. He thought this was a loose end of the trail he could follow up. And, I have to tell you, he was making considerable progress. Before he disappeared . . .'

✠

There was silence when Harper had finished. Eventually, Aunt Jane spoke.

'What do you mean, disappeared?'

'Hasn't young Matt told you?' Harper said.

'Well, yes. But if I know Arnie, he's just wandered off on some expedition and forgotten to mention it.'

Harper smiled thinly. 'Yes, he is a bit like that, isn't he? But I'm afraid it isn't that simple.'

'Perhaps you'd like to explain,' Venture told him.

'Yes,' Matt said. 'Perhaps you would.' He had been caught up in Harper's tale, but now he felt numb, wondering what the point of it really was – how it related to Dad.

'The Treasure of St John has never attracted much real attention, except as a sort of academic amusement,' Harper said. 'But it has always struck me that its worth is far greater than diamonds or gold. Think of it . . .' He leaned forward, his grey eyes suddenly coming alive as they caught the light. 'Think of it, the knowledge and wisdom of the ancients, codified and collected. Oh yes, there might be precious stones and metals and trinkets and relics. But think what we could discover.' He leaned back again, hands out in front of him, as if begging his audience to share in his excitement. 'They say the writings include the secret of alchemy, which of course they won't. They say they include notes on the knowledge held secret by the ancients. How the pyramids were built, the heavens mapped, the purpose of Stonehenge . . . Perhaps even a clue to the location of . . .'

Harper paused, staring past Matt into the distance. Then he blinked, and was suddenly once more in the present. 'Of who knows what . . .' he said. 'But we can be sure that whatever is written in those books and on those parchments will fundamentally change the way we see the ancient world and our place in the modern one.'

'What about Matt's dad?' Robin said levelly.

'I'm sorry? Of course. What am I thinking of?' Harper stood up. He clasped his hands behind his back and paced to and fro in front of Venture's desk. 'I engaged Dr Stribling to find me the treasure. I knew his reputation. I'd read a paper of his about the fall of Nice to the Turk Barbarossa in 1543 and there was a mention in it of Henri Sivel that intrigued me.' He stopped pacing and fixed his attention fully on Matt. 'Your father agreed to work for me. He seemed to be making good progress . . .'

'And then?' Matt prompted.

Harper sighed. 'And then he was gone.'

'But gone where?' Aunt Jane asked.

There was no answer, and instead Venture asked, 'Who else is interested in this Treasure of St John?'

His voice was quiet, but his words were enough to make Harper sit down again. He looked tired and pale. 'You are right,' he said. 'There are others. I don't know who exactly, but it was clear to me almost from the outset that there are others, other . . . forces involved. They also want the treasure. But not for the purpose of wisdom and learning, you can be sure of that. Should they find it, the collection would be broken up, sold off in secret, destroyed.'

His expression changed and Matt realized with surprise that the man was suddenly furious.

'That must not happen!' Harper insisted.

Matt was feeling strangely distant. It was like he was watching Harper on a stage, in a play. Not really there . . . 'And my father?' he heard himself ask, though he already knew what Harper would say. 'What has all this to do with Dad? Who are these other people – these other forces?'

'I don't know,' Harper confessed. 'Not exactly. But I do know that they are people who want to find the treasure for themselves, not for the good of humanity as a whole,' Harper said. 'They are interested in its material value, not what we can learn from it – about the ancient world, and about ourselves. They know of my passion and of your father's progress.' He paused, as if gathering his thoughts. 'In answer to your other question – the more important question for you, I assume . . .' Harper sighed. 'Well, I believe that your father is now working for these misguided people.'

'But he would never do that,' Matt said, feeling the anger rise within him. 'If what you say about them is true, Dad would never agree to help them.'

'I didn't say he was doing it willingly,' Harper told him. 'Your father has disappeared, without explanation or even a suitcase. They have taken him. Whoever these despicable people are, they have kid-napped Dr Stribling to force him to find the Treasure of St John for them.'

'And if he won't help them?' Aunt Jane asked, her voice husky and fearful. 'If he refuses?'

Harper sighed. 'Then I expect they will kill him.'

6

'You didn't know that Matt, or Miss Stribling for that matter, were here,' Julius Venture said. He leaned forward, elbows resting on the top of the desk and hands clasped together.

'That is true,' Harper admitted.

Venture unclasped his hands. 'So why come to me?'

Harper considered this carefully before answering. The room was silent, all eyes on him. 'I have known for some time,' he said at last, 'that there might be – what shall we say? Competition? Knowing that, it would have been irresponsible of me not to warn Dr Stribling. I suggested that he might want to take precautions, as I did myself. I offered him a bodyguard, for example. Which he refused.'

Matt heard Aunt Jane's heavy sigh from across the room. Like her, he wasn't surprised that Dad had refused to have a bodyguard. He would have laughed off the suggestion.

'But,' Harper went on, 'we did discuss what to do in the case of various events. I had my IT people model, *simulate*, several scenarios.'

'On computers?' Matt said. He shouldn't be surprised at this, he realized. After all, Harper had made his fortune out of computer research and manufacturing.

'That's right. Your father was not, I think, as excited as I am at the opportunities the new technologies offer for archaeology.'

'I bet,' Matt said quietly. Dad saw computers as tools. He understood what they could do, but he had never been excited by technology – unlike Matt or Mum. He had once told Matt that when the technology becomes more interesting than what you're trying to do with it, then you're in the wrong business. It was a sentiment that Matt could understand, but he wasn't sure he entirely agreed with it. And Harper seemed to be a good example of how to combine two passions to the benefit of both.

'The long and the short of it is,' Harper was saying,

'that we discussed what to do in the eventuality that Dr Stribling disappeared or was captured. And he was very clear on his advice.'

'Which was what?' Robin prompted.

'First, that I should continue to try to find the Treasure of St John no matter what threats might be made, though I have to say so far there have been none. And second, that I should come to you for help.' He turned to face Venture across the desk. 'Dr Stribling was most insistent that after himself, you are the person best qualified to find the treasure.'

Venture said nothing; his expression remained set and unreadable.

Harper smiled. 'It did rather surprise me, I confess. I had heard of you of course, have even bid against you at several auctions – though I don't think either of us was actually there. But I had no idea of the esteem in which Dr Stribling holds you. No idea of your breadth and depth of expertise. Tell me, are you the man for the job?'

Venture leaned back in his chair. The fingers of his right hand drummed a thoughtful rhythm on the desk. 'You know,' he said at last, 'in archaeology as in so many others areas, there are some things which should be left well alone.'

Harper frowned. 'You mean the Treasure of St John?'

'Who can say? But given that others are not willing to let it lie wherever it is hidden . . . yes, I'll help you. And yes, as Dr Stribling very well knows, I am the man for the job. Not least because – like everyone else here – I want to find him and make sure he is safe.'

Harper exhaled heavily. His smile became a short, sharp burst of laughter – relief rather than amusement. 'Oh, I quite agree. Thank goodness for that. You know Arnold well?'

'We lived locally when we were children,' Aunt Jane said. 'Arnold has known Julius all his life. And Robin . . .' She stopped, shrugged. 'Well, as I say, we grew up here.'

Harper nodded. 'Of course, Robin. Your lovely daughter?' he said to Venture. Matt saw that Robin scowled at the compliment. Harper seemed not to notice. 'Dr Stribling mentioned you,' he said, turning back to look at Robin.

'Did he?' Her frown deepened. Her eyes flicked to her father, just for a split second. Just long enough for Venture to give the merest hint of a shake of the head. 'What did he say?'

Harper was lifting his briefcase on to the desk. It was heavy, metal, like the sort of case a photographer might keep his equipment in. Or an assassin. 'He said to say hello if I met you.' Harper clicked the locking wheels on the case round to set a combination. 'He said to tell you he remembers your mother.'

Matt was looking at Robin now. He wanted to say something – to plead for them to stop the small talk and get on with finding Dad. But something in Robin's expression kept him quiet, as Harper opened the case and went on: 'He said to say he remembers your christening in the church on the estate.'

Robin's face was blank. All trace of the frown was gone. 'That's nice of him,' she said, and her voice was as expressionless as her face.

Across the room, on the other side of the desk, a nerve ticked for a moment in Venture's cheek. His lips seemed to tighten and his eyes narrowed. Then abruptly he was on his feet, reaching across to shake Harper's hand.

'We shall do all we can to help,' he said sincerely. 'You've convinced me that this is of the utmost urgency and importance.'

'Thank you.' Harper had taken several disks from the case. They looked like computer CDs, in narrow slipcases, labelled in black marker pen. It looked like Dad's handwriting. 'This is a copy of everything that Dr Stribling found or noted or sketched. Absolutely everything. I had it all scanned on to DVD for you.'

'Excellent.' Venture took the disks and placed them on the desk close to his computer screen.

Harper handed him a sheaf of papers, computer printouts. 'Here's a list of everything on the disks, with brief explanatory notes. There are facsimiles and scans of everything relevant. There's Dr Stribling's handwritten notes, copies of all the historical papers he referenced, three-dimensional models of artefacts he felt were relevant. Everything. You will keep me aware of your progress?'

'I'll contact you as soon as we find anything,' Venture assured him.

'Thank you. And anything you need – access to anything at all, contacts, money . . .' He left the offer hanging.

'We'll let you know,' Venture said.

Harper shook hands solemnly with Matt and the others before he left. His grip was tight and confident, but his hand was cold and clammy. 'We'll find him,' Harper said quietly to Matt. 'Believe me. We'll get your father back.'

✞

They stood in the porch and watched the helicopter lift ponderously from the lawn. It gathered speed as it rose before swivelling on its axis, dipping its nose and disappearing into the clouds.

'My study,' Venture said. 'I believe there are a few things we need to discuss.'

Soon they were settled back into the seats they had so recently left. The exception was Robin, who took the chair across the desk from her father – where Harper had previously sat.

'Do you believe him?' Aunt Jane asked. 'About Arnie?'

Venture was swinging slowly back and forth in his chair. 'Yes and no,' he said. 'Yes, your brother . . .' He paused to look at Matt. 'Your father . . . . Yes, he's missing and may be in danger.'

'We should call the police,' Matt said. He had shied away from this course of action before as he didn't think there was enough evidence to convince the authorities there was anything wrong. But with a man like Atticus Harper confirming that Dad had been kidnapped, surely they would have to take the matter seriously.

'That does seem like the most sensible course of action,' Aunt Jane agreed.

'It is worth considering, certainly,' Venture said. There was something in his tone, in the way that he said it, that convinced Matt that Venture had already considered it. Considered it and decided against. 'But going to the police might put Arnold in more danger, without achieving anything useful. After all, we have very little to go on, and therefore very little we can tell the police. Where would they start?' he wondered rhetorically. 'With the treasure, surely. And I have to say that we are rather better qualified than the authorities to find that.'

'I suppose,' Matt admitted.

'Indeed,' Venture decided, punctuating the word with a raised finger, 'our best course of action is to follow the trail that your father has left. Follow it, and hope it will lead us to the Treasure of St John before anyone else finds it. With luck we'll find Arnold as well, but if not it gives us something to bargain with.'

He fixed Robin with a piercing blue stare that

made Matt shiver even though he wasn't on the receiving end. 'We can't let anyone else find this so-called treasure,' Venture said quietly. 'Not even Harper. Not without us being there.'

'So why delay?' Matt demanded, upset at having his suggestion so quickly pushed aside. 'We need to load the disks he gave us, see what's on them, and sort it out. Find Dad, or – like you say – something to bargain with.' He had been going to tell them about the intruder at Dad's. About how there had been someone watching the house who had attacked him. Matt had not imagined it, Harper's story had convinced him of that. But Venture's dismissal of outside help, of going to the police, made Matt wary again. Why mention it just to be told he'd imagined things?

'It may not be that simple,' Robin was saying.

'Your father has spent a considerable amount of time looking for this treasure,' Aunt Jane said. She seemed to understand Matt's annoyance and impatience, and he imagined she was sharing it. 'We can't expect to find it quickly or easily,' she said.

'Then we should get started, surely. What's the problem?'

Venture tapped his fingertips rapidly against the

top of the desk. 'Door,' he said to Robin. 'Windows. I want to be certain there's no hint of a draught.'

The girl nodded without comment. She walked briskly over to the door and closed it. Then she checked the windows were shut and sat down again. Matt watched her, feeling uneasy and confused.

'The problem is,' Venture said once Robin was again seated, 'that either Harper was lying to us or your father lied to him. Either way, it's a warning that all is not what it seems.'

'How do you know?' Matt asked. 'What makes you think he was lying?'

It was Aunt Jane who answered. 'Because your father never went to Robin's christening,' she said. 'And he never even knew . . .' She broke off. 'Harper wouldn't make that up. So Arnie told him that for a reason.'

'So that he'd repeat it to us,' Robin said. 'It's a message of some sort.'

'Indeed it is,' Venture agreed. 'He always did like cryptic messages and coded clues.'

'So what's it mean?' Matt asked.

'Maybe nothing,' Venture replied. 'Maybe it's simply a warning. To be on our guard. That there's something wrong.'

'Like we didn't know that already,' Matt retorted. But his mind was working furiously, looking for some clue – anything they'd listen to and act upon. 'Perhaps it's something to do with the message he left me,' he murmured, though he couldn't see what the connection might be.

He thought he'd said it quietly, too quietly for anyone else to pick up. But Robin had heard.

'What message, Matt?'

'He left me a message, on a website,' Matt explained. 'Like when I was a kid, he'd leave me clues. Like a treasure hunt,' he added, and immediately laughed at the irony of that. 'Anyway, the message just said he was in trouble and to go to Aunt Jane's, that she could help. And . . .' He hesitated.

'You never mentioned anything about this,' Aunt Jane said. 'You should have told me.'

Matt shrugged. 'I didn't know *what* to tell you. I wasn't really sure I'd understood, or what I could do. I didn't want to worry you. You know what Dad's like.'

'And?' Venture prompted.

'And I think he was telling me to come and see you,' Matt said to Venture. 'Telling me you could help.'

'Just as he told Harper,' Robin said. 'He's making sure we get involved.'

'But involved in what?' Matt wondered.

'We may be embarking on a dangerous journey, against forces we do not yet know or understand,' Venture said. 'And we must tread carefully.' He got up and went over to the window. He stood with his back to them, looking out across the lawn, watching the wind stirring the trees and playing with the fallen leaves. 'I gather you're pretty good with computers,' he said without turning.

It took Matt a moment to work out that Venture meant him. 'Er, yes. I s'pose.'

Venture turned now, and Matt was surprised to see that he was grinning. He rubbed his hands together. 'Then here's how we proceed,' he announced. 'Matt will transfer the data from Harper's disks to the main computer in the library. That's a network server so we can access that data from any screen in the house.' He paused for a moment, looking at Robin. 'Silicon chips,' he said quietly.

'Silicon is sand,' she replied.

Venture nodded. 'Never mind. We'll have to risk that. Everything's made of something after all.' This made no sense to Matt, but before he could ask what the man meant, Venture was talking again – fast and enthusiastic. 'Once we have access to the data, Robin and I can take a look at how far Arnold got and see where his researches take us. Harper assumes he was close to a breakthrough and the timing of his abduction bears that out.'

'How do you know?' Aunt Jane asked. Matt was surprised how businesslike she sounded now.

Venture shrugged. 'Why kidnap someone who's nowhere near finding what you want? No, they'd wait as late as they dared. The less they have to discover under coercion, the better for the abductor.'

'So there is a time constraint,' Robin said.

'We need more background,' Venture decided. 'And back-up. Jane, I think you should call Mr Smith and ask him if he can spare us an hour or two.'

She nodded, her face grave.

'Who's he?' Matt wanted to know.

Aunt Jane looked to Venture, who took his time choosing his words. 'Mephistopheles Smith,' he said at last, 'is a friend and former colleague of mine. He has a lot of influence in circles I choose not to move in. We go back a long way.'

There were six DVDs to be copied. Matt created a folder for each inside a top-level folder called 'St John'. The files on the DVDs were themselves divided into folders, and Matt was both pleased and saddened to recognize his father's mixture of shorthand and abbreviation in folder and file names. He wasn't surprised that Harper had felt the need to provide an additional crib sheet explaining what each file was.

It took a while to copy the data as the DVDs held far more than an ordinary CD-ROM – which was presumably why Harper had used them. So he'd need fewer disks. Matt spent the time between switching disks in browsing the internet. He did a search on the Treasure of St John and found there was very little about it. He saved what links he did find in another folder. There might be something useful that Dad had missed.

Lunch time came and went before he was done. Aunt Jane brought him a plate of sandwiches and a glass of Coke. It was mid-afternoon by the time he had finished setting up the folders, copying the files and cross-checking them against Harper's printed listing.

There were notes against each of the files on the list – some of which were written in a neat, feminine hand that was certainly not Dad's and Matt was willing to bet wasn't Harper's either. Matt typed these into the properties window for each file. That would save Venture from having to check back on the list. He kept the files in date order, in case there was a progression of thinking through the research. Some of the files were only two days old, he saw – Harper had given them everything he had, obviously keeping them right up to date on the hunt.

The afternoon was turning to evening by the time he finished. Matt ejected the final disk from the DVD drive and replaced it in its case. He found Venture and Robin in Venture's study. Venture was at his desk, reading an old leather-bound book. Several more volumes were open in front of him, and in one hand he held a fountain pen that seemed to be scratching notes on a pad without any attention from Venture as he read.

Robin was lying on her stomach on the floor. Her legs were bent up at the knees, her chin supported in her hands as she stared down at a large piece of parchment. Papers and books and maps and scrolls were spread out round her. She didn't seem to be taking notes.

'Ah, Matt,' Venture said without looking up from his book. 'Are you all finished?'

'Yeah. It's all on the computer now. In a folder called "St John". You should be able to see it from here.'

Venture glanced at the screen on his desk. He laid down his pen for long enough to move the mouse and type quickly into the keyboard. 'Thank you.'

'Anything else I can do?' Matt wondered.

'Thank you, no.'

Matt nodded, disappointed. He shifted his weight from one foot to the other, unsure what to do. Probably he should go.

'Dad,' Robin said. It sounded like a mild rebuke.

'That is, yes,' Venture corrected himself. 'I'm sorry. I'm used to having Robin and your aunt helping me out. I know you want to help too. There *is* something you can do.'

'Anything.'

'There's something I need. I wonder, could you fetch it for me?'

'Dad.' This time she sounded disappointed.

Which was pretty much how Matt felt about being sent to run errands.

✝

Venture's directions sounded straightforward enough. But once Matt reached the top of the stairs and turned left, he began to wonder if he would ever find what he was looking for. A small stone statue, about thirty centimetres high, Venture had told him. It was a carving, apparently of Sir Robert de Lisle, rescued from the Priory of Beauval in France after the buildings were destroyed by the invading Germans in 1939. Venture seemed to recall there was an inscription, or part of an inscription, on the base.

It seemed unlikely to Matt that it would help. But he was keen to show he could be of use. Get a simple task like this wrong and Venture would never trust him with something that did actually matter. He wondered how Venture came to have the statue, but the question fled from his mind as he opened the door to the room where the statue was supposed to be, and found himself looking into a linen cupboard.

There was no space for a statue, even a small one, among the folded sheets and blankets. Matt closed the door again and went back to the stairs. Fourth along on the right, Venture had said. He counted again, and it brought him back to the linen cupboard. He must have meant fourth room, not fourth door, Matt decided, and went to the next door along. Unless some of the rooms had more than one door, in which case . . .

He opened the door anyway. There should be a cupboard to the left of the window. It was difficult to tell if there was or not. The curtains were drawn and the room was a mass of shadows. Matt felt for the light switch and, as he pressed it, found himself staring into a room full of crates and packing cases. There were shelves and cupboards, tables and filing cabinets among the crates. Books were piled precariously in islands among the other odds and ends. There was what looked like a gargoyle staring out from a large chunk of weathered stone leaning against one wall.

And there was indeed a cupboard to the left of the window. It was actually quite a way to the left of the window, but it must be the one Venture had meant. If this was the right room.

Matt made his way carefully across to it. Dust seemed to swirl up around him, stirred into life by the faint breeze as he passed. And the cupboard was locked.

He knelt in front of it and tugged in vain at the handle. His fingers were black with dust and the knees of his trousers had gone grey. He stood up, tempted to kick the cupboard. But as he stood he saw the glint of metal on the shelf above it. A small key. Matt tried it in the lock and was relieved to find it turned easily. The door was stiff and he still had to tug hard at it to get the cupboard open.

But there was no statue inside. At first he thought the cupboard was empty. Annoyed, he reached inside and felt round. His fingers found a wooden box. Maybe the statue was inside a box. Certainly it was heavy enough, Matt thought, as he pulled it out and set it down on an empty patch of floor.

The box was plain, dark wood. But it was only about ten centimetres long and rectangular. The lid opened easily. Inside it looked almost like a CD case – but with just two upright slots. There was a disc in one of the two slots. But it was chunkier than a CD and made of heavy metal.

Matt lifted it out carefully. It was brass, or possibly bronze. Dad had told Matt that you could tell when something was really old, no matter how well preserved it was – you just knew. Matt knew that the disc was old. It was about the same diameter as a CD or DVD, but convex on both sides like a discus. The metal was cold to the touch and Matt could feel the texture of the embossed symbols standing proud of the surface of the disc – concentric circles of small carvings. Some looked like pictures, other were little more than raised dots or lines.

There was a stick figure of a man in the centre of one side and a pattern of wavy lines in the centre of the other. Matt felt the raised symbols with the tip of his index finger. Like Braille, he thought. But whatever it might actually be, it wasn't a stone statue of Robert de Lisle. So he carefully replaced the disc and put the box back in the cupboard.

He finally found the statue in a cupboard to the left of the window in the next room along the corridor. It was weathered and chipped. There were indeed the remains of an inscription along the base, but part of it had snapped off, and it was in antique French, so it meant nothing to Matt. He didn't think it would mean anything to Venture either, but he took the statue to him anyway.

Venture gestured for Matt to leave it on the desk. He didn't look up from his book. Robin was still kicking her legs and now skimming through a book, turning brittle yellowed pages far quicker than Matt could believe she was reading it. She raised a hand in a languid wave without looking.

'Thank you,' Venture said as Matt reached the door.

'No problem.'

'In the library,' Venture went on, still without looking up from his book, 'there is an account of the Siege of Malta. You'll find it in the catalogue on the computer.'

'You want me to get it?'

Venture put down the book and looked at Matt. 'No,' he said. 'I want you to read it. See if it's of any use.'

'The Siege of Malta.'

'That's right.'

'1565,' Robin said from the floor.

'And what am I looking for?'

'Well,' Venture said, 'if we knew that . . .' He was smiling. 'The Knights Hospitallers were expelled from Rhodes in 1523 and in 1530 the Emperor Charles V gave them the island of Malta. In May 1565, fewer than 600 knights held off an Ottoman force of over 30,000. One of those knights was Henri

Sivel.' He returned his attention to the book. 'It may be nothing, or it may be another link in the chain.'

Robin had rolled on to her back and was looking up at Matt, hands behind her head. 'It *is* important,' she said. 'Sivel went secretly to Nice after it fell to the Turks, led by Barbarossa, in 1543. Barbarossa fought the Knights Hospitallers from his youth. He may have been at Rhodes when the knights were forced out. So perhaps Sivel went to Nice to find Barbarossa – to try to retrieve the treasure, as he had vowed. If he succeeded . . .'

'Then the treasure would have been in Malta,' Matt said, to show he wasn't daft as much as anything. 'I'll take a look.'

✠

The book was, mercifully, in English. It was a translation of an older journal and account which might have been in French or Latin. The language was archaic and difficult, but not impossible.

Though it didn't seem to be a lot of use. Matt had the book open on the large, round table in the library. As the evening drew in he found he was leaning closer and closer to make out the faded writing. The library was well lit, but however he angled himself and the book he seemed to be reading in his own shadow.

Aunt Jane came to see how he was doing and, recognizing the problem, she brought him the candelabrum that Matt had seen the previous evening. Mephistopheles Smith was coming to visit Venture tomorrow morning, she told Matt. He nodded and thanked her and went back to tracing his finger down a list of the 592 knights who had defended Malta. The paper seemed even more yellow than before in the flickering light of the candles.

She watched him for a few moments, then Aunt Jane told Matt she'd get some tea ready and see him at home soon. He nodded, only half aware of what she had said. He had found Henri Sivel – a mention, no more. A name on a list. But he was there all right.

But that was where it seemed to end. There was no other mention of Sivel. No mention of a treasure. Even the siege, Matt was disappointed to learn, wasn't quite what he had expected. Yes, there had only been those 592 knights. But they had the help of a few thousand locals defending their island. And while the Ottoman force was indeed over 30,000 strong, that was less than half the number the Sultan had sent to take Rhodes. The Knights

Hospitallers were in the twilight of their time, even though, Matt knew from his internet reading, they remained in charge on Malta for another 200 years and more. They had fought off the attack, kept the enemy at bay until reinforcements arrived from Sicily. But their days were numbered. And reading the tired, almost clinical account of events, Matt sensed that they had themselves known that.

A shadow fell across the page he was reading. A hand closed on Matt's shoulder. He gave a cry of surprise and jumped out of his chair, twisting and turning sharply to throw off the sudden grip.

'Hey, you're jumpy,' Robin said. She held her hands up as if in surrender. 'I just came to see how you're getting on.'

'Sorry.' Matt sat down again, and Robin pulled up a chair to sit beside him at the table.

The candlelight flickered on her face and danced in her deep blue eyes. 'Any luck?'

'A mention of Sivel. Nothing much else, though.'

'Don't worry,' she said. 'We'll find it. And your father.' She put her hand on his shoulder, then pulled it quickly away again. 'Sorry.'

Matt smiled. His heart was still racing. 'That's OK. You startled me before. Like you said, I'm a bit jumpy.'

'Because of your dad.'

'Yeah. And because . . .' Should he tell her? 'Because of something that happened when I went home, to Dad's house.'

'Oh?'

'Probably nothing. Just imagination.'

'Tell me.'

He was afraid she'd laugh at him. But she sounded sincere and Matt was feeling more and more that he could trust the girl. Weird, yes. But friendly and helping him find Dad. Her deep eyes seemed to draw him in still further. So he told her.

'I went into Dad's study. When I first got to the house. I heard him in there. At least, I think I thought I did. I don't remember much. I must have fallen, slipped and banged my head. Or fainted. And maybe it was a dream.'

'What?'

'I thought someone had been there. Going through Dad's stuff.'

'Who was it? Did you recognize them?'

He shook his head. 'I didn't *see* anyone. Well, just a vague figure out the back. Watching the house, I thought. I can't be sure.' He shuddered as he remembered. 'But someone hit me, or smothered me. Put their hand over my mouth. That's why I was jumpy.'

She put her hand on his shoulder again, and this time she kept it there. 'I'm not surprised.'

'It was a rough hand. Not really like a hand at all, the texture I mean. Gritty and sharp.'

As he spoke, Matt was staring at the candle flames. Three tiny yellow shapes, dancing and flickering. They seemed to be leaning towards him, as if anxious to hear what he was saying, or to see what he had been reading. The shadows lengthened across the pages of the book as the flames moved.

'It felt like sandpaper,' Matt said.

He heard Robin gasp. Felt her hand whipped away from his shoulder. With a sudden movement, she stood up, leaned forward and blew out the candles. Thin trails of black smoke curled up from the dead wicks.

Her voice was a fearful, trembling whisper. 'You shouldn't have lit the candles,' she said.

7

At dinner, Aunt Jane alternated between saying nothing and talking non-stop. Nerves, Matt guessed. He felt the same. He wanted to talk about things – about Dad, and Atticus Harper and the Treasure of St John. But he had very little to say. Neither of them ate much and Matt cleared away plates of half-eaten lasagne.

'Didn't your father give you any idea where he was going?' Aunt Jane asked Matt, for the third time.

'I told you, I haven't spoken to him. Apart from the weird message he left me on that website. He's more likely to tell you what he's up to than me or Mum.'

Aunt Jane's expression suggested she didn't think this was really the case. But she didn't say so.

'Anyway,' Matt went on, 'wherever he was, he's not there now. Harper told us that.'

'*Mr* Harper,' Aunt Jane corrected him.

Matt sighed. 'Whatever. He'd done some work from home, I think.' He tried to look on the bright side. 'If we find the treasure first, maybe they'll just let him go, whoever these people are. Or if they find the treasure, they won't need Dad any more so they'll let him go anyway.' Not that Matt was convincing even himself. 'Do you think?' he added, doubtful.

'Let's hope so.'

'About all we can do,' Matt said glumly. 'Apart from help *Mr* Venture and Robin follow Dad's trail through documents and files.'

Aunt Jane looked at Matt sadly. 'Leave that to them,' she said.

'But I might be able to help. I can sort out the computers and organize the data for them.'

She turned away, so he couldn't see her face. 'I told you – I don't want you involved,' she said.

Matt went over to her and put his hand on her shoulder, remembering the warmth and sympathy of Robin's similar gesture. Aunt Jane turned round and he saw how sad she looked. He kept his hand on her shoulder, squeezing gently to reassure her that he wasn't cross or angry. He was sad, like her. 'It's my dad,' he told her. 'I may not see him much. I may not really understand him or listen to him, not all the time. But it's *Dad*. I've got to help.'

She put her hand over his. 'I know. He's an infuriating, stubborn idiot, with no common sense and no idea how any of us feel about him. But he's my brother and I love him, and so do you.' She sighed. 'And you're right. We have to help all we can.' She turned away and he only just caught her last words. 'Whatever the cost,' she said quietly.

✝

Matt thought he'd never get to sleep. He finished the book he'd borrowed from Aunt Jane, then he lay with the light out, listening to the wind howling round the cottage. There was going to be a storm. He thought about Robin closing the door and windows in Venture's study, about her anger and fear at the candles – what was that about? But before he could reach any sort of conclusion he had drifted into sleep. He woke with the wind still clawing at the windows and the curtains glowing with the early-morning sun.

He told Aunt Jane at breakfast about the candles. But she had no more idea about Robin's reaction than Matt did himself. 'Julius asked me to remove the carafe of water from his reading room,' she said. 'He always keeps water there. Perhaps they're just feeling the stress. Like we are.' She looked like she hadn't slept at all.

Further discussion was cut short by the sound of a car outside. In fact, it was two cars, as well as four motorbikes. Matt and Aunt Jane watched through the kitchen window as the convoy of vehicles swept up the drive to the manor house. Two enormous black limousines flanked by outriders in bulky yellow reflective jackets.

'Mephistopheles Smith,' Aunt Jane said. 'This will be his idea of travelling discreetly.'

'At least it isn't a helicopter,' Matt said.

✜

The business of running Venture's affairs had to go on. He was patron of several charities, was invited to give lectures and talks, write papers, review journal articles, meet with the great and the good – or at least the famous. Aunt Jane handled all these commitments and more. She managed his diary, organized his schedule, arranged his meals . . . So once again, despite the urgency of the quest for the

Treasure of St John, Matt would be left to his own devices.

They walked up to the manor house together, struggling against the wind that seemed determined to drive them back, away from the house.

'They say that if the leaves start to fall this early, then we're in for a cold autumn and winter,' Aunt Jane said as they reached the shelter of the porch. 'But then, they always say that.'

Matt did not answer. He was looking at the cars and motorbikes parked outside. Stony-faced motorcyclists, still wearing their helmets, stood almost to attention beside their bikes. He imagined that similarly serious drivers were at the steering wheels of the two cars. But the windows were tinted, so you couldn't see in. Matt assumed they could see out, guessed they were watching him every step of the way to the porch.

Standing at the door was a man in a dark suit. It was a dull blustery day, but the man was wearing sunglasses. Like the drivers in the cars, his eyes watched without being seen. The thin lips pursed into the semblance of a smile and the man pushed open the front door for them.

'Thanks,' Matt said.

The man had already turned away, all trace of the smile gone.

Another man in sunglasses stood outside the closed door to Venture's study. He might have been the first man's brother, they were so similar. Even down to the expressionless face.

Aunt Jane clicked her tongue in annoyance. 'Mr Smith is always so melodramatic.'

'What's he do?' Matt asked.

'Who knows? Some sort of adviser to the government, I think. A spin doctor or a Whitehall mandarin or something.'

'Do you know what Mr Smith does?' Matt asked the blank-faced man at the door.

The sunglasses angled slightly towards Matt. 'I really couldn't say.'

'He doesn't know either,' Matt told Aunt Jane.

She smiled sympathetically. 'He said he couldn't say, not that he doesn't know. Come and find me if you get bored. I'm sure there's lots you can do to help me out.'

She didn't want him spending time with Robin, Matt thought. But he kept his expression as blank as the men in sunglasses. 'Will do. See you, then.'

He found Robin was already in the library, sitting exactly where he had left her the previous evening. The book giving the account of the Siege of Malta was still open on the table, but now it was surrounded by other books and documents. There was a small laptop open in the middle of it all, looking rather out of place. Matt could see that it was displaying images of some of his father's handwritten notes.

Robin glanced up as Matt approached. She looked pale and tired.

'You been here all night?' Matt asked. He meant it as a joke.

But Robin nodded, and, looking at her, Matt could believe she had not actually slept at all. Maybe not even left the room. 'We've made good progress,' she said.

He sat down next to her and surveyed the mass of papers and volumes. 'Tell me about it.'

'We're narrowing the options,' she said. 'Dad was here too, until Smith arrived just now.' She shifted a couple of books, moved a pile of papers. 'It's odd. Weird.'

'What is?'

'Your dad's work. I mean, it seems like it's all there, but he jumps to conclusions in a way that really isn't like him at all.'

'You'd know, would you?' Another joke that she answered seriously.

'So my dad tells me. But anyway, he follows leads that don't seem to be the best option really, yet time and again he turns out to be right.'

'Luck?'

'A lot of it. He also discards what seem like the best leads, again without any apparent explanation. Just gives up on them, or glosses over obvious clues. There's a mention of Sivel being in Brittany in 1567, for example, though he must have been quite old by then. But he just ignores it. Doesn't even mention it in his notes, but he must have known because he's catalogued the diary of the Duc de Malpores that includes the account.'

'So what are you telling me?' Matt asked. 'What are you saying?'

She shrugged. 'I don't know. Maybe we don't have all his notes. Or maybe he didn't write everything down.'

Matt picked up the nearest book. It was a small,

leather-bound journal written in faded ink and in a language he didn't recognize. 'You said you'd made good progress,' he prompted. He put the book down again and gave Robin his full attention.

As she spoke, the tiredness seemed to slip away and soon her deep blue eyes were shining with enthusiasm and energy. 'Henri Sivel vowed to retrieve the treasure after it was taken by the Turks,' she said.

'Yeah, we sort of figured that yesterday. We thought maybe he was in Nice when the city fell to get the treasure back from Barbarossa or something.'

'That's right. Sivel thought – we assume – that Barbarossa had taken it. And it seems that Sivel was successful, that he found the treasure again. There is the fact that you discovered he was on Malta in 1565. Your father also found an entry in a journal kept by one of the knights that mentions his arrival.'

Robin pulled the little laptop towards her and paged through several documents, looking for the one she wanted. 'Here we are. See.' She read from the screen, running her finger under the text as she did so: 'Henri Sivel, of this order, arrived yesterday and with him brought a great gift the value of which cannot be overstated.'

'That's in Latin,' Matt pointed out.

'So?'

'So you read Latin?'

'Obviously. I'm good at languages. I have a good teacher.'

'Where do you go to school?' Matt wondered. He doubted it was nearby. And anyway, the state schools hadn't broken up yet.

'Does it matter?'

'Sorry. Go on. Henri Sivel brought a great gift to Malta. No prizes for guessing what it might be, right?'

'Right. Then Sivel isn't mentioned again. But his gift is. Or at least, your father assumed that it was his gift . . .' She closed the file on the laptop and opened another one. 'Here are his notes. He believes that the reference in 1568 to "certain divers papers and artefacts" that were taken from Malta for safe-keeping refers to Sivel's gift, to the treasure.'

'And why does he think that?'

'You tell me. But assuming he is right, it was taken with a group of the knights who left to found another centre for the order. We aren't told who went, but your father discovered a sort of roll call for all the remaining knights taken two years later, in 1570.'

She sounded excited and Matt was finding himself caught up in her enthusiasm. 'Of course,' he said, 'so we can compare the list of who was left with the list of who was at the siege in 1565, and that'll tell us who's gone off in that time.'

'That's right. And Sivel is not included in the later list. But before you get too carried away, that doesn't mean he went off with these knights to some other centre. Or even if he did that the treasure went too. It just means he was no longer there. He could have left for some other reason, or even died in the meantime. Or the list might not be complete. We just don't know.'

'But it's something, isn't it?' Matt said, trying not to get disappointed. 'It's a possibility.'

Robin nodded. 'And one that your father took to be a probability. He followed it up quite vigorously, and found several mentions of a group of wandering Hospitallers at various times and places across Europe. He even drew a map. Look.'

She dug round in the papers on the table and eventually extricated a sheet of modern paper with a map of Europe on it. 'I printed it out, complete with your father's estimates of the routes they might have taken.'

Matt examined the map. It had a dotted red line running from Malta to Brittany. There the line split into several lines. One headed for Italy, one across the Channel to England and on up to Scotland. Another was dotted across land up into Scandinavia, while a fourth headed back towards the south of France.

'Just some of the possibilities,' Robin said. 'Presumably the ones he thought were most likely, for whatever reasons.'

Each line ended in a red cross. 'X marks the spot?' Matt suggested.

'*Possible* spot.' Robin pointed to the cross in Scotland. 'That's Rosslyn, which he discounted as just too convenient.'

'Why?'

'Supposed to be where the Holy Grail is, according to one set of opinions and legends. There's a fascinating chapel there, and it all relates to the Knights Templar.'

'Wrong order,' Matt agreed.

'And wrong period – the chapel was actually built far too late. But that still leaves these others, though.' She pointed to them in turn. 'Pomponini, an old Roman town. Valdeholm, which is actually a little island with lots of churches on it. And Pont St Jean, which does at least have an echo of St John in its name, but that could be coincidence. And the knights may have moved on from any of these places, taking the treasure with them.'

'Or they may have been to none of them,' Matt said.

'And even if they were there, they might not have had the treasure with them anyway.'

'And you call this progress?' Matt said. He punched her gently on the shoulder and grinned. 'Just kidding.' But there was something at the back of his mind; something that Robin had said stirred the dust in his brain, reminded him of something. Something important, Matt thought. If he could only remember what it was.

Robin stood up. 'I could do with a break.'

'Good idea.' He'd almost had it then, but the memory scuttled away so he barely caught sight of it. Just a shadow in the corner of his mind.

☩

Robin wanted to get some air, probably to wake herself up after the night's work. She had pulled her long black hair back into a ponytail, which made her look younger. Matt wondered again how old she really was. Fifteen, maybe.

They reached the hallway just as the door to

Venture's study opened and a man stepped out. Matt could see that the curtains were drawn and the lights were on, although it was bright and sunny outside now, but his attention was on the small, round man who smiled amiably at him. He had dark hair slicked back from a high forehead and he wore small, round, dark-tinted glasses that hid his eyes. It was only as he blinked that Matt caught anything from behind the lenses. Standing beside the tall, broad-shouldered bodyguard whose eyes were covered by designer sunglasses invited comparisons that did the man no favours.

'You must be Matt,' he said, and his voice was surprisingly deep and rich.

'Yes,' Matt said. 'Hi. You must be Mr Smith.'

The small man nodded enthusiastically. 'I must indeed, yes. And in fact, I am.' He thrust out a podgy hand. 'Delighted to meet you, young man.'

The grip was strong and firm and as Matt shook the man's hand he felt he was being carefully scrutinized.

'I met your father a few times,' Smith said. 'Oh, many years ago now. Be assured I shall do everything in my power to help Julius find him for you.'

'Thanks. That's . . .'

But Matt didn't finish. Smith had already moved

past him to give Robin a hug. She kissed him on both cheeks, and Matt was surprised at how he resented the attention she gave the man. Who was he anyway? He realized that Venture was standing beside him now.

'Having Mephistopheles on our side is a great help,' he told Matt. 'I wasn't sure he would remember your father. He has so many things to deal with.'

'What's he do?' Matt asked quietly.

But Smith heard him and turned with a smile. 'Do? Why, practically nothing. I am a facilitator, an adviser. I tell others what *they* should do. Heaven forbid I should have to do anything myself.' He laughed and clapped his hands on his ample stomach. 'I really don't think any sort of strenuous exercise would suit me at all, do you?' Then, just as suddenly as he had become amused, he was serious again. His glasses seemed to darken as he addressed Venture: 'Take care, Julius,' he said. 'I agree with you that there is more to this than at first appears.'

'Like what?' Matt asked.

'Well, that's the question, isn't it?' Smith told him. 'It depends rather on what the Treasure of St John really consists of.'

'If it still exists,' Robin said.

'Oh, it exists all right. Otherwise there wouldn't be all this fuss and bother. Someone is getting close to discovering the old secrets,' he added darkly.

'You what?' Matt said.

'Be on your guard,' Smith added, ignoring Matt's comment. 'How long has it been windy outside?'

It seemed a ridiculous question in the circumstances, but Venture answered it seriously. 'Several days.'

'Since before Harper came to you?'

'Yes.'

Smith nodded, as if his worst fears had been confirmed. 'Then someone knows. They know about Harper and they knew he was coming to you. And they know something already of what they hope to discover when they find the treasure.'

'And what's that?' Matt asked.

'Ancient knowledge,' Smith said. 'Matters that are best left untouched.'

'How do you know?'

'It's elementary,' Smith told him. He smiled as if this was a joke. 'You take care now. All of you.' He shook hands with Venture, gave a brief wave to Matt and Robin, and then left. His bodyguard followed without comment or expression.

'What an odd man,' Matt said as soon as he had gone.

From outside came the sound of the cars and motorbikes starting up.

'He probably thinks you're weird too,' Robin said. Which was pretty rich coming from her, but Matt didn't say so.

'Keep the curtains drawn and the doors shut,' Venture told Matt and Robin. He seemed not to have heard their brief exchange of views about Smith. 'No candles, no naked flames. Drink only when you have to, and well away from your notes and researches.' He went back into his study and closed the door.

'What's he on about?' Matt asked Robin. 'What is it with the candles?'

Robin looked pale. She pulled nervously at her long dark hair. 'Just . . .' She shook her head. 'Just be careful,' she said.

8

Doors stayed closed and curtains drawn. It made the large house seem oppressive and claustrophobic despite its size. Matt found that he was getting nervous and jumpy – paranoid, more like, he thought. He too closed doors behind him, saw vague faces in the patterns of rain spattered against the windows and quickly drew the curtains. He felt draughts in rooms where the air was still and warm, and he caught his breath anxiously as dust stirred when a door opened.

By the afternoon he was ready to leave the books and papers that Venture and Robin had set him to catalogue and return to Aunt Jane's cottage. It looked more like autumn than midsummer outside. Leaves were strewn across the lawn and the trees looked brittle and bare. The sun seemed to be struggling to make an impression through the skittering clouds and Matt wished he'd worn a coat.

Another sound mingled with the gusting wind and creaking trees, a deep throbbing that Matt could feel reverberating inside his chest. He could see a car speeding up the driveway as if it was still on the main road. A low silver sports car with headlights that bulged up from the sleek bonnet like the eyes of a frog. The sound of its engine grew louder and deeper as it swung round the outside curve of the drive and started up the incline towards the house.

Matt stepped back into the porch and let the car screech to a halt outside. A shower of gravel flew from its braking wheels. The engine gave a final roar, then faded. The driver's door opened and a woman got out. She made climbing out of the low seat seem easy and natural. She was wearing black trousers and a bright red leather jacket that perfectly matched her lipstick. She was tall and slim and confident, striding towards where Matt was standing. Her pale features were narrow and angular and her green eyes were shaped like a cat's. The most striking thing about her was her hair. It was cut into a neat bob just above her shoulders, the ends curling back on themselves, so it seemed moulded rather than brushed into shape. It was so blonde it was almost white.

'You must be Matt,' the woman said. She reached out to shake Matt's hand, and he was surprised how icily cold her grip was. The woman tilted her head to one side as she looked at him. 'You're the image of your father.' She didn't wait for a reply, but walked briskly past him and into the house.

+

Two hours later, Matt was on a plane.

The woman's name was Katherine Feather and she was Atticus Harper's Personal Assistant. Matt could hear the capital letters as she said it. She spent twenty minutes with Venture before they all gathered again in the study.

'Mr Harper is concerned,' Katherine Feather explained. 'It seems that somehow news has leaked out that you are working for him.'

Venture held up his hand to stop her. 'We are not working for Mr Harper,' he said quietly. 'We are working *with* Mr Harper. Helping him. That isn't the same thing at all.'

Katherine smiled thinly. 'Whatever you say. But the point is, the opposition will now know about you.'

'This mysterious opposition we hear about so much and know so little about,' Venture said. 'And what can you tell us about them, Miss Feather?'

The thin smile did not falter. 'Not much, I'm afraid. We hear rumours, half-truths. I think Mr Harper believes it is an organized crime syndicate from Eastern Europe.'

'Why would they be interested?' Matt wondered.

Katherine shrugged. 'Money? It's not my area. But the important point, surely, is that we should be on our guard.'

'Are you saying we're in danger?' Robin asked.

'Does it matter if they know?' Matt asked. He was torn between feeling that the woman was being melodramatic and the knowledge that Dad was missing and probably in danger. 'We're not giving up, not stopping.'

'Of course you're not,' she said. 'But Mr Harper feels that it might be appropriate at this point if he offered you his hospitality and his protection.'

'Does he?' Venture seemed amused at the idea. 'And why is that? At this point.'

'Several reasons.' If she was irritated by the question, she gave no sign of it. 'Mr Harper's facilities are likely to be more secure than your own home.'

'That will be the facilities where Matt's father was working, will it?' Robin said sarcastically. 'He was really safe.'

'And he wasn't there when he went missing,' Katherine said without looking away from Venture. 'If he had been there, I imagine he would still be working, quite safely, for Mr Harper. He extends that promise of safety to you as well. As you'll discover, our enemies – whoever they are, and however organized and well resourced they might be – won't be able to interfere once we arrive at Mr Harper's residence. It is quite, quite safe and secure, I promise you.'

'You seem very certain of that,' Venture said. 'How well placed is that confidence, I wonder?'

'Come with me and you'll find out,' she replied calmly. 'And, of course, you will have the added benefit of being able to see at first hand the documents and notes that so far you have only had copies of.'

'And,' Venture told her levelly, 'Mr Harper will have the added benefit of being able to keep an eye on us and see how the work is progressing.'

The thin smile returned. 'He would like to keep in touch with your progress, that's true. You can hardly blame him for that.'

'And where is Mr Harper based?' Aunt Jane asked. 'Assuming Mr Venture decides to accept, there will be travel arrangements.'

'He has a facility in South America. In the depths of the rainforest. As I said, it's hardly on a normal travel agent's itinerary, and anyone looking for you is unlikely to find us. The arrangements are all taken care of. One of Mr Harper's private planes is already at Staverton on the assumption,' she said to Venture, 'that you accept his invitation.'

'That's quite an assumption,' Venture told her.

'It's quite an invitation,' she replied.

Matt frowned. Something she had said had struck a chord deep in his memory. Again, it was just out of reach, but it was there. Whatever had worried him earlier was close to the surface, but still not quite close enough.

'The Itzacan Palace?' Venture was saying. He sounded impressed. 'I'd heard Harper was working on its restoration. I would be very interested to see how his project has progressed. So, in that case, Robin and I shall be delighted to accept.'

'Good. Then I shall let Mr Harper know that he has two guests for dinner tonight.'

'Three guests,' Matt said firmly. 'I've got my passport in my bag. I'm coming too.' He met Aunt Jane's stare, saw the sadness and resignation in her eyes, and knew that while she didn't want him to go she wouldn't stop him.

☩

The plane was more like a hotel suite than a jet liner. Rather than rows of seats jammed in, there were several large leather couches arranged round the walls and a large conference table in the middle of the cabin. A steward brought drinks and food during the long flight, and there was a huge plasma-screen television hooked up to a DVD player.

Chatting to Robin, and with the prospect of watching DVDs of the latest blockbusters, Matt could almost forget about Dad's plight. Almost.

'Have you heard of this place we're going to, this palace?' he asked Robin while her father and Katherine Feather were talking quietly at the conference table.

She nodded. 'Oh yes. It's also known as the Waterfall Pyramid.'

'Why?' Matt asked.

'Because it's a step pyramid. And it's beside a waterfall,' Robin said levelly.

'Imaginative, then.'

'It's been hidden in the depths of the Amazon jungle for centuries. Millennia, probably. Until Harper found it a few years ago. It caused quite a stir in the archaeological world. It's spectacular.'

'That why it caused a stir?'

'Not entirely. It was the way he found it that ruffled a few feathers.'

Matt was intrigued. 'Go on.'

'There's a theory that many ancient sites were built in specific places around the globe.'

'Aligned with the sunrise and all that?'

'More than that. Have you heard of ley lines?'

Matt had. Ley lines were supposed to be lines of some sort of force or magnetism that linked ancient sites and might explain why they were built in particular places. Some people claimed to be able to find them by dowsing, while others said they were all a load of nonsense.

'Well,' Robin went on, 'it's a step up from ley lines, if you like. The theory suggests there might have been some ancient blueprint or plan, and that important ancient sites are built on specific points of longitude and latitude according to that blueprint.'

'Sounds crazy to me,' Matt said. 'I mean, weren't

some of these sites built centuries apart?'

'Thousands of years apart. You know the North Pole has moved?' she asked.

Matt seemed to remember something about it. 'Didn't it used to be over in northern Canada or something, in Hudson Bay? Like thousands of years ago.'

'That's right. And if you measure the angle between the old pole and the current position of the North Pole from Stonehenge, you find it's 46 degrees.'

'So?'

'So Stonehenge is located at a latitude of 46 degrees.'

'Coincidence.'

She shrugged. 'Perhaps. We mentioned Rosslyn this morning. The angle from Rosslyn is 50 degrees.'

'And am I right in guessing that Rosslyn's latitude is also 50 degrees?'

'Absolutely. So maybe the newer monuments are built on sites that were already identified and special. Like Canterbury Cathedral, which gives an angle and a latitude of 45 degrees, and is built on the site of an ancient pagan temple. Or maybe . . .'

'What?' he prompted.

'Maybe they really were according to some grand plan or other.'

Matt laughed. 'You can probably take a dozen sites and prove there's some sort of relationship between their locations,' he said. 'You can prove anything with numbers and maths.'

'True. Which is why Harper tried a different approach. There have been a few people before, like Rand Flem-Ath, who have worked out where key positions should be and then checked to see if there's an ancient site there.'

'Sort of reverse engineering.'

'Sort of. What Harper did was to take a site in the middle of nowhere, a set of coordinates where, according to the model, there should be something but there isn't. Or at least, no one could tell that there was, not from satellite pictures anyway. And you couldn't easily go there and see.'

'Why not?'

'Because,' Robin said, 'the site was in the middle of the South American jungle.'

'Ah.' Matt understood now. 'This place we're headed to now, that's how he found it?'

'He spent a fortune on an expedition. Everyone,

or nearly everyone, said he was mad. He went there, and sure enough, underneath what turns out to be the third biggest waterfall in the world, he found the Itzacan Palace.'

Matt was grinning, suddenly excited. 'And we're going there?'

Robin was grinning too. 'We're going there.'

✠

Matt had been on planes before, but apart from a holiday in Florida with his mum a couple of years before, he'd not been on such a long flight. He doubted that twelve hours in a commercial airliner would have passed so pleasantly as the time in Harper's jet. He was tired and they were flying through the night. He knew there would be a long journey once they left the plane, so after talking to Robin and watching a movie on DVD – a block-buster that wasn't even out in the cinema in Britain yet – Matt tried to get some sleep.

The lights were dimmed for the middle hours of the flight. But Matt found his mind was alive with the excitement and novelty of it all. He felt guilty at enjoying himself when Dad could be in deadly dan-ger. But there was nothing he could do about it.

Everyone else seemed to have gone to sleep. Robin must be exhausted after working through much of the previous night, and even her father seemed to be taking a nap.

At last Matt slipped into a doze. He woke several times and thought that he could not have slept much at all. But when he woke again and checked his watch he found he'd been asleep for nearly three hours. The main cabin lights had come back on and the sound of the engines changed as the plane started to descend towards Rio de Janeiro.

Through the windows, Matt could see the famous statue of Christ standing, arms out-stretched, above the city. Skyscrapers rose against a backdrop of ragged mountains. Modern and ancient thrust together.

Matt was disappointed that they weren't spend-ing any time in the city. But that disappointment was tempered by his desire to get on with finding the Treasure of St John – with finding Dad. He fol-lowed Robin down the steps from the plane and the heat hit him with a physical intensity. He hoped that Harper had installed air conditioning in his ancient palace.

After a brief wait in a private lounge in the airport, they continued the journey by helicopter. The contrast could not have been greater – from relaxing, luxurious space to a noisy, cramped cabin. Matt was jammed between Robin and Katherine Feather. Whenever he moved, he rubbed against one of them and became more and more embarrassed. When he felt the urge to scratch his ankle, it became a major operation watched by the others with undisguised amusement.

But the view was worth the discomfort of a few hours. Right from the noisy, shuddering take-off, Matt was transfixed. He was glad he was sitting in the middle now, as he had a good view out of both sides of helicopter. On the one side he could see the golden sand of the beach, covered with tiny people sunbathing. On the other was the view of the mountains. It seemed to take for ever to rise up high enough to fly over the hills and mountains and leave Rio behind. The roads became fewer and narrower, the mountains even more craggy, the open spaces larger and wider. Soon any sign of civilization was rare. Matt had lost all track of time as they dipped between mountains, flew along a narrow valley, over a lake . . . And there, stretched out in all directions, was the green and brown carpet of the rainforest.

They had been flying low over the jungle for a while. It was like skimming above heads of broccoli, the vegetation was so dense. There were occasional breaks, rivers and streams, even once a narrow road snaking through. But for the most part the jungle was uninterrupted.

Then suddenly the vegetation seemed to surge towards them. A mountain thrust up out of the jungle, its top a ragged plateau as if it had been bitten off. The jungle clung to the slopes, so that until they were relatively close it was hidden against the backdrop of the jungle floor. There was what looked like a small rectangle of grey at the base of the mountain. It was only as they approached that Matt realized how enormous this clearing was – like a giant patio in the middle of a neglected garden.

Closer still, the rotors throbbing through the thick earphones Matt was wearing, and the grey resolved itself into stone. And on the stone stood broken walls and ruined buildings. The helicopter banked, throwing Matt heavily against Robin. But neither of them noticed. They were staring out of the cabin window.

Because now, as they angled round the mountain,

they were close enough to see the white, foaming torrent of water that gushed from the upper slope of the mountain and crashed down in a tremendous waterfall into a clear blue lake beside the grey stone ruins.

'Where does the water come from?' Matt wondered in amazement.

She could not have heard him, but Katherine shouted the answer above the sound of the engines. 'The mountain is an extinct volcano. The plateau might look solid, but under the vegetation is a huge caldera – the mountain is almost hollow. Several streams and small rivers feed into it and the rainwater builds up. It's forced out through the waterfall. Spectacular, isn't it?' she added unnecessarily.

Now they had passed the waterfall, the helicopter turned again and headed back towards it. From this side, they could now see behind the waterfall, into the space between the water pouring out and the mountainside. The sun was shining through the water, making it sparkle like solid silver. It arced out from the lower slopes of the mountain and there behind it, below the point where the water emerged, the mountain had been carved away. On a shelf of rock hidden behind the waterfall was a huge pyramid. Its four sides were massive steps of rock, like a staircase leading up into the very heart of the volcano.

The Waterfall Pyramid.

And as the helicopter swung in towards the shelf of rock, the sunlight filtering through the surging water cast the shimmering shadow of the edge of the pyramid against the naked rock behind it – the stepped walls echoing the shape of the waterfall, created out of light and shadow.

The helicopter was dwarfed by the pyramid as it came to rest on the shelf of rock. Matt was amazed it had fitted behind the waterfall. They had been so close he reckoned he could have reached out of the cabin window and touched the water. The whole side of the glass bubble that was the cabin was spattered with drops of water. It reminded Matt of the window of the train on the way from school – the patterns and shapes of water on glass . . .

Two enormous stone archways stood alone and impassive between the helicopter and the pyramid. They framed a huge doorway into the massive structure. And standing in the doorway, a tiny figure in the middle of the ancient grandeur, was Atticus Harper.

Katherine in particular was keen to get out of the heat and hurried them inside. Once through the heavy, polished steel doors, Matt found himself inside a structure that was a strange mixture of ancient and modern. Whereas in Venture's house the old and the new seemed to coexist side by side, here the contrast was so marked that he wondered if it was deliberate.

The doors opened into a large foyer from which a massive stone staircase rose to the floors above. It looked more like the sort of thing you'd find in a National Trust property than in the middle of an ancient South American pyramid.

The floors were slabbed with stone, like a medieval castle. Windowless stone walls were hung with modern art as well as photographs of archaeo-logical sites and paintings of ancient monuments. Katherine Feather's voice echoed as she told them this was Atticus Harper's centre of operations and corporate headquarters.

'Not that there are many people here,' she said as she led the way up the stone staircase. 'But the building provides accommodation and recreation facilities as well as office space. When the city on the plain outside has been mapped and excavated, we might move some of the people out there.'

'Wouldn't that destroy the archaeology?' Matt wondered.

'The secret is to use the space sympathetically,' Venture said. 'I doubt this staircase, for example, is an original feature.'

'Hardly,' Robin agreed.

'Mr Harper will do whatever is best,' Katherine said. 'He is in the business of preserving and enhancing the past, not destroying it.' She led them from the stairs along a corridor. 'We have given you rooms just down here.'

The flagged stone floor of Matt's room was covered with a deep, soft Persian rug. A plasma-screen television even bigger than the one on Harper's private jet was hung on the wall opposite the bed. The bed itself was surrounded by velvet curtains and might have come from a five-star hotel, while the furniture – wardrobes and cabinets – was polished wood. The bathroom was modern, with marble tiles, a shower, a deep bath that was almost a mini swimming pool, and chrome taps and fittings.

His bag was already at the foot of the bed, and

Katherine Feather told him that she would collect him for dinner in half an hour.

After only twenty minutes, there was a knock at the door. It was Robin. The door opened normally from the inside, but outside was a numeric keypad on which you had to enter a code to get in.

Robin looked round the room. She didn't seem terribly impressed. 'Mine's pretty much the same,' she said. 'I'm next door, that way.' She pointed through the TV screen. 'My code's 0118.'

'And why are you telling me that?' Matt asked.

She shrugged. 'I don't like locks and bolts and codes. It's for information, not an invitation.'

'Fine. The code for my room is –'

'0116,' Robin interrupted confidently.

Matt smiled. 'No, it isn't. It's 1601.'

But Robin didn't seem upset to be wrong. She nodded as if this made perfect sense. 'They reverse the pairs so it isn't a progression. Makes sense.'

'Not to me,' Matt admitted. 'What are you on about?'

She sighed, like a teacher trying to be patient with a slow pupil. 'My room is the ninth along this corridor, which you'll have noticed runs the length of the first floor of the building. The system they use to derive the codes is that they double the room number – so double the nine and you get 18. Floor 01, room 18. So it's 0118.'

'And my room is the eighth. Double that is 16. So it should be 0116. Like you said.'

'Except they must swap the pairs of numbers every other room so there isn't such an obvious progression. Instead of floor one room eight, you're room eight on floor one. So double the eight and it's 16, *then* add the floor number 01 after that. You get 1601. Simple.'

'Yeah. Simple.' Anyone else and he'd have suspected they were making it up as they went along. But somehow he knew that Robin was right. 'You worked that out pretty quickly,' he said.

She brushed off the comment. 'I didn't work it out at all. It's obvious.'

Katherine found them a few minutes later. 'It's nice to see you two children getting along so well,' she said.

Robin's lips tightened and Matt guessed she wasn't happy being called a child. But Katherine seemed not to notice, and led them back along the corridor to the impressive stone staircase they had climbed from the entrance hall.

'So how much of this was already here?' Matt asked her. 'I mean, were all the rooms and everything just like this?'

'Oh no.' Katherine didn't look back as she led them down the stairs. 'The pyramid was completely hollow. A single huge chamber. Empty.'

'So Mr Harper built the internal structure.'

'Completely.'

'Impressive,' Matt said.

'I'm sure he'll be pleased you think so.'

'Why did he bother?' Robin asked.

Katherine's foot hesitated over the last step. 'What do you mean?'

'Like Matt said, it's impressive. But why go to all the trouble? Why bother?'

She did turn to face them now. 'You can ask him that as well. But this is Mr Harper's base of operations. He runs all his businesses from here, and all his archaeological work too.'

'Not many staff,' Robin said.

'You'd be surprised. Just because you haven't seen people doesn't mean they're not here. This is a big place. There are offices, kitchens, accommodation. The whole of the sixth floor is a computer suite, housing the servers that control and monitor and record every aspect of Mr Harper's work through-out the world. All his other subsidiaries and offices and employees can link into here.'

'I'd like to see that,' Matt said.

Katherine nodded. 'Yes, I'm sure you would. I'll see what we can arrange. But later. Now, you must be hungry. I know I am.'

╬

They saw the first of the 'staff' when they arrived at dinner. Katherine led them down the stairs and then through the entrance foyer, along a wide stone-walled corridor until they reached a set of double doors. The corridor continued, but the doors were obviously where they were headed. Two large men dressed in khaki-coloured camouflage uniforms stood one either side of the doors.

'Expecting trouble?' Matt asked.

'Not at all,' Katherine assured them. 'Mr Klein's security team is here for just that. Security. There is not a lot of official law and order out here. We had a bit of trouble with one of the local tribes when we first arrived. Nothing serious, and they soon moved on to another part of the rainforest. They keep well away now and leave us to our own devices. But it's as well to be careful.'

'And Mr Harper is an important man,' Robin said.

'Indeed,' Katherine agreed. 'He has many business rivals. Some of them have very questionable business practices.'

'Unlike Mr Harper,' Robin said.

Katherine seemed to take her at her word. 'Quite.' She gestured for them to go in to dinner.

Atticus Harper and Julius Venture were already seated at the dining table and deep in conversation. The room was like the banqueting hall of a medieval castle, dominated by a long wooden table and with a gallery running round the upper level. There were alcoves round the stone walls under the gallery, and in each of these was a painting or photograph spot-lit by a bright halogen lamp set into the stonework above.

'The pyramid is formed of seventy-two steps in all,' Harper was saying. 'I'm sure I don't need to explain the significance of that.'

'And I notice that the area outside, where we landed, is composed of 366 stone slabs,' Venture said. 'One of which is a quarter the size of the others. Representing the 365 and a quarter days in a year.'

'You must count very quickly,' Harper said. 'But

yes, the ancient people, who originally built this structure, knew more than most people credit.'

Katherine led Matt and Robin to seats next to each other at the table, which was covered with bowls and dishes containing fruit and salad and cold meats.

'What's so special about there being seventy-two steps?' Matt asked as he began to help himself to food. He hadn't realized till now how hungry he was.

'Precession,' Robin replied.

'You what?'

It was Robin's father who answered. 'The earth wobbles very slightly on its axis as it spins,' he explained. 'So the point at which the sun rises and sets and the constellations too all appear to move very slowly back and forth across the sky as the earth tilts back and forth. It's called precession.'

'And the sky moves one degree every seventy-two years,' Robin finished.

'You really think the people who built this place knew that?' Matt asked.

'Undoubtedly,' Harper told him. 'And not just because of the seventy-two steps. That could be coincidence, though it is a number repeated often enough throughout ancient architecture. The number seventy-two crops up again and again, along with pictograms of the constellations, at various points in history. But then there is also the way the pyramid is aligned exactly on the points of the compass, as are certain of the carvings in the outer stonework, and the buildings in the town below. This building and the associated town are a message passed down through history.' He leaned forward, resting his arms on the table, fixing Matt with a piercing gaze. 'And everything about it speaks of the passage of time. The number of slabs in the causeways equals the days in the year – the earth's journey round the sun, as Julius mentioned. Also the blocks in each layer of the pyramid are multiples of twenty-four – the hours in each of those days. The buildings in the town are laid out in sets of seven. And it was all constructed close to fifteen hundred years ago.' He leaned back and smiled, his point made.

'I suppose the real surprise,' Venture said, 'is that the site isn't older. At this position, with the level of astrological and temporal detail you describe, I'd have expected remains dating back rather further.'

Harper's eyes narrowed. 'Really? And how much further, would you expect?'

Venture smiled. 'Oh, about 11,000 years. What's for dinner?'

The enthusiasm Harper had for his pyramid palace was obvious throughout the meal. Venture and Robin quizzed him on all aspects of the pyramid and the details of how he had discovered and then renovated it. Matt soon bored of the details, and instead tried to make out each of the pictures in the alcoves, guessing what they might be. Katherine Feather said little, probably having heard it all before. She caught Matt's eye and smiled. He smiled back.

There was only one picture that Matt had not been able to examine surreptitiously. He had spot-ted paintings of ancient Egypt, photographs of the pyramid they were in being cleared of creepers and jungle plants, and a map of the world with dots on it to represent ancient sites or maybe Harper's offices. But he had not turned to look immediately behind him, and Matt knew there was a picture there. He had glanced at it on his way in. He twisted in his chair in an effort to see it without attracting attention.

He failed dismally. Harper saw at once what he was doing and called down the table, 'That is Lieutenant-Colonel Percy Fawcett.'

Matt didn't bother trying to pretend he hadn't been looking. He twisted round properly in the chair to look at the picture. It was a black and white photograph of a man in a heavy coat and fur hat. He had a dark beard and eyebrows that spiked up at the ends. A pipe was clamped in his mouth and his hands were thrust into his coat pockets.

'So who was he?' Matt wondered.

'He was an explorer,' Venture said. 'He disappeared somewhere along the border between Brazil and Bolivia, or so it's thought, in 1925. Am I right?' From his tone, he knew he was.

'Indeed,' Harper agreed. 'He was following in the footsteps of other lost explorers. He found an account of an eighteenth-century Portuguese expedition that claimed to have discovered a lost city in the jungle.'

'He was searching for a lost city?' Matt said.

Harper laughed. 'For a lost civilization. He thought the survivors of some ancient cataclysm were scattered across the world and had perhaps passed on some of their knowledge.'

'It's a mystery, for example,' Robin said, 'how the ancient Egyptians transformed themselves from groups of warring factions into a kingdom with such technology and learning in such a short space of time. There's no evidence for the evolution of the hieroglyphic language. It just appears, fully defined. Maybe it evolved somewhere else. Maybe they had help.'

'And the Mayans too,' Harper added. 'Or so Fawcett thought.'

'He's a hero of yours?' Matt wondered. 'A romantic explorer chasing a dream?'

'I suppose so. But more than that.' Harper stood up and tossed his napkin down on the table beside his empty plate and wine glass. He walked slowly over to look at the picture. 'When we finally opened this pyramid,' he said, 'when we managed to clear the plants and debris from the entranceway and force open the stone gates that stood there . . .' He reached up and brushed the back of his fingers gently against the glass over the photograph. 'We found a skeleton. A human skeleton, trapped inside by a rock fall that jammed the doors closed. Someone who got here before us, got into this building. But he never got out again.'

'Fawcett?' Robin said.

Harper turned to face them and his eyes were sad. 'DNA testing suggests that the skeleton belonged to a European. It was male. It dated from the right period. What was left of the clothing would seem to bear that out. Of course, we can never be absolutely sure, but I like to think it was him. That he succeeded at least in that part of his great treasure hunt.'

He strode back to the table. 'And speaking of such things,' he said, 'I think perhaps now is the time for you to tell me how our own treasure hunt is going. Although of course it is not the treasure as such that I am interested in. It is the knowledge, the wisdom, the information that is contained in the ancient documents that Sir Robert of Lisle rescued from Constantinople all those years ago. Knowledge I can add to what I have already gleaned from other sources. So many other sources. Perhaps with that we can finish what Lieutenant-Colonel Fawcett started.' His eyes were gleaming with enthusiasm as well as sadness now. 'I believe that when we find the Treasure of St John, we will discover the truth in those scrolls and parchments. We will know at last for certain that such an ancient people existed.'

9

They left Julius Venture to explain their progress so far. Both Katherine and Harper himself seemed to assume that neither Robin nor Matt was much involved in the investigation. Matt could see that Robin was irritated by this, but although he was anxious to find his father he was happy to leave the discussions to Venture.

'Can I see this computer facility?' he asked Katherine.

'Aren't you tired?'

'Not yet.'

'All right, then.' Katherine turned to Robin. 'Are you interested in computers?'

'As a means to an end,' she said. 'As tools. But not for what they are. Not really, no.' Robin yawned. 'I think I'll get some sleep, if that's all right.'

Katherine smiled. 'Fine. It's been a long day for you, I expect.'

She turned back to Matt, so she couldn't see the face that Robin pulled in reply. It wasn't like Robin to be tired. Matt remembered she had been up all the previous night, but she had slept on the plane. Jet lag perhaps – after all, while it was early evening here, it was the middle of the night back home.

An unobtrusive polished wooden door under the main staircase turned out to be the entrance to a lift. Robin left them at the first floor, and Katherine and Matt continued up to floor six. The lift door opened to reveal a bare stone passageway, lit by electric wall lamps that were in the shape of burning firebrands. The lights flickered, sending shadows eerily back and forth across the pale stone floor and walls. A flight of stone steps emerged next to the lift, continuing up to the next level.

'He likes to contrast the old and the new, doesn't he?' Matt said, meaning Harper.

'Mr Harper sees technology as a way of unlocking and utilizing the mysteries of the ancients,' Katherine said. She led the way along the passage. 'A way of illuminating the past – literally so here.' She smiled at her own joke.

Matt wondered if she ever actually dared to laugh. With the shadows and light flashing across her pale face and her platinum hair, she might almost have been made of ice.

The passageway ended in a large door of dull metal studded with rivets. There was a keypad beside it, but Matt couldn't see what number Katherine punched in. The door sprang open.

'Wait here a moment.' She seemed suddenly unsettled, as if she had thought of something that should have occurred to her earlier. 'Let me check that . . .' She hesitated. 'That the staff aren't busy with something. There shouldn't be anyone here at the moment, not at this time. But I want to check, all right?'

Matt shrugged. 'OK.' He waited in the passage, staring at one of the fake firebrands and trying to see how the flickering effect worked.

There were half a dozen lights inside, each shining through a different section of the fake wooden stave. They flashed in what seemed to be a random sequence to create the effect of flickering flames, but in fact the pattern was repeated every so often. But since this light was not synchronized with any of the others, the pattern was obscured.

Matt knew that nothing technological was completely random. When a computer program created a random number, it needed a seed number to start from – a number on which it performed some calculation to generate an apparently random result. That seed number was often taken from the computer's clock. So, if you knew the exact time the program instruction was run, then in theory you could work out the result. Which was cheating, so far as Matt was concerned. If you could predict it, then it wasn't truly random. Not like the way the air molecules moved when the wind blew, or the drops in the ocean were affected by the tides and currents . . .

His thoughts were interrupted by Katherine's return.

'There's no one about,' she said. 'So I can give you a quick tour. Come on.'

It was indeed an impressive facility. It was hard to believe that Matt was inside an ancient stone pyramid in the middle of the South American jungle. The computer suite must occupy most of the floor, apart from the narrow passage from the lift to the doors. It stretched almost out of sight – lines and lines of computer system units. Racks of circuit boards and memory arrays.

Matt could not hear any noise from outside, so he guessed it was soundproofed. Certainly, from the blast of cool air as he stepped through the doors, it was air-conditioned. The hum of the ventilation added to the sound of the computers.

Along one wall was a line of desks – plain, pale wooden office furniture – with computer screens on them. A stylized letter 'H' twisted and turned and spun and spiralled on each screen apparently at random, but in fact following the directions of a program which Matt knew was anything but.

'Impressive,' he said.

'Yes,' Katherine agreed. 'Mr Harper likes to do things properly.'

'So I see. Have you worked for him for long?' Matt wondered.

'One of his companies sponsored me through university,' Katherine told him. 'My parents could never have afforded it, and I was lucky enough to get on to the sponsorship scheme Harper was running. I didn't think Mr Harper would know who I was, but when I got my degree he sent me a personal letter asking me to come and work for him.'

'Perhaps he does that with all the students he sponsors,' Matt suggested.

She smiled thinly, not amused. 'They don't all get a double-first. He offered me a job and here I am.'

'You owe him a lot, then,' Matt said.

'I suppose he made me what I am.' She started walking down one of the aisles between the rows of equipment, the subject evidently closed. 'I gather you know something about computers, so let me show you round.'

She led him between banks of servers and disk drives, explaining which machines serviced which of Harper's industries and connected to which continents.

'Do you have a lot of systems programmers and stuff?' Matt wondered. Even though everything was running smoothly on its own, he knew it was a lot of work to keep systems up to date and install new software and so on.

'A few. Mostly it's done remotely. Our technical people access the systems from wherever they happen to be on high-speed access lines. There's a microwave link through the rainforest as there are no phone lines. But we have a few hardware engineers here in case of failures. And our chief technical executive is here too, with an office on another floor.'

'He must have his work cut out for him,' Matt said.

'I'm sure you're right,' Katherine said. 'They're new, but settling in well.'

There was a bleeping from somewhere nearby and Matt assumed it was one of the computer systems they had just passed. But it was Katherine's mobile phone. She flipped open the cover and read the message she'd just received.

'We have to go now,' she said. 'Mr Harper is asking for me. It doesn't do to keep him waiting.'

'Can I stay here for a bit?' Matt asked. 'It's fascinating. I'd like to look round some more if I may. I won't be long.'

Her eyes narrowed slightly as she considered. 'All right,' Katherine decided. 'But just ten minutes. And don't touch anything. You can find your way back to the lift?'

'Through the doors and down the passage. I don't think I can get very lost.'

She nodded without comment. The click of her heels was still audible long after she was lost to sight behind the racks of servers and computer storage.

Matt waited until he had heard the door close at the far end of the huge room before hurrying back in the same direction. He sat himself at one of the desks and moved the mouse. The spinning 'H' on the screen was replaced with an administrator's user interface.

But overlaid on it was a window demanding a password. The user's access code was already entered, so at least he didn't have to guess that. But what could the password be? He tried 'Harper' but, not surprisingly, it wasn't that simple. It wasn't 'Atticus' either. Or 'waterfall'. Probably not a word at all, Matt decided. Probably a jumble of letters and numbers. He drummed his fingers on the desk as he thought about it.

Mum had once told him she used a system for her administrator passwords that was based on the current month and changed every month. Her own passwords were never so predictable, but it was a system she used if other people had to remember them. It was a pattern on the keyboard starting from the number of the month and preceded by the first letter of the month. So the password for January started j1 and for September it started s9. Maybe it was a system lots of computer administrators used, though that didn't sound very safe and secure. But then who was going to get inside a pyramid in the middle of the jungle to try?

It was July, so Matt typed j7ygvcft6, taking the letters y g v from down the keyboard under the 7 And then c f t back up to the 6.

And the screen bleeped. The window changed to say:

Password accepted: login in progress

Matt grinned. He could almost believe Mum had set up the systems ready for him. Almost. Amazed at his good luck, Matt set about finding out how Harper's computer network was arranged. He wasn't really hacking in, he told himself. He wasn't doing anything *wrong*. Just looking, just interested. He was soon absorbed in his work.

There was a whole section – a set of servers and a network of client computers – to do with Harper's archaeological work and ancient research. Matt found a map of the world with ancient sites marked on it. If you hovered the mouse pointer over a site, a set of coordinates popped up, giving its longitude and latitude. A pop-up menu from the right mouse button gave him access to data about each site – both archaeological data and details of the state of the site today. It even listed who owned it, and Matt found that many were owned by 'AH', followed by a date. When Atticus Harper had acquired it, he guessed.

He glanced at his watch and was amazed to find that it was almost half an hour since Katherine Feather had left him. Probably time to log off and head back to his room. He reached for the mouse.

And a shadow fell across the screen.

'What are you doing?' a soft female voice asked.

☩

'I nearly died!' Matt told her when he'd recovered from the shock.

'You might, if Harper finds you,' Robin said. She'd told him it wasn't difficult to work out the code for the door and apologized – while grinning – for surprising him. In return, Matt showed her the data he'd found.

'What do you mean?'

She shrugged. 'Just that I don't trust him. Or that woman.'

'Just because she called you a child,' Matt teased.

Robin didn't try to deny it. 'Not just that,' she said. 'When she left you here, she actually checked on me. Came to my room and opened the door to see if I was asleep. Probably had some plausible excuse ready and waiting in case I wasn't.'

'But you weren't,' Matt pointed out.

'She doesn't know that. The light was out and I was in bed.'

'You expected her to check up on you, didn't you?' Matt realized. 'Blimey, you're devious.'

'Blimey, I'm right,' she told him. 'Why don't you see what it says about this place?' She pointed to the map that Matt had brought up on the screen.

'She's just concerned that you're OK. Probably,' Matt said. Not thinking, he clicked the left button on the marker for the Waterfall Pyramid, not the right one. And instead of a pop-up menu, the screen changed completely. He cursed and moved the mouse, wondering how to get back.

'No, leave it,' Robin said. 'What is that?'

It was a three-dimensional model. A wire-frame representation of a building – all lines and corners, with none of the walls or floors or detail filled in.

'It isn't the pyramid,' Matt realized. 'It's the wrong shape.'

'It's all curves . . . Can you get it to paint the rest of it so we can see the thing properly? What do you call it when the computer paints it all in – rendering?'

There were some controls and buttons on a panel at the bottom of the screen. Some of them, Matt knew, would tilt the picture or move the screen's point of view through the model so it would look as if you were walking through the real place. He experimented with a few of the controls and after a while managed to get a picture of the whole structure. It was still just a framework, but it was more obvious now that it was a building.

'Looks like Roman architecture or something,' Matt said. 'Circular, like the Colosseum.'

'Older than that,' Robin said quietly. 'I wonder why it's on here.'

'Some ancient site. Just got linked to the wrong point on the map, that's all.'

'Could be,' she agreed.

'There's a link button here, with an arrow on it. Probably takes us back to the map.' Matt clicked on it.

The screen changed again, to show another wireframe model. But this was not a building.

'Looks like a person,' Robin said. 'Why's that linked in?'

'To give an idea of scale?' Matt suggested. 'Or maybe they're building a recreation of the place when it was in use, centuries ago or whatever. They

can populate it with models of people. Like the figures in those simulation games. They're called
avatars,' he tried to explain. 'Those are . . .'

'They're computer simulations of people or creatures that have some behaviour and habits that the
computer generates. So you can simulate an environment. Like those games you get recreating cities or
battles or whatever.'

'Yeah, that's right,' Matt said, a bit disappointed
that she knew.

Robin nudged his shoulder. 'So stick him in the
model and see what he does.'

'We can try.'

It took Matt a few minutes, playing around with
the mouse and the keyboard, before he was able to
do it. In the process he discovered how to make the
building a solid, real-looking structure with stone
walls and floors. They could see now that it was in a
poor condition – walls were broken and the floors
were scattered with sand and rubble.

'Right, I think I've got the hang of it now,' he said.
'Let's put our little man in this area here, beside the
wall.'

Matt positioned the mouse pointer on a section
of sandy floor beside a stone wall. The detail in the

wall was impressive now it was fully rendered – a thick creeper was hanging down, large, veined leaves gripping the crumbling stonework as the creeper looped in a lazy 'S' shape towards the sandy floor.

In response to Matt's click, a figure shimmered into existence beside the wall. It had the shape of a man, but it did not look like a man.

✛

Away from watching eyes, wreathed in shadows, the sand had lain on the stone floor for centuries. It stirred, as if worried by a breeze. But no breeze disturbed the large, veined leaves of the creeper hanging down the wall and gripping the crumbling stonework.

On the ground, the sand shimmered and shifted, slowly at first, but gradually it rippled and moved. Grains rolled together, coalescing into a shape. A flat image on the floor, like a relief carving . . .

Then the figure filled out, rose up, gathered more and more of the sand into itself as it rose. It didn't climb to its feet, but flowed upwards – sand forcing its way like water bubbling from a spring.

Into a crude approximation of a man.

'I think there's a problem with the program,' Robin said. She sounded strangely anxious.

'Looks like he's picking up the same texture map as the floor or something,' Matt agreed.

The man's shape was filled in with a rough, pale brown texture. His face was a crude approximation and his whole form seemed lumpy and misshapen – as if he was made of sand. The sand man took a step forward as Matt moved the mouse again. Flecks and particles dripped and rubbed from him as he walked, leaving a faint trail across the screen behind him.

'Make him walk through that door.' Robin pointed to an open archway on the screen. 'Let's see where it goes.'

The man followed the pointer through the arch. Into blackness.

✛

The figure made of sand lurched forward, towards the archway. As it moved, feet dragging slightly, grains of sand rubbed off, fell away, eroded from its body and dripped to the ground. Leaving a faint trail of sand and dirt across the ground behind it.

'Must be the edge of the model,' Matt said. 'They haven't built any more of it. Unless there's another model linked into this one, to extend the world. You might be able to plug them together like a jigsaw. Let's see.'

He clicked away for a few moments and, sure enough, another environment sprang into existence, replacing the blackness. More stone walls and sandy floors. And a studded, metal door.

'That can't be right,' Robin said. 'Pull back a bit. Let's see what it is.'

The figure was walking again, still heading in the direction that Matt had sent him – through the door and up a set of stairs beyond. The picture pulled back, and the man and the staircase became smaller as the image zoomed out.

The figure was walking out of the building and up into another structure that seemed to be built above it. Or was it upper floors of the same building perhaps? Further back and the figure was a moving dot on a winding staircase. The circular building filled the bottom half of the screen. The top half was the other building.

The trail of sand dusted the steps that wound up out of the ruined building. The figure moved slowly and deliberately on its journey, towards its appointed destination.

✠

'That can't be right,' Matt said.

The building above, joined to the circular structure by the winding staircase, was a stepped pyramid.

'That's here, that's us,' Robin said. 'The circular building or whatever it is must be buried below this pyramid.'

'It's only a computer model,' Matt told her. 'It's not real.'

Robin was still staring at the screen. 'I suppose not. Bring him up here,' she said.

'What?'

'The man – make him walk up to the sixth floor, to this room. Let's see if the computer suite is part of the model or if it's just an old empty pyramid.'

✠

On the ground floor of the Waterfall Pyramid, a heavy steel door was hidden behind a large tapestry that showed a medieval map of the world. The countries were angular and misshapen.

The tapestry moved as the door opened and a figure stepped through into the pyramid.

A figure that was misshapen and clumsy – barely recognizable as the shape of a man . . .

✠

Matt clicked the mouse a few times, then sat back to watch the progress of the tiny figure as it made its way to the top of the winding staircase and into the pyramid. 'We'll give him a minute, then set the computer to show us his point of view, so we see him come into the pyramid.'

✠

The shadows in the corridor outside deepened as a large figure appeared at the top of the stairs. It paused for a moment at the end of the corridor, then started slowly towards the computer suite. The flickering firebrand light threw distorted shadows against the walls and across the floor, making the figure seem misshapen, like a crude approximation of a human being. It moved slowly but deliberately towards the door at the end of the corridor.

The door opened. The figure stepped into the room and headed towards the boy and the girl sitting at the computer screen.

10

Atticus Harper was seething. 'How dare you?!'

Matt leapt out of the chair, such was the force of
the man's anger. Harper was striding across the
room towards Matt and Robin.

'Sorry,' Matt stammered.

'We were just looking,' Robin said coolly. She had
not flinched at Harper's anger. 'We're not doing any
harm.'

Harper leaned across and grabbed the mouse.
'No harm! You abuse my hospitality and break into
my computer system . . .' He moved the mouse
pointer quickly across the screen.

'Sorry,' Matt said again. 'Look, the screen was
already on.' That much was true. 'We didn't know
we were doing anything wrong. Just looking, like
Robin said. It's such neat kit.'

On the screen, the tiny figure of the avatar walking stiffly up the stairs faded, as if dissolving. The model of the pyramid and the building below it disappeared and the screen returned to the main database.

☩

A thin trail of sand led up the stairs, barely more than a scattering of grains. As if someone carrying a bag of sand with a small hole in it had just passed that way.

The small lights set into the wall at each third step threw a misshapen, clumsily drawn shadow of a man on to the stone wall. Then, abruptly, the shadow was gone. Disintegrated. Turned to flecks and specks that fell to the floor.

Anyone coming down the stairs would have found no one there. Just a pile of sand and dirt strewn across several of the steps, fading into a thin trail that continued downwards . . .

☩

'Are you saying that this screen was logged into the system?' Harper demanded.

Matt glanced at Robin. He didn't want to tell an outright lie, but it was a way out of trouble.

'Katherine was showing me round, and she got a message from you and had to leave. I stayed here and the screen was on. I was just playing.'

Harper's eyes narrowed. 'And you?' he asked Robin.

'Me too,' she said. She was smiling at him – all sweetness and innocence. But Matt could see a determination in her eyes.

'I understood you were asleep in bed,' Harper said.

'Then you obviously understood wrong.'

'Obviously . . .' Harper logged off the system and the monitor once more showed the stylized 'H' like the other screens. 'As you say, there's no harm done.' He straightened up and regarded Robin and Matt with something approaching appreciation. 'You did well to navigate through the data. And I do know that you're something of an expert with computers, young man,' he told Matt.

'Oh?'

'Yes. But in future, please ask before you tinker. I am happy for you to look through the data, of course, and to see how we operate. But with permission and within certain limits. The screen in your room is connected to the system and will give you access to the files and folders you need. But some of the other information on the systems is rather sensitive. Confidential business data and so on.'

'I understand,' Matt said, relieved that they seemed to be getting off so lightly.

'And what about that model we were looking at?' Robin said. Matt nudged her to shut up, but she ignored him. 'Was it supposed to be this pyramid? What was the structure underneath? Like cellars or something. And why the models of people – people made from the elements, from the earth?'

Harper's expression seemed to have frozen on his face. 'So many questions,' he said quietly. 'What an enquiring mind you have.'

'Do I get any answers?' Robin demanded.

Matt felt he wanted to curl up and die. 'Come on,' he said quietly. 'We ought to be going. Like Mr Harper says, we shouldn't really be here at all.'

'People made from the elements,' Harper echoed, ignoring Matt. 'Yes, I suppose it might seem like that. Just an artefact of the computer program.'

'That's what I said,' Matt told him. 'A problem with the texture mapping.'

But still Harper ignored him. He was staring intently at Robin, who met his gaze without seeming at all intimidated. 'Golems perhaps?' Harper said. 'They were supposed to be made from the very earth itself, animated by the will of another. Do you believe the ancients really had the power to manipulate the elements, then?'

'Do you?' she countered. 'They moved blocks of stone to make the pyramids with such precision no one really knows how it was done. All across the ancient world you find religions based on the theory that the elements are entities – gods – in their own right. Earth, air, fire and water.'

'Which hardly sits well with atomic theory, does it?' Harper said. He seemed amused now. 'Atoms and molecules, that's all the air and the earth and the water are. Fire is simply a reaction, albeit one that gives off heat. There is no sentience involved – no thought or feeling or guiding intelligence.'

'You're made of atoms and molecules, and I *assume* your body has some guiding intelligence.'

'Be careful, young woman!' he snapped.

But Robin smiled. 'You're giving off heat too,' she said. She stood up at last, turning to Matt. 'You're right. We should go.'

'Yes,' Harper said. He was apparently calm, but Matt could see his hands were clenched tight and he looked pale with anger. 'You need your sleep. Tomorrow will be a long day as we assess Mr Venture's progress and decide how best to proceed.'

'I'm sorry,' Matt said quickly. 'We'll see you in the morning. I really do want to find my dad.'

Harper seemed to relax slightly at this. 'I know,' he said. 'We all want that.'

'I thought you wanted the Treasure of St John,' Robin said. 'The documents and notes.'

'It comes to the same thing,' Harper told her.

'Don't push it,' Matt murmured.

'We'll go to bed now,' Robin said meekly. 'Like good young people. It's all right.' She held her hand up to tell Harper not to follow. 'We can find our own way back to our rooms, thank you.'

'I'm sure you can,' Harper said, and there was a cold edge to his voice that Matt did not like at all.

☩

The screen on the wall of Matt's room turned out to be a computer monitor as well as a TV, just as Harper had told him. There was a keyboard slotted into a space below the screen. It popped out when Matt pressed it. The keyboard was connected to the screen by infrared or wireless, so there was no cable attached. A joystick at the top right of the keyboard replaced the mouse.

He intended to go through some of the data and explore the part of the system to which he did have access. But as soon as he flopped on the bed, Matt realized how tired he was. So instead he turned off the screen, pushed the keyboard back into its slot to keep its battery charged and tumbled into bed. His mind was a whirl of computer models, historical information, treasure and ancient maps.

Why did Harper have a computer model of the pyramid, with another building linked into it? Was it some structure he believed had existed on the same site before the pyramid was built? And what was the deal with the modelled figures – the avatars that seemed to be textured from sand or earth? They did-n't seem to be there for any reason, except perhaps as a programmer's whim or a trivial amusement.

And Harper had gone on about golems and crea-tures made from the elements. Robin seemed to know what he meant, but it was lost on Matt. Except . . . There was something, some connection there. He remembered the dark figure watching Dad's house – shapeless and shadowy. The rough hand over his mouth, like sandpaper . . . And something else too. A paper? A document? Something at the edge of his mind.

But, whatever antagonism there was between Harper and Robin, the most important thing as far as Matt was concerned was to find Dad. Not the documents and notes that Robin had said Harper was after. Documents and notes . . . Notes . . . Without even realizing it, Matt slipped into a deep sleep. In moments, he was dreaming.

Dad was in his study, working at his desk. Matt was there too, watching. A rough hand was clamped over his mouth from behind and he couldn't shake it off or make himself heard. But Dad was talking to him, not seeming to notice Matt's plight. He couldn't hear exactly what his father was saying, but he was holding a piece of paper, waving it excitedly at Matt. Notes – handwritten notes . . . Then, suddenly, Dad was gone. The French windows were blowing open and shut, papers gusting round the room. Matt struggled free, turning to see his attacker.

There was no one there. And suddenly he was looking down at dad's desk, and it was exactly as he had found it a few days ago. Matt saw himself picking up the book of ancient maps. A sheet of paper fell from it – Dad's handwritten notes on one side.

On the other, a computer printout. Matt picked it up and stared at it.

And now he was somewhere else. Still holding the paper, he felt the cold wind in his hair and tugging at his pyjamas, and he wished he'd been wearing a coat. He was standing on the edge of a cliff. Below him, frothy waves crashed into the dark, ragged rocks.

'So you found me, then,' Dad said. He was standing right beside Matt on the cliff.

✛

The room was completely dark. Usually there was some light – filtering in from the outside world or under the door. But here there was nothing. The darkness was so close and complete that Matt could feel it pressing in on him. He sat up, fumbling for the light, and hoping that it would be there. And that when he turned it on, he would find himself in the room in the pyramid where he had gone to sleep and not in a cave or a dungeon or a sealed box or . . .

The lights faded up in response to his push of the button by the bed. The room was just as it had been when he faded the lights down and fell asleep. Nothing had changed.

Nothing except the excitement in Matt's stomach as he recalled the dream, remembered the printed paper from Dad's study and realized that he knew why it had been left there. Without pausing to check the time, he pushed back the covers and leapt out of bed.

Robin opened her door almost at once, which meant that she couldn't have been asleep. In fact, she was fully dressed and Matt wondered if he'd overslept. Not that he cared.

'I know where it is,' he gasped. 'The Treasure of St John – I know where it is.'

'Then you'd better come in.'

The voice wasn't Robin's. It came from the room behind her. She stepped aside and Matt walked slowly in.

Julius Venture was sitting in a chair, the keyboard for Robin's screen on his lap. 'Get your breath back,' he said. 'Then tell us all about it.'

Matt sat on the bed, with Venture in the one upright chair and Robin cross-legged on the floor. Robin and her father listened attentively while Matt described how he had found Dad's house empty when he arrived there. 'It seems so long ago now,' he said. He described the muddy hallway, and saw that Robin and Venture exchanged glances at this. Then he told them about the intruder who put a sandpaper-like hand over his mouth.

'He's gaining control,' Robin interrupted. 'He knows a little already.'

Matt wanted to ask her what she meant, but Venture was talking again: 'Ancient knowledge. I wonder how much Harper really knows and understands. We've been using Robin's access to the computer,' he explained to Matt, 'because they already have her marked down as curious. You too. But so far as Harper is aware, I am the perfect guest and taking everything at face value.'

'You think we shouldn't?'

'Ancient knowledge,' Venture repeated. 'Remember what Harper said about control of the elements. Remember the wind and the rain, the feel of sand and dirt across your face . . .'

'The candle flames, watching you work,' Robin added quietly.

'You're kidding, right?' Matt looked at their serious expressions. 'You're not kidding. Look, it's just the weather. There's some weird things going on here, but it's not, like, spooky or haunted or anything. I mean, what are you saying? That somehow the, what

213

'– the elements? The elements are being controlled. Earth and wind and fire.'

'And water,' Venture said quietly.

'That's just daft,' Matt told her.

'See if you still think that when we find the Treasure of St John,' Robin said.

'But that's what I'm telling you, I have found it. You see, Dad had a printout from a travel agent's – journey information, an itinerary for a trip he was going to make. And I bet that's why he was snatched when he was, before he could go.'

'Go where?' Venture asked. He was leaning eagerly forward in the chair.

'He was flying to Copenhagen. I remember that, because I went there with Mum once on some business trip. Had to stay in the hotel on my own all day. Dead boring.'

'Copenhagen?' Robin's blue eyes were wide, realizing what was coming next.

'Yeah. And then he was set to go by train and then boat to an island.'

'Valdeholm,' Venture said quietly.

'That's right. So that's where the treasure must be!'

Robin was grinning. 'Well done, that must be it. Matt, you're a hero!'

Matt grinned back.

But Venture was less elated. 'Wait, wait, wait,' he cautioned. 'Just because your father was going there doesn't mean the treasure is there. It implies – heavily implies – that he *believed* it was there. But he might have been wrong.'

'Oh, come on, father,' Robin said. 'When was Arnie ever wrong about anything like this?'

'Let's take it as a working hypothesis, then.'

'A what?' Matt said.

'Let's assume for the sake of argument that your dad was right,' Robin said. 'What then?'

'We go and get the treasure.'

'An island is a big place,' Venture said slowly. 'And there are other considerations.'

'Such as?'

'Such as, what do we tell Atticus Harper?'

'You really don't trust him, do you?' Matt said. 'Just because he got stroppy with me and Robin for hacking into his computers. You can't blame him really.'

'I don't blame him at all. And I don't necessarily mistrust him either. But trust has to be earned, and whatever he really knows and whatever his motives truly are, he hasn't been entirely honest with us. Look.'

Venture tapped away on the keyboard and Matt turned his attention to the screen on the wall. It showed a list of files and documents.

'That's the stuff he gave us to work from,' Matt said.

'Exactly so. The very same files. But with just one slight difference. Let me list them here in date order, so you can see which were created or modified most recently. And you'll see there are even a couple of new files here, created just yesterday. Files we've not seen before. Other files have been altered, updated, recently.'

The list reorganized itself as Matt watched. Each file had a date printed beside it on the screen. He could see from the clock at the bottom of the screen that it was just after seven in the morning. 'So?'

'So, explain to me how some of these documents were changed, or even created, *after* your father apparently disappeared?'

Matt stared at the screen. 'Maybe they're notes and things that someone scanned in afterwards.'

'Some of them. But not all. There's some original work here. Which means . . .'

Matt hardly dared to think what it might mean.

'He lied about when Dad vanished?' he said.

'Possibly, but why do that? It's more likely, don't you think, that Harper has someone else still working on finding the treasure.'

'So, we aren't the only people he's got looking for it?'

'At the very least,' Venture said quietly, 'Mr Harper is not telling us the whole truth. I'd like to know what else he isn't telling us. And I'd like to know why he has what Robin describes as a very accurate computer model of this pyramid that shows another ancient site buried beneath it.' He clicked a key and the screen went blank. 'Wouldn't you?'

'So what's the plan, then?' Matt asked.

'I shall tell Harper of our deductions, though I think I shall be vague about why we think Valdeholm is the most likely location for the treasure. While I keep him occupied with that, you and Robin can take a look round and see what you can find rather closer to home.'

'Sounds like a plan,' Robin said.

Matt agreed. 'But can we have breakfast first?'

✝

'I don't know what you think we're going to find down here,' Matt said. 'Apart from maybe a wine cellar and the dustbins.'

After breakfast, Venture had gone with Harper to his study to explain their theories about the island of Valdeholm. Robin and Matt had managed to slip away while Katherine Feather was taking a phone call, and now Robin had led Matt to a narrow, winding stone staircase that descended from the ground floor into the depths of the pyramid.

'If we knew what we were going to find, we wouldn't have to come looking,' she told him. She stopped abruptly on the stairs and Matt almost cannoned into her. 'I wonder where this came from,' she said, pointing down at her feet.

The steps were sprinkled with sand. They were lit at floor level by tiny, bright lamps set into the wall and Matt could see the lines where someone had made an indifferent job of brushing the sand away.

'Probably fell from the ceiling,' he said.

'I doubt it.' Robin continued down.

The stairs led to a large area with passages leading off. A pile of cardboard boxes stood against one wall. Matt found the top box was full of tinned fruit. He guessed the others were also food and provisions. 'I told you – storage. This is where they keep the food and toilet rolls.'

But Robin wasn't listening. She was standing in front of a large tapestry that hung on one of the walls, reaching right down to the floor. 'According to Harper's computer model, this is where the steps down to the ruins should be.'

'You don't think it was just a model?' Matt had pretty much decided the same himself. But he wasn't expecting to find much evidence of an earlier building – the pyramid must have been built right over it. He looked up at the tapestry Robin had meant – a faded, almost threadbare map of the world. It was obviously very old and the landmasses were distorted and out of shape. It reminded him of the book of maps in Dad's study. 'Anyway, how can you be sure? It could have been any of these other doors.'

'No,' she insisted, 'it was here. You saw the model. You know that.'

'I don't remember it down to the last centimetre, though.'

'Don't you?' She sounded surprised.

'No. And obviously neither do you. Because you've made a mistake.'

'Have you looked at the floor?' she asked.

'The floor?' Matt looked down, wondering what she meant. He knew at once when he saw the thin trail of sand scattered from the bottom of the stairs. It ran across the flagstones, ending at the tapestry. 'Like in Dad's study,' he said quietly.

'Let's test a theory,' Robin said.

She reached out and grabbed the large tapestry, pulling it to one side. It was heavy and she struggled to shift it. But even so, it moved enough for Matt to see the door hidden behind.

☩

The room could have been in a modern office block. The desk was pale wood and the fittings chrome and steel. The desktop was clear apart from a computer screen, a mouse and keyboard, and a telephone. But Harper's attention was focused on Venture.

'So on balance,' Venture was saying, 'we think the most likely location would seem to be this Scandinavian island.'

'But you're not 100 per cent sure?'

'You can never be 100 per cent sure in this game,' Venture told him.

'Maybe not, intellectually speaking.' Harper

clapped his palm over his chest. 'But you can tell, you can feel it here. You just instinctively know sometimes when things are *right*.'

Venture did not reply.

⊹

The hidden door opened into a narrow stone-walled corridor that led downwards, into the depths below the pyramid.

'We'll be under the mountain itself if we keep going much further,' Matt said. 'Where do you suppose this leads?'

'Let's find out,' Robin told him.

Matt wasn't at all sure he wanted to. Harper had already told them off for prying where they shouldn't. 'Maybe it's just abandoned. Maybe no one ever comes here.'

'Yeah, right.' Robin paused and turned to look at him. 'That'll be why there are lights.'

Matt hadn't thought about that. There was lighting at floor level, like on the stairs down into the basement of the pyramid. Obviously, now Robin pointed it out, the tunnel was in use. At its far end was a warm glow which might be sunlight.

'It's just another way in and out of the pyramid,'

Matt said. 'It probably comes out on the other side of the waterfall.'

'Tradesman's entrance?' Robin said. She didn't sound convinced.

'OK,' Matt admitted as they reached the end of the tunnel. 'Not the tradesman's entrance.'

The tunnel emerged on to a wide ledge. One of the tunnel walls continued, while the other was gone, affording a view out over the incredible sight below. The ledge was a paved walkway that was part of the top of a ruined structure that had been built into the rock.

A huge amphitheatre. Matt and Robin were standing at the back, on the top level, looking out over rows and rows of curved terraces that led down eventually to a circular area at the bottom of the structure. The terraces were interrupted by entrances and exits cut into them – tunnels leading off from the amphitheatre and disappearing into darkness. The terraces stretched round about two-thirds of the structure. The last third, behind the circular stage, was a sheer rock wall. Between the stage and the rock wall was a black mass that seemed to shimmer and move. Water, Matt realized – an underground river running lazily through the ancient structure.

'How old is this?' he murmured.

'Older than the pyramid,' Robin said. 'Much, much older. The pyramid is built on top of it. This is what Harper's calculations actually led him to when he worked out where there was an undiscovered ancient site. The pyramid above isn't old enough to have been important.'

'You think he knows this place is here?' Matt realized how stupid a question that was as soon as he said it. He put his hand up to stop Robin pointing it out. 'OK, OK. Of course he does. You could hardly miss it. And there are the lights.'

'And people have been working down here,' Robin said. 'It's being excavated – look.'

The whole place was bathed in a yellow light cast by enormous floodlights standing on metal gantries and poles arranged at intervals along the terraces. They were almost lost in the scale and grandeur of the place. The sheer size of it had impressed Matt so much he hadn't noticed that some areas were roped off, divided up into squares like on an archaeological dig. Whole stretches of terrace were buried in sand and rubble. Broken pillars of stone lay where they had fallen, probably centuries if not millennia ago. Roots and creepers had grown through from the forest far above and snaked across the whole site. In some places they had obviously been cleared away, but in others they stretched across the terraces and up the walls like dark veins against the pale stone.

'Have you seen this?' Robin asked. She was pointing to the stone wall behind them, at the end of the tunnel.

'What about it?'

A thick creeper was hanging down the wall close to them. Large, veined leaves gripped the crumbling stonework as the creeper looped in a lazy 'S' shape towards the sandy floor. It reminded Matt of something. He felt suddenly cold. 'It's just like the wall in the computer model. Where we created that avatar figure.'

☩

'Before the ancient world as we know it,' Atticus Harper said, 'there was another civilization.'

'It's an interesting theory,' Venture told him. 'One that is gaining some credibility, I believe.'

'It is the only theory that fits the facts. Yet still the academic world as a whole refuses to accept it.'

Venture nodded. 'It steps on too many academic toes. Too much of the current thinking would be invalidated if your theory were true.'

'Hardly my theory, Julius. Since the geologist Robert Schoch suggested the erosion on the Sphinx was due to rain and not sand back in 1991, the establishment has sought to discredit anyone who backs a theory that doesn't match their cosy view of the ancient world.'

'Schoch has to be wrong,' Venture agreed, 'as do West and Hancock and Brennan and all the others. Because if the Sphinx was standing when there was such heavy rain in Egypt, then it must be far older than the historians would like to think. It doesn't fit, so it can't be right. In short, *they* cannot be wrong.' He watched Harper carefully as the big man tapped at his keyboard for a few moments. 'Is that why you're after the Treasure of St John?'

Harper was frowning at the screen. He returned his attention to Venture. 'Yes,' he said simply. 'I'm sure there are other papers and articles and relics of note in the so-called treasure. But most of all, I am after whatever was rescued from the library at Alexandria. If I can prove – really *prove* – that a civilization existed long before any other and passed on its knowledge . . .' His eyes were shining and his brow creased with an intensity and passion. 'If I can find proof of that, then it really will be remembered as my theory. My discovery.'

'You want to be remembered as someone who changed archaeology,' Venture realized. 'Someone who changed how the human race sees itself in the light of history. Someone who changed the world.'

Harper smiled, the intensity fading. But the passion in his eyes was still there. 'Everyone wants to change the world,' he said. 'If you can't control it, surely that's the next best thing.'

Venture swallowed, his mouth suddenly dry.

✛

The terraces were like enormous steps, each about a metre high. They jumped down from one to another, towards the flat circular area that must be the stage.

'It must be Roman,' Matt said. 'Or Greek.'

'In South America?' Robin said.

'A copy, then.'

'It's older than the pyramid. Much older.'

'Ancient Greece was hundreds of years BC,' Matt pointed out. 'That's older.'

'This is older than that,' Robin said. 'I'd say 10,000 years older.'

Matt gave a low whistle. 'That *is* old. How do you know? How can you tell?'

She had turned away. 'I just know.'

Matt thought about this. She had to be wrong, but she'd never admit it. 'So how come it looks Greek if it's that old?'

Robin jumped down another huge step, then turned back and looked up at him. She spoke slowly and patiently, like Matt's history teacher at school. 'Before the ancient world as we know it, there was another civilization. I mean thousands of years – perhaps as many as 20,000 – before ancient Greece and Egypt.'

Matt had heard this from Dad, though he'd never paid much attention to it. He had been surprised his father gave it so much credence. 'That's just a theory.'

Robin ignored him. 'Its ships sailed the world from China to the South Pole,' she said. 'They had advanced knowledge of science, maths, astronomy and geometry long before anyone else.'

'It's just a myth, you know. There's no proof. It's just a story.'

'But it's a story of a civilization that was wiped out by a great catastrophe – floods and earthquakes or whatever. It doesn't really matter, not any more.

But what if the survivors escaped to Egypt and to other places? Including South America. It is their knowledge that informed these ancient societies. That enabled the pyramids to be built, and not just the pyramids . . .' She opened her arms and turned a full circle.

'So you're saying this place was built by some ancient lost civilization?'

'I'm saying it might have been built using knowledge that was passed on from that ancient civilization. Knowledge that enabled them to move stones weighing thousands of tonnes; to map the heavens and the earth with terrific accuracy without ever going into space; to hollow out stone to make vases with necks so narrow a child can't get its finger inside.'

'That's crazy,' Matt told her. 'No one's ever going to believe that.'

Robin stared at him, her pale face framed by her black hair. He thought she was about to lose her temper, but instead she smiled. 'You're probably right,' she said. 'Come on. I'll race you to the bottom.'

✠

Harper was concentrating on the screen. He barely listened to what Venture was saying; almost all his attention was focused on the graphic the computer was displaying. He angled the screen to be sure that Julius Venture could not see it.

'The author Robert Graves made a distinction between what he called *lunar* knowledge and *solar* knowledge,' Venture said. 'That's really what we're talking about here, isn't it? Lunar knowledge, the knowledge of the ancients if the theories are born out, wasn't based on calculation and synthesis of data which underlies the modern so-called scientific method.'

'I'm sure you're right,' Harper said, without looking away from the screen. He moved the mouse and the wire-frame model he was examining shifted and turned.

'No, this ancient knowledge system was all to do with intuition, to do with having a unified view of the universe and of our own existence.' Venture gave a short laugh. 'And there's talk now about a unified theory, as if it's something that can be calculated or discerned, rather than something that just *is*. You know,' he went on, 'some children can tell you how many sweets there are in a pile just by looking. It's a vestige of that knowledge system, before it evaporates under the pressure of modern teaching. The children simply *know* how many sweets there are just by glancing at the pile from a distance. They don't need to count them individually.' He paused, as if sensing that Harper was not listening. 'Or how many paving slabs there are in a causeway just by glancing at it from a helicopter.'

✠

The circular stage was far bigger than it had seemed from the back of the amphitheatre. The sand was so deep across it that, with the water the other side, Matt felt as if he was walking on a beach.

From one side of the stage, Robin waved to him to join her.

'What have you found?' he asked.

'There's a narrow ledge running along the side of the river,' she said, pointing to where a shelf of rock disappeared into the shadows.

'So?'

'So you were right. Well, sort of. Judging by the orientation of this amphitheatre, that leads to the back of the volcano.'

'If it goes all the way.'

She smiled, tilting her head to one side. 'Want to find out?'

Matt smiled back. 'Yes,' he said. 'But I think we should be getting back. Goodness knows what Harper would do if he knew we were down here. He'd go ape.'

╬

'Ah, Katherine.' Still Harper did not look away from the screen. 'It seems we are all off to Scandinavia. Perhaps you and Julius could make the necessary arrangements?'

'How soon are we travelling?' she asked.

'As soon as possible. If that is all right with Julius and his . . . party?'

'I'm sure Matt will be keen to bring things to a satisfactory conclusion,' Venture said. He stood up, sensing that the meeting was at an end.

'I'm sure he will,' Harper said. 'He'll be keen to find the treasure in the hope it will bring his father back to him.'

Katherine Feather gestured for Venture to pre-cede her out of the study. She waited a moment – just long enough for Harper to look up at her from his computer.

The screen showed a wire-frame computer-gen-erated model of an amphitheatre. In the middle of the picture, two small stick-like figures were clambering up the steep terraces towards the tunnel leading out. If he had zoomed in on them, filled in the texture and rendered the data fully, Harper would have seen that one was a tall, thin boy and the other a girl with long black hair. But he already knew that.

Harper nodded to Katherine and she followed Venture from the room. Leaving Atticus Harper alone with his thoughts.

11

A few days ago, Matt had never been in a helicopter. Now it seemed as if he was spending most of his life in one. The trip back to Rio was every bit as spectacular in reverse, and it lost none of its beauty and interest with the repetition. Matt hoped they would have time to explore the huge city, but Harper's plane was already waiting to take them on to Copenhagen.

Passport checks and security were barely a formality, and it was clear that the authorities were more than happy to have Harper as their guest. Even with the air conditioning full on in the aircraft, Matt could feel the heat. He was still tired from the last journey and it wasn't long after they were airborne before he was drifting off to sleep again.

He woke feeling refreshed but with a bitter taste

in his mouth and realized he was hungry as well as thirsty. Robin was sitting close by, eating a salad. He went to the galley to get himself some food and then joined her. Venture, Harper and Katherine Feather were sitting round the conference area in the jet, talking about the island and how to go about researching where to look when they arrived. So Matt took the opportunity to talk quietly to Robin about the amphitheatre under Harper's pyramid.

Outside, the sky was a deep blue with wisps of clouds drifting past. If there were shapes in the clouds, then it was probably just the water vapour reacting to the air currents and the temperature. If there were faces, peering in at the windows, then Matt did not notice them . . .

✠

There was a limo waiting at Copenhagen to drive them from the airport into the city centre. Katherine had booked them into a large, modern hotel right in the middle of the city. It was impersonal and unremarkable and reminded Matt of where he had stayed for a day when he came to Copenhagen with his mum. It was late afternoon when they arrived, and Matt and Robin left the others to their discussions and walked through the nearby Tivoli Gardens.

In one of the buildings, there was an exhibition of holograms that fascinated Matt. They were lit by bright spotlights that enhanced the three-dimensional effect. Pictures of faces, vehicles, flowers, even a model of a dinosaur. He was intrigued by the way the images seemed both real and unreal at the same time. The way that light could be so clever.

'You know,' Robin told him, 'all the information about the image is held in every part of the hologram.'

'So what does that mean?' he asked.

'It means that if you break one, shatter it into pieces, then each piece will show a smaller version of the complete image. Not a fragment of the picture, but the whole thing. Order out of apparent chaos.'

As the evening drew in they had dinner together on the terrace of one of the restaurants overlooking the spectacular gardens. It surprised Matt that Robin had a credit card.

She shrugged. 'Makes things easier,' she said.

They lapsed into silence, looking out over the lawns and flowerbeds as the shadows of the trees lengthened.

'You think we'll find the treasure?' Matt asked.

'I don't care about the treasure,' Robin said. She turned to look at him, her deep blue eyes fixing on Matt. 'Neither do you.'

'No,' he agreed. 'No, I just want to find Dad.'

Robin reached across the table and took his hand. 'Me too,' she said. 'Let's hope that we find the treasure and that brings us a step closer to your dad. But . . . But just don't expect him to be waiting there with it. All right?'

Matt hadn't really expected that at all. But all the same he felt his eyes stinging with disappointment. 'We should be getting back to the hotel.'

✝

They had a section of the hotel to themselves, including a conference centre with several meeting rooms. Matt slept well in a huge, soft bed. When he woke the next morning, he was surprised to see how late it was. He was served breakfast in the dining room that was part of the conference centre, and Robin joined him for coffee.

'Dad and the others are discussing what we do now,' she explained, leading him through to the largest of the meeting rooms.

They passed Katherine Feather in a seating area outside. She was deep in conversation on the phone, but smiled and waved them through into the main room. Harper and Venture were seated either side of a large conference table. The lights were turned down low and a map of the tiny island of Valdeholm was displayed on a plasma screen from Harper's laptop computer.

'The population,' Harper was saying, 'is virtually zero – just a few shepherds and fishermen and their families. But the island is apparently remarkable for having six medieval churches.' He paused to welcome Matt and Robin and gestured for them to sit down.

They found themselves seats further down the table as Harper explained that the churches were themselves out of the ordinary in that they were of a circular construction – unusual apparently for Scandinavia.

'Not so strange if they were on Malta,' Harper went on. 'But it does seem likely that the Knights Hospitallers were here long enough to have some influence.' He rubbed his hands together in satisfaction. 'I feel that the treasure awaits us.'

'The island may be tiny,' Robin said, 'but it's still a

very big place to have to search.'

'They will have left clues for those who followed them to retrieve the treasure,' Harper said. He was exuding confidence.

'Let's Find Treasure,' Matt said.

'What?' Robin stared at him in surprise.

'Just something Dad used to say,' he explained.

She nodded. 'Of course,' she said, though there was no way she could have known that. Probably trying to make him look less daft in front of her father and Harper.

But they hadn't noticed anyway. Venture was studying the map displayed on the big screen. 'Can you mark the churches on here?' he asked.

'You think their positions might be important?' Harper asked.

'Possibly.'

'Well, you wouldn't be the first,' Harper told him. He tapped at the keyboard and the picture changed to show another map of the island, marking the locations of the six churches. The island itself was shaped like a ragged lozenge and the churches were all close to the edge.

'Makes sense,' Robin said. 'They're probably close to the fishing communities.'

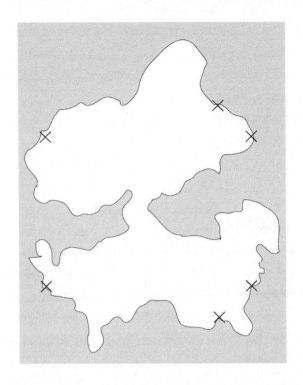

'They are,' Harper agreed. 'But even so, their distribution is interesting. Several are exactly the same distance apart. There have been studies that have tried to discern a relationship between their positions. The most plausible explanation, so far as it goes, is that they form a pentacle.'

'But it's not that simple,' Harper went on with a laugh. 'And I don't think it's very helpful either. He operated the keyboard again and a series of lines appeared, joining four of the churches to a point halfway between the other two. 'Why these two should be different and merit a single point on the star halfway between them is not something that the theory really explains,' he said.

'And the pentacle isn't perfect by a long way,' Robin pointed out.

'Wouldn't it make a big difference which part of the church you drew the lines to?' Matt asked.

'Indeed it would,' Harper agreed. 'But each church has a Maltese cross engraved on the floor at the centre of its circular structure.'

'And the lines are drawn from the middle of the crosses?' Venture asked.

'In theory. But again it is flawed. To make the pentacle even begin to work, the professor who first suggested a pattern had to argue that some of the churches are built in the wrong places.'

'Which rather makes a nonsense of it,' Venture agreed. 'You can hardly argue that the people who built them had a geometrical knowledge out of keeping with the era if you also say they got it wrong.'

'He makes a good stab at it, though,' Harper said. 'He argues that the churches are in fact built on older, ancient sites of worship and that the exact location of *those* sites is now lost. So the churches approximate to them, which is why the pattern is flawed.'

'Finding excuses,' Robin said.

'Is there any evidence of older sites?' Venture wanted to know.

Harper shook his head. 'In fact, there is evidence only for a seventh church which has since fallen into the sea when the cliffs collapsed. Another problem with a very flawed argument. There are other geometric theories too, but mostly based on patterns that need to include notional points out to sea or in the middle of nowhere. They are even less plausible.'

The door opened and Katherine Feather joined them. She smiled and nodded to Harper, and Matt guessed that her telephoning had been successful – whatever she had been arranging was now sorted out.

Venture was standing close to the screen, examining each of the locations of the churches in turn. 'A Maltese cross, in the floor of each church,' he said quietly.

'Isn't that what firemen in the USA use as their symbol?' Katherine said.

'That's right,' Robin replied. 'And the St John Ambulance Brigade.'

'St John?' Matt said. 'Is that significant? I mean, can it be?'

'Oh yes,' Venture said, without turning from the map. 'Tell them, Robin.'

'Both organizations use it,' Robin said, 'because the Maltese cross was the symbol of the Knights of the Order of the Hospital of St John. The Hospitallers. The St John Ambulance – well, that's obvious. And the knights were originally an order dedicated to medical help.' She drew a Maltese cross on a piece of paper as she spoke and held it up for them to see – four triangles, their points meeting in the centre.

'And firemen?' Matt asked. 'What's that about?'

'The Turks threw bottles of naphtha at the knights in battle. When they were covered with it, the Turks threw firebrands and ignited it, burning the unfortunate soldiers alive. The knights who weren't on fire dragged their fellows clear and tried to help them. The first firemen. Sort of.'

'Which is of academic interest,' Harper said, 'but hardly helpful.'

'I think you're wrong about that,' Venture said. He took a felt pen from a flipchart stand at the side of the room and started to draw on the surface of the plasma screen.

Katherine gave a gasp of astonishment and got up to stop him, but Harper stopped her: 'Wait.'

Venture was drawing a line connecting two of the churches. Although he drew it freehand, the line was perfectly straight. Then he drew lines from each of them to a point in the middle of the island, forming a triangle. Then he did the same with two more of the churches. The result looked like a bow tie.

'Half a Maltese Cross,' he said.

'But only half,' Harper told him. 'And, strictly speaking, the Maltese Cross has spayed ends to each of the arms. You've got a straight line.'

'And I'll bet the Maltese Crosses in the floors of the churches have too,' Venture said. 'This is an earlier version of the Maltese Cross. They'd want to keep it simple, and it's the symmetry that's important. Now, where exactly was the seventh church before it fell into the sea?'

Harper worked the keyboard, and a small 'X' appeared just off the edge of the island. Venture was already holding his pen over the exact spot. He connected the point to the last but one of the surviving churches, and again drew a line from each of these into the middle – another inward-pointing triangle. 'Three quarters of the cross.

But that only leaves you one church,' Katherine said.

In answer, Venture drew a line from the last church into the middle of the unfinished cross. 'We'll have to measure it out exactly,' he said. 'But to complete the Hospitallers' symbol, the Maltese cross, we need to use a point just here.' He drew another 'X' on the screen, then drew dotted lines from that point to the last church and into the

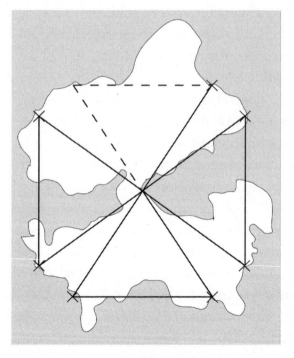

middle, completing the cross. 'This is the point they wanted us to find,' he said, tapping the pen on the X he had drawn. 'This is the missing point in the picture. The one point we need to add ourselves in order to complete it.'

'So?' Katherine said, still puzzled.

'So that,' Robin told her, 'is where the treasure is.'

They all stared at the cross that Venture had drawn in silence for a while. Then Harper said, 'You've ruined the screen, Julius, and I imagine the hotel will charge me for that. But it sounds as though it was well worth it.' He turned to Katherine. 'Are all the arrangements in place?'

'I just need to let them know the exact point where we wish to dig. Sven will sort out any problems with local landowners.'

Harper clapped his hands together in satisfied delight. 'Then I think we should be on our way. No point in wasting any more time.' His voice was almost trembling with excitement. 'How soon can you arrange the travel?'

A mere four hours later, in a noisy helicopter, with the island of Valdeholm just minutes away, Matt was just beginning to feel the same excitement welling up in his stomach. Was there really an ancient treasure down there, just waiting for them to come and get it?

✝

The reach of Harper's influence was apparent as soon as they landed. Matt had guessed that they would have to spend several more days finalizing permission to dig – finding local equipment and help, organizing accommodation and transport from the mainland . . . He could not have been more wrong.

Katherine Feather's time on the phone had obviously been well spent. Now Matt could see what she had been doing. The pilot set the huge helicopter down on the cliffs, close to where they believed the treasure was hidden. As they flew in over the sea, Matt and the others had a good view of the grassy cliff top. There was no sign of habitation at all and normally there would be nothing to suggest anyone lived on the island. It was like looking across a huge grassy plain, except that the side of it had been sheered off and dropped away almost vertically to the sea.

But today was not a normal day for the island. Matt could see at once where they would be dig-

na

ging. It was a small, low hill, bulging up from the flat plain like a medieval burial mound or barrow. Clustered round it, like metal insects, were several yellow diggers and earthmovers and two off-road, four-wheel-drive vehicles. Harper was serious and he was in a hurry.

It was cold on the cliffs, despite the bright morning sunshine. The long grass was blowing in the wind which whipped round Matt's body, tugging at his coat and freezing his ears. He stood with Venture and Robin while Harper and Katherine spoke to a man in a suit who had been sitting in one of the four-wheel-drives.

After a few moments, the man in the suit nodded and walked back to his vehicle. Harper turned towards Matt and the others and gave them a thumbs-up. Everything was in place; all the paperwork was already processed. They could begin.

The man in the suit drove away. The other four-wheel-drive belonged to a man called Sven, who had a neatly trimmed red beard that matched his fierce red hair. He was extremely tall and as thin as the metal rods being hammered into position round the site. The seats in the back of his vehicle were folded down to form a low table, over which was spread a large-scale map of the area. From Katherine's directions, he had already marked on the Maltese cross, and he told them he'd double-checked the measurements using GPS satellites before coming over from the mainland to meet them.

Venture and Harper examined the map, and discussed with Sven where best to start digging. As they spoke, another man arrived with a computer printout.

'Ground-penetrating radar,' Harper explained, taking the long, folded sheet of paper. 'No time to get the most modern equipment, I'm afraid, but this will probably do.'

Matt had seen similar printouts before. It looked like a sonar trace from a submarine and worked in much the same way. Radar was used to map out the rock and any other solid structure below the surface of the ground that would reflect back radio waves – metal, different types of soil even . . . He left Venture and Harper with Sven as they plotted the results of the radar trace over the map.

'You really think it's in there somewhere?' Matt asked Robin.

She was standing just inside the staked-out area, sheltering from the worst of the wind behind one of the enormous diggers. They had looked so small from the helicopter, which was itself perched like a metal fly on the cliff top 100 metres away.

She shrugged, pulling her coat more tightly round her. 'We'll know soon enough.'

'You been on a dig before?' Matt asked her.

She looked at him with ill-disguised sympathy. 'Just a few.'

They huddled into their coats and watched as Katherine directed the diggers into position, relaying instructions from Harper and Venture. Before long, the first chunk of grassy earth was bitten out of the ground and moved aside, revealing the rich, dark soil beneath.

✝

Harper had transferred the data from the radar into his laptop and used it as the basis for a computer model of the mound. It showed densely packed material – rock or stone – forming two intersecting double-lines through the mound. A cross. They set the diggers to work at either end of one of the lines.

'Why not just dig down in the middle?' Matt wondered. He was getting bored watching. The diggers seemed to have been at it for hours, peeling back layer after layer of topsoil. It was amazing how delicate the huge machines could be.

'We want to preserve the context,' Venture told him. 'We dig along, making a trench, then we can see the history and what else is going on. The radar image shows what looks like two parallel lines forming each of the arms of the cross. I'd like to know what they are.'

'What do you think they might be?' Matt asked.

Venture's reply was interrupted by a shout from one of the men supervising the diggers. They ran to see what had been uncovered.

It was an opening – a rectangular hole leading into the darkness. Weathered stone walls on either side formed a corridor into the very heart of the mound. Venture smiled and nodded, as if this was exactly what he had expected. Perhaps it was, Matt thought – it made sense. A way into the treasure house. There was a shout from the other side of the mound and Matt guessed that the other digger had uncovered something very similar.

Sven brought torches. Harper inspected the tunnel opening, rubbing his hands together in delight. 'I suggest we approach the problem from both ends,' he said. 'Julius, perhaps you and Robin would like to explore this tunnel, while, Sven, would you take the other end?' He turned to Matt. 'I assume you'd like to go with him and see what your father has been searching for so diligently, hmm?'

'Of course,' Matt agreed. He felt both excited and nervous at what they might find inside. Would there be treasure, or just a short tunnel ending in a wall or earth?

'What about you?' Robin asked Harper.

'Oh, I'll wait here for you to report back.'

'You don't want to see for yourself?' Matt asked, astonished.

Harper was already sitting down on the raised edge of the mound and opening his laptop. 'I'll see soon enough, and I should hate to miss the excitement by being in the wrong tunnel. If you find anything, come straight back and tell me. Anyway, you're the ones who've done all the real work here.' He turned his attention to the screen. 'I shall write up my account while events are still fresh in my mind, unpolluted by memory and emotion.'

'You're sure?' Venture asked him.

'Hurry back.'

Venture nodded. 'See you in the middle,' he told

Matt and Sven, and together with Robin he stepped into the tunnel.

Sven walked quickly to the other end of the mound. It was about fifty metres and Matt had to almost run to keep up with the tall man. 'They'll be there before us,' Matt said. Sven did not answer, but Matt could see his eyes were gleaming with excitement.

They reached the very similar opening on the other side, the other end of the tunnel. Sven switched on his torch and shone it into the darkness. The walls, floor and roof of the tunnel were all made of stone. But between the stones, Matt could see the thin, dark lines of earth trying to break through.

'I think, from what Mr Harper says, that you deserve to go first,' Sven said.

Matt was surprised. 'Thank you.' He wondered if Sven was willing to let him take the lead as the tunnel looked about ready to collapse under the weight of the soil and earth above. But he switched on his torch and stepped into the tunnel without protest. Immediately the air felt damp and stale, the fresh wind cut off. He had to stoop slightly to avoid bumping his head. Glancing back, he could see that Sven was bent almost double.

'Have you worked for Mr Harper for long?' Matt asked as he moved slowly forward into the gloom.

Sven laughed, the sound echoing in the tunnel. 'Since his people called me at six o'clock this morning,' he said. 'I am curator of a small museum in Dorpfelt, about eighty kilometres away as the blackbird flies.'

They made their way slowly forward, Matt shining his torch on the ground ahead. The floor was lined with slabs, but they were old and uneven. In places, the stone had lifted and the ground seemed to be forcing its way through into the tunnel. The walls were the same – old and broken. Here and there stones had fallen or crumbled away, leaving debris on the floor and holes for earth to trickle through.

Matt ran his hand along the wall to steady himself as he picked his way over a pile of debris. He could feel the old, damp texture beneath his fingers – indentations, flaking stone and then, suddenly, a straight edge. Surprised, he stopped and shone his torch directly at the wall.

'Look at this,' he breathed.

'What is it?' Sven was shining his own torch at the same spot. At the indentation in the wall where a small cross had been carved out of the stonework. 'There's another one here,' Sven said, shining the torch further along, ahead of them.

'And another,' Matt realized, looking back towards Sven. 'All along the wall.' He turned and examined the opposite side of the tunnel. 'Both walls,' he said. 'Leading us onwards. Marking the way.'

The torchlight seemed to be swallowed up by blackness when Matt shone it ahead of them. As they moved forward again, he saw why. A whole section of the tunnel roof had collapsed. The passageway ahead of them was nearly filled with earth and debris, creating a huge mound that reached almost to the remains of the ceiling.

'We shall have to go back,' Sven said, disappointed.

Matt was not so sure. 'There's space at the edge. We might be able to squeeze through. If it isn't too densely packed.'

'You think so?' Sven sounded dubious.

'Worth a try,' Matt told him. He shone his torch round the edge of the pile of debris and could see the stone floor disappearing into the gloom on the other side of the obstruction. He turned the torch off and stuffed it into his pocket.

With only half the amount of light, the tunnel

seemed to close in around him. Matt tried to push himself sideways through the narrow gap. Sven was right, there just wasn't enough room. But the gap got wider higher up. Matt reached his arms over the pile of stone and earth and felt for something on the other side, something to grab hold of so he could pull himself through.

It was strange, Matt thought, as he stared up at the murky darkness of the collapsed roof – the hole in the tunnel ceiling was just about the same size as the space he was now trying to wriggle through. It looked like something had pushed its way through, forcing the ceiling and the earth behind it down into the space below. Had someone got there before them?

'Careful!' Sven warned as more earth fell through the ruptured ceiling and slid down the pile.

'It's OK,' Matt gasped, heaving himself up and into the gap. 'It's not blocked for long. I can get through, then we can maybe shift some of this and make the hole wide enough for you.'

He was nearly there now. Emerging head first from the mass of dirt and debris into darkness. His body was filling the gap and blocking out the light from Sven's torch. He could feel the grip of the earth round him. It seemed to tighten as the dark-ness deepened. Then, with a last heave, he was through and tumbling down the other side of the mound of earth.

But even as he did so he was aware of a roaring in his ears – Sven was shouting, and the whole tunnel seemed to groan and move. Then dirt and darkness came crashing down over Matt. The roof was collaps-ing, what little support had been left for it pulled away by Matt himself as he broke through the blockage. He could feel the earth and stone falling down around him, knocking him sideways. His nose and eyes were full of gritty blackness. He fumbled desperately for his torch, and managed at last to switch it on.

The beam of light was misty with falling dust and dirt. And behind Matt the tunnel was completely blocked. He could hear Sven's muffled voice from the other side of the blockage, shouting to him that he would get help and dig Matt out.

Matt sat on the cold, damp tunnel floor, shining the torch helplessly and hopelessly at the mass of debris clogging the passage behind him. All he could do was wait.

Or was it? Surely, if he kept going, he would meet Venture and Robin coming the other way – he might even find the treasure. Matt scrambled to his feet and set off quickly along the tunnel.

Only to find that there was another blockage further along. One of the walls had fallen into and across the tunnel, blocking the way forward with huge, heavy chunks of stone.

☩

The wind was blowing Katherine Feather's ice-blonde hair round her face as she stood at the end of the tunnel. She was peering into the darkness. There was no sign now of Venture and his daughter. She waited patiently, listening for any sound, watching for any indication that they had found something.

Sitting on a lower part of the rising mound, Harper was still engrossed in his laptop. He was smiling thinly, oblivious to the cold wind, angling the screen so he could see it despite the bright sunlight.

There were two windows open on the screen. One showed a basic wire-frame model of the mound itself, with the information from the radar added in so that the tunnels formed a cross through the middle. It was the second window where

Harper was working. An image solidified slowly from its own wire skeleton – surfaces and textures gradually filling it out like a child's colouring. A dark, mottled, rat-like creature revolving slowly inside the window. Its eyes glinted darkly.

Satisfied, Harper clicked on a control and the creature stopped turning. It stared back out of the screen at him. Harper's fingers traced across the touchpad and the pointer on the screen moved to another control. An entry box opened and he typed in a number: 10. He hesitated, then added another 0, making it 100. The box closed and the window was suddenly full of the creatures, jostling and fighting for space, disappearing behind the edges of the window. They seemed to scratch at the glass of the screen, trying to get out. Screeching and shrieking erupted from the little speakers at the sides of the laptop and Harper adjusted the volume.

Then he closed the window. It shrank back down to a small icon on the desktop. Slowly, carefully, Harper picked up the icon with the pointer and dragged it over to the wire-frame picture of the mound. The pointer, loaded with the icon, hovered for a moment over a point two-thirds of the way along a tunnel – a point where a black web of lines traced out an obstruction. Harper lifted his finger from the touchpad. And the icon tumbled into the tunnel.

✚

It was the noise that Matt noticed first. A scratching, scraping sound.

'Hello?' he called. 'Is that you?' Had Robin and her father reached the other side of the cave-in? Were they trying to get through? 'I'm here!' he shouted, shining the torch at the wall of fallen stone in the hope that some of its light might penetrate to the other side for them to see.

The sound was getting louder, a high-pitched shrieking and squealing as well as the scratching. It seemed to be coming from all around him. Matt swung the torch away from the wall. A shape caught in its beam – it hesitated, then darted into the blackness. Shadows moved and trembled all around him.

Something landed on Matt's shoulder. Instinctively he brushed it away, looking up in case the roof was about to fall. His hand had brushed against something cold and rough, like fallen earth. The torchlight seemed to be absorbed by the black of the roof – dark shadowy stone. It rippled and moved as the torchlight shone across it. As if it was alive.

And another shape detached itself from the ceiling and dropped on to Matt's shoulder. Caught full in Matt's torch beam, dark eyes gleaming, the shape stared back at him. A rat. Claws raked savagely at his face.

Matt shouted, thrashed at the thing on his shoulder, and crawled back as more of them fell from the roof. They were landing all around him – *on* him. The scratching and shrieking got louder and louder. A black tide was flowing across the ground, clawing its way up his legs as he struggled away as quickly as he could.

The back of his head met something hard and gritty, and Matt turned and lashed out. The torch went flying, its light dancing crazily across the scene before landing with a thump. It went out. Darkness.

But Matt had already seen the wall of earth behind him and the mass of creatures scurrying towards him. He was trapped.

Without thinking, he was lashing out again, thumping at anywhere on his body he felt – or thought he felt – one of the creatures. He expected them to be soft, oily, warm . . . But they were hard and brittle, rough and gritty, like the earth piled behind him. And cold as stone. He could feel their sharp, brittle claws scraping through his trousers, tearing at his coat. Their teeth nipped at his ears and face as he desperately fought and thumped and ripped them off him. The sound was unearthly – echoing and reverberating in the confined space. No longer the high-pitched shriek of the creatures, but Matt's own shouts and cries for help and the thumping of his heart.

Without the light, he could only imagine where the animals were, how many were attacking him. He was breathing in short, sharp, panicked gasps as the blackness itself seemed to take on texture and become a living thing. He could feel it pressing down on him. Dragging him into oblivion.

✝

'Matt is trapped,' Sven gasped. 'There was a fall – the roof . . .' He paused to get his breath back.

Harper glanced up. 'But he is all right?'

Sven nodded. 'We need to get him out.'

'We can reach him from other end of the tunnel, I'm sure,' Harper said. He was smiling as he returned his attention to his computer.

'I'm afraid not.' It was Venture's voice, and Harper looked up again, surprised.

Venture and his daughter were standing with Katherine Feather. Their faces, hands and clothes were dusted with mud and earth.

'Problem?' Harper asked.

'The tunnel's blocked,' Robin said. 'We went as far as we could, but there's no way through. It's completely collapsed.'

'We can get through from my end,' Sven said. 'We just need a couple of shovels.'

'Come on, then,' Venture said.

Harper tapped his fingers thoughtfully on the area below his keyboard. Then he closed down the program he was running and snapped the lid shut. 'The poor boy will be terrified,' he said. 'We must help him, of course.'

✛

Matt found the torch by accident – rolling over it as he desperately thrashed and crawled, trying to get away from the attacking creatures. He scooped it up, thumbing the switch without much hope. Incredibly, the torch wasn't broken. It must have just switched off when it hit the ground.

A beam of yellow light shot out, illuminating the passageway and the dark mottled shapes of the creatures as they hurled themselves out of the darkness at him like a black wave. Matt gave a shriek of terror and swung the torch, smashing it into one of the dark shapes. The creature exploded in a shower of dry fragments.

But Matt didn't stop to think about that, didn't wait to see the dry earth that fell to the ground tremble and gather itself back into a new, identical creature – stone-black eyes glinting malevolently. He was tearing at the mass of earth and stone blocking the tunnel. He couldn't go back, but he could try to dig his way forward, further into the mound.

Coughing and choking and gasping, tears streaming down his frightened face, he had nothing to lose. He pulled desperately at the rubble, scraping away the smaller stones, leaping out of the way of the larger ones that fell down after them. He jammed the torch under his armpit so he could use both hands to rip away the obstruction.

With a scraping roar, the whole bank of debris collapsed. A falling lump of stone caught Matt on the shoulder and knocked him backwards. He stumbled away, stamping one of the creatures to powder, not noticing. The tunnel was full of dust, like an eerie mist. He almost dropped the torch again. It slipped from under his arm and he scrabbled to catch it. As it fell, the light cut through the opening in the rock wall ahead of him, showing him the hole that he had cleared. A hole large enough to climb through.

He hurled himself towards it and scrambled through into the tunnel beyond.

On the other side, he waited only long enough to realize that the rat-like creatures were not following him. He didn't stop to wonder why, he just ran. Head down, he charged along the tunnel, the torch-light swaying drunkenly over the floor and walls.

Behind him, the small, shadowy creatures fell back into the darkness from which they had come. Scattered across the tunnel floor. Dirt and earth and mud and sand . . .

✝

The rock fall was not as deep as it looked and, with help from Sven, Venture managed to shovel the earth aside quite quickly. As soon as there was room, Robin was past them and pushing through the gap.

'Matt? Matt, are you all right?'

She turned to take the torch that Sven held through the gap for her. The ground was covered with small piles of earth, like molehills, but otherwise the tunnel ahead seemed empty. She reached the second rock fall and, like Matt before her, climbed over the fallen lumps of stone from the roof.

'Here!' a voice called from ahead in answer to her increasingly worried shouts.

Further on, the tunnel widened out into a large circular chamber with a domed roof. The floor sloped gently down into the middle of the chamber, which must reach almost to the top of the inside of the mound.

The floor was grey with the dirt of ages, but even so Robin could see that some of the stones were black in among the light grey that was used everywhere else. A pattern, inlaid in the floor – a large Maltese cross with the centre directly under the middle of the dome.

Sitting cross-legged on the floor in the middle of the chamber was Matt. He looked pale under the dirt that smeared his face and his clothes were torn and caked with mud. There were trails down his face where tears had run, but now he was grinning in the light from the torch resting in his lap.

'I think this is it,' he said. His voice was trembling, and Robin could sense it was from fear as much as excitement. 'Here, help me.'

The centre of the cross, the tips of the four inward-pointing triangles that formed the pattern, was set into a single circular stone. Like a tile, it rested in the middle of the floor, about half a metre in diameter. Matt had his fingers in the narrow crack between the circular shape and the stone next to it. He had managed to lift it just slightly.

Putting down her torch, angling it so she could see what they were doing, Robin reached down to help. The stone was cold and unyielding, but together they managed to nudge it slowly upwards. At last, there was darkness beneath as the stone lifted away to reveal a dark circular well.

Robin picked up her torch. She was only vaguely aware of her father and Sven arriving beside them and barely noticed Atticus Harper and Katherine Feather entering the chamber.

Like Matt, she was looking down into the hole they had revealed. Staring at the cracked rolls of parchment, the leather-bound volumes, and the glint and gleam of metal.

12

There was nowhere on the island for Matt to clean
himself up, so he had to wait until they were back in
Copenhagen. He was cut and bruised, but elated at
finding the treasure. However, just as Robin had
warned him, there was no sign of Dad – or even any
indication that he had ever been there. Harper gave
instructions that the site was to be preserved and left
it to Katherine to organize the purchase of the land
from the farmer who actually owned it.

'Buy the whole island if you have to,' he said, and
gave her the names of three Danish officials and
politicians she could talk to if there was a problem.

Nothing was touched except for the artefacts and
relics and documents that Matt and Robin had
uncovered in the central chamber. These were carefully crated up and put on the helicopter to return

with Harper and the others to the Waterfall Pyramid. Harper brushed aside the objections of Venture and Sven, both of whom argued that everything should be left intact and *in situ*.

'We have to know if this is indeed the Treasure of St John,' Harper insisted. 'And if it is, then we need to take it into safe-keeping. Who knows what might happen to it otherwise – we're not the only people interested in it, you know. But we are the most trustworthy.'

Venture said nothing, and Sven was silenced with some quiet words from Katherine. Matt did not hear what she said, but he could guess – a grant for his museum, a pay-off of some sort. It seemed to be how Harper did business. To Harper, everything *was* business.

At Copenhagen airport, money also greased the wheels. But Matt did not object – Harper had organized rooms at a luxury airport hotel and Matt was at last able to soak off the mud and dirt in a hot, deep bath. His whole body stung like hell from thousands of tiny scratches. They had three hours before Harper's plane would be leaving for Rio and their luggage had been sent over from the other hotel. Matt spent over half the time just lying in the bath, occasionally topping it up with hot water, and gradually feeling less of the pain. He tried not to think about how he had come by the scratches and bruises. It was over now, that was what mattered. Just . . . rats. But a part of his mind couldn't help but wonder if that was really what they were. Where had they come from? Where had they gone?

When a car arrived and took him back to the runway, Matt wasn't surprised to find that Harper himself, together with both Venture and Robin, did not seem to have left the plane at all.

'There's a shower,' Robin pointed out as they strapped in for take-off. 'Everything we need. Why bother with the hotel?'

'Oh, wish I'd thought of that,' Matt said sarcastically.

'Well, you're a special case,' she told him.

'Thanks a bunch.'

'I mean, you really *did* need a bath.'

On the flight, Matt tried to tell Robin about the creatures in the tunnel. It was the first chance he'd had to talk to her without other people around, but the further he got with his story, the more improbable it seemed. Was he starting to imagine things, he wondered? Was it some sort of nervous problem brought on by the strain of the last few days?

'Rats?' she said incredulously. 'I didn't see any rats.'

'No, well, they were there. Hundreds . . .' He sighed. 'A lot of them.'

'Something must have scared them off,' Robin said. From the way she said it, Matt guessed that she didn't believe him.

'You, probably,' Matt grumbled.

'Thanks a bunch,' she said, echoing his earlier tone.

✠

The crate was standing in the main cabin, and it wasn't long before Harper had it opened and, together with Venture, began to unpack the artefacts on to the conference table.

Robin, Matt and Katherine helped. Matt could feel the age of the leather-bound books as he lifted them out of the packing and placed them carefully alongside rolls of parchment. The paper was thick and dry and brittle. The writing was faded and none of it was in English.

'Just a fraction of what was there in Constantinople,' Venture said sadly. 'It seems they managed to save even less than we thought.'

'Or else Sivel didn't retrieve it all,' Robin suggested.

Harper, strangely, did not seem interested in the papers and parchments and books. Almost at once he had picked up one single artefact, ignoring jewelled crucifixes, bracelets, swords and daggers and even gold and silver coins. He sat alone on a large sofa and examined a disc that looked like it was made of terracotta.

The others continued to sort through the materials on the table, except for Venture. He was standing motionless close to Harper, watching him intently through narrowed eyes. He was so still and stern that seeing him made Matt shiver.

'What have you got there?' Venture asked after he had been watching for a while.

Harper did not look up. 'I wonder,' he said. 'Any ideas?' He held the disc out and Venture took it.

Venture cradled it carefully in his palm as he examined it closely. 'It's just a bit of pottery,' he said in a level voice. 'Anyone else?' He handed the disc to the nearest person, as if deciding it was of no value or interest at all.

The nearest person happened to be Matt. He took it, turning it over in his hands, feeling the weight . . . For a moment, just a second, he imagined himself back in Dad's study. Something about the disc was so familiar. The size, the shape, the weight . . . Then he remembered the box he had found in Venture's house when he'd been sent to get a statue. A wooden box containing a metal disc . . .

Matt was aware that Venture was watching him closely, as if he had guessed what Matt was thinking. The slightest shake of the head – almost imperceptible. The man's expression was still set and stern. Matt shrugged and handed the disc to Katherine Feather.

'I've never seen anything like it,' he said.

✝

The gentle motion of the plane eventually lulled Matt to sleep. He dozed and woke and dozed again. Sometimes when he woke, Robin was sitting beside him, sometimes he was alone. Snatches of reality in between dreams of darkness.

He was aware of Katherine stretched out cat-like and asleep on one of the sofas. None of the others seemed to sleep at all. Harper in particular was wired – examining the strange disc through a magnifying glass, going through the parchments and papers, talking earnestly and urgently to Venture.

An hour out from Rio, Matt woke to find Robin once more in the adjacent seat. Her father was beside her, crouched down so they were on the same level to talk.

'I've told him it's not my field,' Venture was saying. 'But he's becoming worryingly insistent. Just be careful.'

Robin nodded, and Matt wondered what they were talking about.

Venture was looking across at Matt now, seeing that he was awake. 'You need to be careful too,' he said.

'What of?'

'Of Harper. He wants me to help him translate the symbols on that disc.'

'And you can't?'

'I won't,' Venture said softly. 'He may ask Robin. He may even ask you. Be careful how you reply. That disc is *unique*.'

Matt frowned, remembering the very similar disc he knew Venture had in his possession. 'But surely –'

Venture cut him off. 'As far as Harper is aware, it is unique. It is obviously that disc he's been after, not the rest of the treasure. He thinks it will lead him to a treasure far greater than the one we have already found for him. That's the trouble, isn't it? We're never satisfied. The more we have, the more we want.'

'I just want Dad back,' Matt said. 'We've got the Treasure of St John now. Do we bargain, or will they let him go, or what?'

Robin took Matt's hand and held it between both her own, just like she'd held his hand in the restaurant in Copenhagen. 'We'll find him,' she promised.

'I think we're now much closer to finding Arnold,' Venture agreed. 'Though perhaps not in the way you imagine.'

'Meaning what?' Matt demanded.

Venture smiled, but it was a sad, sympathetic smile. 'Just a theory. It is perhaps surprising we've heard nothing from these mysterious opponents of Harper's. Seen nothing of them. No evidence that they even exist. Except for the fact your father's missing. The treasure was undisturbed and Harper never suggested that there might be anyone else in Denmark after it. He seemed to take no precautions. And now, well, Harper's sudden insistence that I help him further worries me. His quest for more of the ancient knowledge . . .'

Matt shifted in his chair, stretching. 'I think that's just a lot of mythical rubbish. Ancient knowledge and powers.'

Robin looked to her father for the answer. 'It doesn't really matter what *we* think,' Venture said quietly. 'It's what Harper thinks that matters now. He has the disc, he has a dream. And he's offered me a very large amount of money to help him interpret the disc and realize that dream.'

'Worrying,' Robin agreed.

'Not as worrying as the fact that he described it as his "final offer",' Venture told them. 'We could jump ship in Rio, but I doubt we'll get the chance. And better to extricate ourselves amicably if we possibly can. Stay on good terms. He's a powerful man and it wouldn't do to upset him if we can avoid it. Get some sleep,' he went on before Matt could ask him again what he meant. 'We're all going to need our wits about us.'

Looking over Venture's shoulder, Matt could see Harper staring at the disc, his forehead creased with concentration.

✠

The helicopter back to the Waterfall Pyramid was as noisy as ever. Both Harper and Venture seemed preoccupied. Harper's eyes were gleaming with excitement and enthusiasm. Venture, by contrast, was solemn and serious.

Despite having seen it before, Matt was still as impressed as ever with the spectacular view of the approach to the pyramid. The sight of the water cascading down the side of the extinct volcano was almost hypnotic.

As soon as the helicopter landed, the moment the noise of the engines had died and the rotors had spun to a lazy stop, Venture said to Robin and Matt, 'I've been thinking some more about that disc. And I'm convinced that Harper is now very close to what he is actually after. The rest is a diversion. It's the knowledge he thinks he can get from the disc that is really driving all this. First thing you do when you get inside is pack. We're leaving just as soon as I can persuade Harper we're no longer useful to him.'

But Harper, it seemed, would not be persuaded.

'I really can't agree to let you go,' he said, as if he was refusing them some minor request. He stood by the helicopter, watching as men in khaki uniforms unloaded the crates into which the various artefacts had been repacked in Rio and carried them to the pyramid.

'It isn't a question of agreement,' Venture told him. 'We came here to help you find the treasure, which we have now done. I really can't spare any more of my time. I have other things to see to, other work to do. Of course, if you'd like my help again I can try to schedule something. But not for a while. So we are leaving. Now.'

Harper shook his head. 'I don't think so.'

One of the men in khaki had paused beside Harper. He was a tall man, solidly built and with a completely bald head. His skin was tight on the face, his eyes sunken so that his head was a thinly wrapped skull.

Harper nodded to the man. 'Have you met Mr Klein?' he asked Venture. 'He is my head of security. So very efficient.'

As if to prove it, Klein slipped something off his shoulder and caught it easily in his massive hands. It was a machine gun, and it was pointing at Venture, Robin and Matt.

'You really will have to accept my hospitality for just a little while longer,' Harper said. 'I was hoping that you'd help me decipher the disc willingly. But if not . . .' He shrugged. 'Well, so be it. Mr Klein, will you show my guests to their rooms? I think that for the time being Mr Venture should share with his daughter. Perhaps that will help him to get matters into perspective. She needs such careful looking after.'

Harper smiled, his whole face creased and wrinkled as if with the effort. He reached out a hand, running the tips of his fingers down Robin's cheek. She stared back at him impassively, not moving.

And quicker than Matt would have believed possible, Venture's arm shot out. Quicker than either Harper or his head of security could react, Venture knocked Harper's hand away. His voice was low and dangerous: 'Don't you dare touch my daughter. If anything happens to her . . .' He left the threat hanging heavy in the air between them.

Klein recovered quickly, swinging the gun round so it was pointing directly at Venture.

Harper was shaking with anger, but he put up a hand to stop Klein. 'Then you had better make sure there is no reason for anything to happen to her,' he said, furious. 'By cooperating.' He stood for a moment, staring Venture down. But Venture's eyes were cold and unflinching and it was Harper who looked away.

He turned to Klein. 'Take them inside,' he said.

✠

Several other armed men in similar khaki uniforms joined Klein to take Matt and the others to their rooms. Matt was bundled back into the room he'd had before. He could hear Robin and her father being pushed into the room next to his before his door slammed shut. There was no sound of a key or a bolt, so he guessed there was a guard outside. He tried the door to check.

It wouldn't open. There must be some way of programming the door so it could only be opened from the outside. He was trapped – locked inside a stone-built room with no other way out. Matt put his ear to the door and could hear nothing from outside.

But, he realized, he could hear *something*. From somewhere else, ever so faintly, he could hear music. There had been no music a few moments ago. Where was it coming from? He walked round the room, trying to work it out. But it was so faint that it was impossible to tell.

So Matt gave up. He flopped on to the bed and stared at the ceiling. Then he got up and switched on the huge plasma screen on the opposite wall. The computer desktop appeared – just as he had left it. And still he could hear the music. It was a different tune now, a pop song he recognized from last year. Still so faint he wondered if he could be imagining it.

He shook his head and switched the screen from the computer to television. Somewhere, maybe down in the ruined town below, Harper must have one hell of a satellite dish to pick up the channels from here, he thought, as he flicked through them. An American news channel, news again only in Spanish or Portuguese, a documentary, adverts, someone explaining how exciting a steam cleaner could be, a film, MTV, more adverts . . .

Matt stopped. He stared at the advert – a woman driving a big car through a mountain stream and along a narrow road in the middle of nowhere. Then he changed back to the previous channel. MTV – music. The *same* music as he could hear, accompanied now by the video. He muted the sound and watched the dancing. Yes, it was exactly the same music, exactly in time. He could hear a television somewhere. He turned off the screen and sat on the bed, thinking.

☩

The television was tuned to a music channel and turned up loud so that Robin and Venture could talk quietly without the risk of anyone hearing them. Of course, there was no one else in the room, but Venture was pretty sure that Harper had microphones installed. He had searched carefully for hidden cameras and was as certain as he could be that there were none. But microphones could be built into the walls themselves. They didn't need to be visible; they didn't need to see and therefore be seen.

'There doesn't seem to be any way out apart from the door,' Robin said.

'Then we must get out when the door is already open,' Venture told her. 'A different problem.'

'Harper will take you to help him decipher the disc soon. Maybe you'll get an opportunity to escape.'

'We are in the middle of the rainforest,' Venture pointed out.

'So we bring someone else here. To get us. Though I don't know how,' she admitted.

'Smith?' Venture smiled. 'He'd love that.'

'He'd be interested in this place,' Robin said. 'And the disc.'

'Yes, the disc.' Venture tapped his fingers together. 'That's another strange thing . . .'

'What is?'

Venture was frowning now. 'That's an odd drum-beat.'

'Modern music,' Robin told him, smiling. 'We'll never understand it. The youth of today.'

But Venture was on his feet, checking the door and then the walls. 'Definitely coming from the screen,' he decided. He clicked the remote and the music faded.

Yet the thumping sound they had taken to be a drumbeat continued.

Venture turned up the music. 'Great beat,' he said loudly as he did so. 'Hear that rhythm. No other drummer like him.'

Robin watched, her head tilted to one side so that her long black hair hung away from her head, as her father felt round the plasma screen. He beckoned for her to come and help. She managed to work her fingernails, then the very tips of her fingers behind the screen. Together they edged it away from the wall.

'It must come out for maintenance or replace-ment,' she said quietly. The screen was moving easily now, as if someone was pushing from the other side.

Wires and cables trailed behind the screen. The sound of the music was almost deafening and the thumping had stopped. The thin screen came clear of the wall panels and they stepped carefully back – to reveal the empty space behind the screen. Empty apart from Matt, climbing through from the hole in the wall. A hole that went right through into the other room beyond, which was a mirror image of theirs.

'Makes sense,' Venture said as they pushed the screen back into place. They did not push it right back, so it would be easier to remove next time. 'A single set of cables for both screens. Like when you plumb hotel bathrooms back-to-back.' He dusted his hands together and said to Matt, 'You did well to work it out.'

'Thanks,' Matt said. 'Why's the telly on so loud?' Robin explained about the microphones and Matt shook his head. 'You're just paranoid,' he said. But he said it quietly.

'We are locked up,' Robin pointed out.

'First things first.' Venture spoke as if this was not a problem. 'It won't be long before Harper sends his thugs to take me to help him with his disc, so we had better make this quick.'

'Why's the disc so important?' Matt said. It was tempting to shout to be heard above the sound of the music. He had to struggle to hear Robin and Venture, though they didn't seem to find it a problem. 'You've got one very like it, only yours is made of metal.'

'And don't tell him *that*, whatever you do,' Robin said, then paused before asking, 'How do you know? Anyway, it's different.'

'It certainly is,' Venture agreed. 'Though I'm not certain if that's a good thing or a bad thing. Harper thinks,' he told Matt, 'that the disc is a message. A message from the past. As I told you on the plane, he thinks it is the key to a great treasure. He believes that it contains clues that hold the secret of that great treasure, or that can lead him to that treasure. The treasure he is really after.'

'And what's that?' Matt laughed. 'Ancient gold and silver?'

'In a sense. He's after what the ancients *knew*. Their ancient knowledge and wisdom. The way they thought, the way they controlled their lives. That is what he is after, and it is far more valuable and infinitely more dangerous than any ordinary treasure. Now he has the disc, he believes it is within his grasp.'

'So, how do we stop him?' Robin asked. 'He'll

decode the disc. With or without your help.'

'I'm afraid you're right,' Venture said. 'Even the fact he can't decipher the disc won't slow him down for long. It may be the disc itself that he is after, or the disc may point the way forward to the next stage of his journey. He's on the trail and he knows where it leads. He's desperate to reach the end of the journey and it seems that he's already a good way along it.'

'The rats,' Robin said, her voice almost swallowed up by the music.

'What about them?' Matt demanded.

'Later,' Venture said. 'There is a lot you need to know, but later. Now we have to get out of here. Or, more accurately, we have to get you two out of here.'

'What about you?' Robin said, her concern evident.

'I must try to stop Harper, or slow him down. And I'm afraid I don't see a way that I can get out of here as well as you two.'

'And how do we get out?' Matt asked. 'The door's locked, the hole in the wall only leads back into another locked room. The walls are solid stone – well, except for the hidden microphones – and the plughole in the bath is too small even for Robin.'

Venture smiled and nodded. 'All you see is the problem. You must learn to see the solution. See the wood despite the trees. Trust me, there is a way.'

✝

The waiting was the worst. Matt could hear nothing, and he hoped that Robin would have a better idea of what was going on. In the event, he need not have worried. Without warning, the door to his room was yanked open and the skull-headed Mr Klein strode into the room.

He stared at Matt through malevolent eyes, without saying a word.

Matt had been lying on the bed, reading. Though he had little idea what he'd actually read. Really he was just staring at the pages.

'What?' he said.

Klein still did not reply. He turned on his heel, stormed out of the room and slammed the door shut behind him.

'Wonder what's rattled his cage,' Matt said out loud. 'Think I'll put the telly on.'

With the music channel once more blaring out it was easier to pull the screen away from the wall than it had been to manhandle it back into position earlier. But now Matt had the help of Robin pushing from the other side – from the space where she had been hiding between the two screens.

'There's not a lot of room in there,' she complained. 'Let's hope they left the door open.'

'Did you hear what happened?' Matt asked as they pushed at the screen in Robin's room from the space behind.

'It was that Klein man,' she said. With both screens playing loud music, it was hard to hear her at all.

'Mr Baldy,' Matt said. 'Yeah, he stomped in, looked at me and then stomped out again.'

'Checking you hadn't disappeared too.'

'What did your dad say when they found you'd gone?'

Robin smiled. 'He said I'd just popped out for a bit and would be back later. That didn't go down too well actually, although it's the truth.' Her smile was gone now and she was biting her lower lip. 'I think they hit him. I heard them searching the room, checking I wasn't hiding. Then they took Dad to Harper.'

The screen almost fell into the room. But between them they managed to keep hold of it and lower it gently down the wall as far as the connected wires and cables would allow. Then they climbed through into Robin's room. It was a mess – drawers pulled out of the cabinets and books and papers and clothing strewn across the floor. But it was empty.

And the door was open.

'Let's put the screen back,' Matt whispered. 'Keep them guessing.'

'They'll guess the truth as soon as they look in your room and see the screen's out there. It's a pity we can't put it back from this side.'

It was Matt's turn to be smug now. 'Then we'll do it from the other side. The door will open from the corridor. You can hold it open while I put the screen back. In case we need to play the same trick again.'

'They aren't going to lock me up again,' Robin said, and Matt could tell that she meant it.

'Got your passport?' he asked.

'The main exit will be guarded,' Robin said quietly as they made their way carefully along the corridor towards the stairs. 'They may not know how I escaped, but they know I'm on the loose.'

They had both had the same idea. If the main entrance was now guarded, then they should get down into the hidden amphitheatre. Either they could take refuge there, or – with luck – they could get out into the ruined town at the foot of the mountain. Then they could look for some way of escaping from the jungle and getting back to Rio and modern civilization.

The narrow, gloomy stairway took them down to the storage area, Matt remembered. Fortunately Harper's guards did not seem to be searching for Robin down here and Matt guessed they were concentrating on the more obvious escape routes. The two of them heaved aside the old tapestry and made their way warily through to the ancient ruined structure.

'Which way?' Matt wondered. 'They'll be looking for us soon, even down here. Maybe we should find somewhere to hide till the fuss dies down.'

'If it ever does. I don't think Harper is the forgive-and-forget type who doesn't bear a grudge or remember an insult.' Robin was looking round for the best way to go. 'We could head down to the river and see if we can get out along there, through the tunnel,' she said. 'Or while we're here we can see if there's a better way out.'

The place was vast and there was a lot of it they had not explored. Matt had not realized how much was in darkness. The lamps only illuminated the area round them, pools of light in a huge cavern of blackness. They made their way slowly down the terraced tiers towards the circular stage and the rushing water far below. There must be fifty of the huge steps leading to the tiny-looking area at the bottom. But as they got closer, Matt realized that the stage was actually as big as any he had seen before. He stared off into the gloom, trying to make out the limits of the place – the walls he knew must be there.

He saw only darkness. And then, about two-thirds of the way down to the stage, off to the far side of the amphitheatre, he saw a distant light.

'What's that?'

Robin looked where he was pointing. 'I'm not sure. Must be another part of the complex, but I don't remember it being lit up before.'

'Let's take a look.'

'Let's just get out of here,' she countered.

'I want to see,' Matt insisted. 'It might be a way out.' He walked towards the light, picking his way carefully through the ruins in the gloom.

Robin sighed and followed.

The light was coming from behind the ruins of a low wall. As they got closer, Matt could make out more of the area on the other side of the wall. He could see desks and office furniture. He could hear the hum of computers. The light was coming from several lamps suspended from tall metal poles, but also from desk lamps.

'Talk about open-plan,' he said.

As they rounded the wall, they found themselves in an area laid out like a modern office, complete with desks and workstations, filing cabinets and metal cupboards. And there were people working there. They looked up as Matt and Robin approached.

Two people. Sitting next to each other at a desk, working together at a computer. One of them was Katherine Feather, her platinum hair almost glowing in the light from the computer screen. She looked at Matt in surprise.

But not as much surprise as the man next to her showed. Not as much surprise as Matt himself was feeling. It was as if he was detached from his body, seeing things from a distance. His feet were like lead, unable to take another step forward, and his voice sounded like it was filtered through water. He stared at the man at the desk, the man now standing up and staring back at him, and said just one incredulous word: 'Dad?'

13

The room looked exactly as it had when Venture was taken from it. Now he stood just inside, his arms pinioned by two of the khaki-clad security guards. He watched with amusement as Harper walked slowly all round the room. Beside Venture, Klein was scowling.

'Nervous?' Venture asked quietly, his voice barely audible above the sound of the television.

Klein did not answer, but one of his men twisted Venture's arm viciously.

On the other side of the room Harper switched off the screen. He stared at it in the ensuing silence. Then he turned to Klein. 'This is exactly how you found it?'

'It's exactly as we left it,' Klein said. 'He was here.' He nodded at Venture. 'The girl was gone. We checked everywhere.'

'You can't have checked *every*where,' Harper said. He strode across the room and stood immediately in front of Venture, staring into his blue eyes. 'Where is she?'

'I don't know.'

'Where was she hiding?'

'Under the bed.'

Harper turned sharply towards Klein. 'Did you look under the bed?'

The man blinked. 'Yes, sir.'

He had hesitated only a second, but it was enough. Harper's arm lashed out and he slapped the man hard across the face. 'No, you didn't.'

'She wasn't under the bed,' Klein insisted.

'I know that, you fool.' Harper went to the bed and pulled up the covers. The bottom section of the bed below the mattress was solid, with drawers in it. There was less than five centimetres between the bed and the floor.

'We did look in the drawers, sir,' one of the men holding Venture said.

'It doesn't matter.' Harper seemed suddenly bored with the conversation. 'I really don't care where she was hiding. That isn't important.'

'Sir?' Klein said.

But Harper was again talking to Venture. 'Is it?' he said quietly. 'But never mind. I can find her again, quite easily.'

'Really?' Venture said. 'It seems not everything is as predictable as you think.'

Harper turned back to Klein. 'Bring him to my study.'

'Yes, sir.' Klein gestured for the men to take Venture out.

Harper waited until they were out of the room, but Venture could hear his fury, could hear him shouting at his head of security: 'What matters is that *you left the door open!*'

✝

'I'm so sorry, Matt. I wanted to tell you. I really did.'

Matt hardly heard Katherine's words. All his attention was focused on the wiry figure of his father. The face he knew so well – round and friendly with laughing eyes and thinning brown hair.

'It's good to see you,' Dad said. 'I knew you were here of course. Harper enjoyed telling me that.' He turned to Robin, and Matt was surprised how pleased Dad seemed to be to see her.

'Hello, Arnie,' Robin said. 'It's been a long time.'

She held out her hand. But to Matt's astonishment, his dad pulled Robin into a hug.

'Why are you here?' Even as he asked the question, Matt knew the answer. 'He's had you working on finding the treasure, hasn't he? That's why some of the data was so new. You never left.'

'Oh, I left,' Dad told them. 'Well, I was working from home, but I told them I quit. Took them by surprise, that did. But they soon came looking for me. I thought that would be the end of it, I could just refuse. Maybe I was a bit naïve.' He clicked his tongue, as if considering this. 'Yes, well, I *was* a bit naïve. They came and got me – brought me here. I tried to refuse to have anything more to do with Harper's researches, but they made it very clear what would happen if I didn't cooperate.'

'He threatened you?'

'No.' Dad sat down at the computer again, looking suddenly tired. 'He threatened *you*. That's why I couldn't leave. That's why I had to help him find the Treasure of St John, though I did my best to point them the wrong way. But now Harper wants me to try to decipher the disc you found on Valdeholm.' He looked up and, to Matt's surprise, he was smiling. 'I'm so proud of you,' he said.

'I don't know what you have against Mr Harper,' Katherine said. 'I can't say I approve of his methods or the way he has treated you. But why refuse to help? He offered you a good salary.'

'And that's what you think it comes down to, is it?' Dad asked her. 'Money? Is that why you stand and watch and do nothing? Afraid of losing your job.'

She looked away, avoiding his stare. 'Yes,' she said quietly. 'I'm not proud of it, but I have parents who depend on me to keep them. And, all right, I enjoy what I do. I like having a good job with travel and a big salary. You didn't answer my question,' she added. 'Why refuse to help?'

It was Robin who answered: 'Because of what Harper is trying to discover.'

'The truth about the past?' Katherine said. 'He wants to discover the secrets of lost civilizations, that's all.'

'That's *all*?' Dad echoed. 'That's *everything*. The secrets he is after could change the world, could make him even more powerful than he is already.'

'You're exaggerating.'

Matt was inclined to agree with Katherine. 'I don't like being locked up or used as a hostage,' he said. 'But Harper can't change the world just by deciphering some old disc, can he?'

'This disc is just –' Dad started to say.

But Robin interrupted him. 'It's a means to an end. He wants knowledge and knowledge is power. Literally so in this case. He had a good start even without the disc, from what we've seen. But now, once he understands it all, he will have it *all*. Literally. No one should have that power. The secrets of the ancients remain secret for good reason. They knew things we can only guess at, things that would fundamentally change the world. They knew things that destroyed them.'

'Like what?' Matt countered. 'No, don't tell me – it's secret. So you can't know that, not for sure.'

'No?' Robin said. 'Think about it.'

'Harper's power is growing,' Dad said. 'He's able to predict behaviour to a degree. And I think he's gaining control over the elements. Just a start, but the more knowledge he gets, the better he understands, the more power he will have.'

Katherine was incredulous. 'What are you talking about? He's a businessman. A very shrewd businessman. He knows how people will react; he can predict what the markets will do as much as anyone who's successful in his line of work.'

'And what's this about the elements? What do you mean?' Matt asked.

'Earth, air, fire and water. The basic stuff of the world. Remember the candles,' Robin told him. 'And the hand that felt like sandpaper over your mouth.'

'Yes, but –'

'And the rats.'

Matt hesitated. The rats. Or whatever they were. He could remember them attacking him so clearly, he could almost feel them pressing in on him like the earth itself. 'You can't control the elements,' he said. 'Not like that. That'd be . . . magic.'

'That's undoubtedly how the ancients saw it,' Dad said. 'But it isn't. It's perfectly feasible. We just don't know how to do it. Or rather we didn't, until now.'

'You really think Harper can manipulate fire and earth in some way?'

'The basic elements of the world. Earth, air, fire and water,' Robin said. 'It isn't coincidence that they were seen as gods, or the gods were given control of them.'

'But it's ridiculous,' Katherine said.

Matt nodded in agreement. 'I can light a fire, just

as anyone can. I can control it, to an extent, feed it stuff to burn. But that isn't what you mean, is it?'

'No,' Robin said. 'It isn't. We're talking about fashioning the elements into forms we determine, organizing them to do what we will.'

'Like remote control?' Matt said.

'If you like,' Dad told him. 'That was how the ancient world worked in many ways. Everything was a proxy for something else, a representation. The Nazca Lines, not so far away from here, are an ancient map of the stars, a grid. The locations of the lines on the earth are dependent upon the positions of the stars above. The pyramids were a copy of the stars the Egyptians saw in the heavens.'

'But they didn't change and manipulate the stars in the heavens,' Matt pointed out.

'They believed they could,' Dad said. 'Everything on earth had a heavenly counterpart, and vice versa. The Maya, who lived near here, reckoned the very end of the world was predicted in the skies. Their Feathered Serpent was a beast made of the air itself. OK, so maybe they couldn't influence the stars, but think of Egyptian ushabti figures – little dolls that represented real people and went on the journey to the afterlife for them. People in other cultures had worry dolls that they could transfer their problems to.'

'That's like voodoo,' Matt said. 'You can't tell me it really works.'

'All right, think about voodoo if you like,' Dad said. 'You make a representation of a person, a real person – a voodoo doll – and what you do to the representation happens to the real person even if they're a vast distance away.'

'Which is obviously impossible,' Katherine said.

'You think so?' he replied quietly. 'I know you've got some scientific training. Have you ever heard of quantum entanglement?'

'Of course. Einstein called it "spooky action over a distance". But I don't see that . . .' Katherine's voice tailed off and the colour seemed to drain from her face so that it was almost as pale as her hair. 'You can't be serious,' she whispered.

✛

A click on a control added people to the model. The wire-frame representation of the pyramid was suddenly speckled with dots – each one of them a person in the real world. They moved and interacted and went about their business.

Harper was typing into a search field at the bottom

of the screen. 'You can't escape, my friends,' he murmured.

Venture, still held by two guards, watched impassively. Klein was standing close by, waiting for orders.

The image spun and changed – zooming in as the system found what Harper had asked for. It panned down beneath the pyramid, into the amphitheatre, across the terraces and towards an open area off to one side.

Four dots became vague shapes, became outlines of people. Two male, two female. Two sitting, two standing . . .

'Got you!' Harper said. His hand reached again for the mouse.

'I'll go and fetch them,' Klein said, turning to leave.

'Oh, I'm sure that won't be necessary,' Harper told him with satisfaction. 'I think it's time our young friends had a practical demonstration of my abilities.' He glanced up at Venture. 'Don't you?'

✟

'What are you talking about?' Matt demanded. He looked at Robin and saw that she seemed as grave as his father.

'Basically,' Dad said, 'quantum entanglement is a

process that allows scientists to tie together molecules, so that what happens to one molecule happens to the others linked to it. They say the molecules are entangled.'

'And they can be many kilometres apart, it still works,' Robin said. 'You think that's how Harper is working things? How he has managed to get control?' she asked Matt's dad.

'Possibly. I'm not an expert. I'm not sure how it works, just that it does. He creates models on his laptop – computer models, representations of things in the real world. Those things are made from earth, air, fire or water. Or a combination of them. And Harper has somehow "entangled" his computer models with the real world. He manipulates the model and the real things respond.'

Matt's mouth dropped open. '*Computer* models,' he said. 'We've seen them.'

'And you probably understand them rather better than I do,' Dad told him. 'But there has to be some grounding in the real world. In voodoo it's a lock of hair or a bit of fingernail that provides the link, the *entanglement*, between the doll and the real person.'

'Like DNA matching,' Robin said quietly. 'You'd need a unique pattern to identify the target – to be able to link the right model to the specific person. Harper's models do the same, but by being exactly to scale in every dimension. So accurate they are unique and specific with no ambiguity. This far Harper's been able to manipulate relatively small things, like grains of sand and candle flames. But what he really wants to do is to create a model to control the whole world. The universe, run like a program code on a computer.'

Matt held his hands up. 'OK, OK. Never mind how he does it, I'll accept that he does *something*. I've been attacked by rats that crumble to powder.'

'Back to earth,' Robin said. 'Dust to dust.'

'Whatever. But never mind that. The thing now is we have to get out of here. Then we can worry about how to stop him, assuming he needs stopping.'

'He needs stopping,' Dad said. 'What you've experienced is just the beginning of what he's hoping to do.'

'Fine, then let's get moving.'

'Why not just go to Harper and tell him to stop?' Katherine said. 'Tell him what he's doing is dangerous. He'd listen.'

'No, he wouldn't,' Robin told her. 'Matt's right. It's time we were going.'

Harper sat back, swinging gently in his chair as he watched the screen. 'Oh, I'm so sorry.' He leaned forward again and moved the screen slightly so that Venture could see better.

It showed a picture of what looked like an open-plan office, except there were no walls. The furniture was blocky and crudely coloured, like a computer game. The people were also rough approximations, but immediately recognizable – Katherine Feather, Dr Stribling, Matt and Robin.

Harper moved the mouse and the image moved with it. The point of view changed as if the camera was moving, pulling back to a low stone wall. And behind that, the rough, rocky side of the cavern itself.

As they watched, the wall of the cavern shimmered and moved. The surface seemed to ripple and melt. Then it bulged and grew as a shape began to force its way out of the wall . . .

✛

'I'm staying,' Dad said.

'You what?' Matt couldn't believe it. 'But you

don't have to stay here for me any more. I only just found you – I'm not losing you again. We can get away.'

'Only if we're quick,' Robin pointed out. 'Once they've searched the pyramid, they'll come looking down here.'

'I'm staying,' Dad repeated. 'Sorry, Matt, but I have to. From what you tell me, Julius is still here, and together perhaps we can keep Harper in check. Maybe we can slow down his work. And while I think of it,' he said, smiling, 'this disc he has us all working on . . .'

'Yes, I was thinking about that,' Matt said. 'There's something you need to know about the disc, something important . . .'

But Robin stopped him. She was holding his arm tightly. 'Come on!'

'I think,' Katherine said, 'that you may already be too late.'

She was pointing past them, towards the main amphitheatre. Matt and Robin both turned to look. It was dark between the area where Dad and Katherine were working and the main structure. But silhouetted against the distant lights, shapes were forming, shadows were deepening. It was as if the walls and the floor were erupting, spewing out dark, earthy creatures. Lumpy and misshapen figures that were lurching towards Matt and the others.

If they waited, they would be trapped. 'We have to get past them,' Matt shouted. 'Dad – it's now or never. I can't just leave you here.'

But Matt's father was shaking his head. 'You can,' he said emphatically, 'and you must. There's no time to explain or to argue. Just believe me, it's for the best. Now, go on – get out of here while you can.'

'If we can,' Robin muttered. 'Leave him, Matt. Once he's decided something you can't make him change his mind.'

'Like you'd know,' Matt said. He felt close to tears, but he was determined not to show it. He took Robin's hand and they ran. 'See you, Dad,' Matt shouted back over his shoulder. 'We'll get out of here – I'll come back for you. We'll bring help!'

'Be careful!' he heard in reply. As if he hadn't thought of that.

The ground at their feet was rippling and moving. In the dim light, Matt could see the earth and grit between the slabs of stone bubbling up like spring water. It was coming together, coalescing, forming into a puddle of sand that flowed *upwards* –

another figure that turned to face them, lumbered after them, misshapen arms stretched out to grab them as they passed . . .

Coarse, gritty fingers snagged at their clothes and clawed at their faces. They put their heads down and charged through. Matt lashed out, felt his hand thump into earth. It came away wet and muddy.

They were in the light now, leaping down the terraces towards the stage. But the creatures were hurrying after them, leaving trails of sand and earth behind them. Matt did not dare to look back, did not dare to look too closely at the things that were after them. Were they really made from the earth itself?

Robin had pulled her hand free and was running just ahead of Matt. 'That's what I call empirical proof,' she shouted to him.

'It's what I call a nightmare,' he gasped back.

They reached the stage and Robin charged onwards, heading for the river that roared past on the other side of the circular dais.

'What now?' Matt asked. 'Swim for it?' He was struggling to keep up with her.

'Don't be daft. Down the tunnel.'

The river ran past the stage and out of the enormous chamber through a tunnel it had eroded from the mountain rock over the millennia. Along the edge of the water was a lip of rock – little more than a ledge. It ran like a path beside the river. Matt followed Robin into the tunnel.

'We won't be able to see where we're going,' he pointed out. The light was already fading. He could see the water like oil surging past them, its rush and roar almost drowning out his words.

A tiny light. Not much, but enough to illuminate Robin's face. 'Keyring torch,' she said. 'Don't know how long it'll last.'

'Or what good it will do,' Matt said. 'If this ledge just stops we'll be in the water before we know it.'

'Oh, you're a bundle of optimism,' she told him. 'Come on.'

But Matt had stopped dead, rooted on the ledge just metres down the tunnel.

'What?' she demanded.

He could only nod dumbly at what he saw behind her.

Slowly, Robin turned, holding up her keyring. The tiny blue light glimmered faintly, throwing shadows across her face. Barely enough light to see.

Barely enough light to illuminate the wall of water rising up from the river and curling over at them. Barely enough to show the way the water split, like arms reaching out. The wall of water was hanging in the damp air, holes torn out of it that might be eyes. A raging mouth. A face that Matt had seen before, he realized with horrified fascination – staring at him from the window of a train. Had Harper been watching him for so long?

Another dark, wet shape was forcing its way up out of the river. Glistening and rippling, arms first, then head and shoulders – a figure heaving itself up on to the ledge in front of them. A figure made of water. Feet slapping on the rock floor, puddles escaping from its every step, cold wet hands reaching out for Robin and Matt. Behind it, the whole river was still curling upwards, towering over them.

They turned and ran, as the huge wave crashed down on the ledge and watery dank figures pushed through it and sludged after them towards the cavern.

Out into the light again – to find the earthy creatures almost at the stage, trails of sand and mud like seaweed behind them.

'Back up to the pyramid?' Matt wondered, so winded he was almost retching.

'Reckon so. You got your breath back?'

'No.'

'Come on, then,' she said. Robin grabbed his hand and dragged him after her.

Back the way they had come, up the steep steps. Shoulders down, smacking into one of the figures, sending it spinning away – mud and earth showering from it like water shaken off a dog. Another figure loomed ahead, reaching out, so close that Matt could smell the fetid stale earth it was made from. He could see roots and plant filaments knotted through its clutching hands.

Matt grabbed the pole holding one of the lamps as they passed and pulled. The lamp crashed down, exploding in a shower of glass as it hit the ground. But Matt held on to the metal pole and swung it hard at the creature reaching out for them.

It scythed into the figure, sending earth flying. The pole stuck – buried in the creature's side as if he had thumped it into the ground. But it slowed the creature enough for Matt and Robin to sprint past.

On, up the terraced steps – enormous leaps, chest-bursting breathless running. The dark opening of the passageway leading up to the pyramid now within sight. Matt looked back, saw how close the things were and ran faster. He glanced anxiously across to where Dad had been, but could see noth-

ing and no one through the gloom and past the broken outer walls. 'I shouldn't have left you,' he said.
But his words were little more than breathless gasps.

Into the passage. No more steps, but uphill. Their
breathing echoing off the walls. Sand slipping from
between the stones and pooling on the floor – rising
up. Matt kicked viciously at every little pyramid of
sand he passed, sending the grains flying apart again.

Then, suddenly, they were out – through the tapestry and into the lower level of the pyramid. Ahead
of him, Robin skidded to a halt. So abruptly that
Matt piled into the back of her and they almost fell.

'We made it,' he gasped, almost laughing with
relief.

Then he saw the grinning skull-like face of Klein
looking down at him and the dark muzzle of the
gun like a tunnel leading into blackness. 'Mr Harper
would very much like a word with you,' he said.

Klein gestured with the gun for them to go ahead
of him up the narrow stairway. Matt did not dare to
look back, but he could hear the head of security
talking into a radio, telling his men that the search
was over and they could return to their normal
duties.

They emerged into the entrance hallway, under

the main staircase. Klein ushered them onwards, down the corridor, and Matt glanced longingly at the now-unguarded main exit from the pyramid. So close to freedom. But there was no way he was getting out now.

Even as he was thinking this, even as he turned back, he caught a flash of movement out of the corner of his eye. Robin had seen it too and they both looked at the same time. They both saw Klein glaring malevolently at them, gun levelled threateningly. And they both saw a dark figure step out from the shadows of a doorway. A figure holding what looked like a frying pan.

It was a frying pan, and it connected loudly and painfully with the back of Klein's head. A split second of surprise registered on his face, then his eyes flickered and closed and he slumped to the floor.

'That jarred right up my arms,' Katherine Feather complained. 'Those things . . .' She shook her head incredulously. 'All right – you convinced me. Harper's really lost it big time. I should have seen it before, when he forced your father to help him. I just put it down to a bit of persuasion, convinced myself your dad was being daft or in breach of contract. But with what I've just seen . . .' She broke off, sighed and inspected the frying pan. 'I never liked that man,' she muttered, dropping the frying pan on top of Klein's unconscious body.

'Thanks,' Matt said. 'But what now?'

Robin was pulling at Klein's gun. But he had fallen on top of it and the shoulder strap was still wrapped round his arm. She gave up trying to drag it from underneath him. 'Helicopter, out the front,' she said.

'Good idea,' Katherine agreed. 'I think we need to get a long way away from here as fast as we can.'

'Thanks for helping us,' Matt said to Katherine as they hurried back to the entrance and out into the sunshine.

'No problem. Like your dad says, there's a point where money isn't enough of an excuse. Maybe I've just taken it for too long without really thinking.' She hurried across the causeway, leading them towards where Harper's helicopter was resting massively on its landing area. 'What were you about to say to your dad about that disc?' she asked.

'What? Oh, that. Just . . .' Matt shook his head. 'Doesn't matter. I'll tell you later, when we're away from here.'

The helicopter door was unlocked. Katherine

dragged it open and they jumped up inside. There was no sign of the pilot.

'Tell me about the disc,' Katherine said. 'In case we get separated or captured again.'

'No way,' Robin said. 'We are out of here.'

'You kidding?' Katherine said. 'How's that, then?'

*Outside a wind was whipping up.*

'You can fly us to Rio,' Matt told Katherine.

*Sand and grit blew across the massive slabs.*

'We'll get a plane from there somehow,' Matt said. 'We can call for help.'

*The sand whirling into a frenzy, gathering, accumulating, coalescing . . .*

Katherine was staring at him in shock.

*Forming into shapes . . . Figures . . .*

'That's your plan?' she said in disbelief.

*The figures turned towards the helicopter. Started towards it.*

'Who do you think I am?' Katherine yelled at him.

*Earthen fingers reached for the door.*

'I can't fly a bloody helicopter!'

14

The first of the creatures formed from sand and earth was clawing at the helicopter door. Dirt smeared down the window as it tried to force its way in. The wind was howling across the open plateau, rocking the helicopter on its wheels.

Matt stared at Katherine in disbelief. He had to shout to make himself heard above the wind outside. 'Why didn't you tell us before we got in?'

A massive, heavy hand thumped into the window. Then another.

'You didn't ask,' she shouted back. 'I didn't know what your plan was. I'm Harper's PA, not his pilot.'

'I thought that's why you led us here!' Matt yelled back. 'You said it was a good idea.'

The window cracked – lines crazing out from

the point of impact. A thin trickle of sand ran down the inside.

'I thought the pilot would be here. I don't fly helicopters,' Katherine insisted.

'Then move aside for someone who does,' Robin told her. She pushed past Katherine and Matt towards the pilot's seat at the front of the cockpit. 'You'd better get strapped in. This could be bumpy with that crosswind.'

'What are you doing?' Matt demanded. 'Don't be stupid.'

'You'll get us all killed,' Katherine yelled at her.

'As opposed to what?' Robin said without looking back. She was strapping herself into the seat, pulling on the pilot's helmet, examining the controls in front of her.

'It's no good,' Matt told Katherine. 'You can't argue with her. Just pray she has some idea.' He sat down and pulled the safety straps over his head, snapping the ends into the central buckle.

'Here we go,' Robin called.

The sound of the wind seemed to increase as the rotors swung lazily into life. Slowly at first, but picking up speed, they turned and rose and the helicopter shifted again on its wheels. Gently, laboriously, it lifted into the air.

'She can do it!' Katherine said in astonishment.

'Of course I can,' Robin told her, still concentrating on the controls. 'I don't know this type, though, so don't get too complacent.'

The helicopter continued to rise and the rough, dark hands slipped away from the windows as it lifted into the air. It turned slowly on its axis, nose angled down. Then, as Robin eased the main control stick forward, the helicopter picked up speed.

Over Robin's shoulder, Matt had a good view of the open plateau. He could see the half-dozen misshapen figures lurching uncertainly from side to side as they seemed to watch their prey getting away from them. One of them reached out and its arm stretched, thinning to a sharp point as it stabbed up at the cockpit window high above it. Instinctively, Matt flinched. Beside him Katherine did the same.

But Robin didn't seem to notice. She pushed the stick further forward and the nose of the helicopter dipped so that it was almost standing on its nose. The rotor blades were now spinning in front of it, like an electric fan. They sliced into the extended arm, sending earth and grit swirling into a sandstorm. Through the dark blizzard Matt caught a confused glimpse of two of the sandmen stumbling into the path of the rotors – being sliced apart, strewn across the flagstones.

The helicopter lurched upwards, buffeted by the wind, righting itself. And suddenly it was clear of the debris and the wind dropped. Far below, the ancient, ruined town at the base of the mountain grew smaller as they left it behind and flew onwards over the green and brown blanket of the rainforest.

✝

At Rio, Harper had two men waiting for them when the helicopter landed. They escorted Matt, Robin and Katherine to the main airport building. Katherine took them to one side and spoke to them – Matt could hear her insisting they should talk to Harper again and get proper orders and what did they think they were playing at?

'I'll keep them in the executive lounge while you find out what's going on,' she told the two thugs. 'Go on!'

No sooner had the two men gone than Katherine led Matt and Robin to the British Airways ticketing desk.

'Next flight to Europe,' she demanded. 'Anything

with three spaces. Then on to London, though I'd rather not a direct flight.'

Matt glanced over his shoulder, expecting Harper's men to be back at any moment. But for now at least there was no sign of them.

The first flight they could get on was to Amsterdam. They had to run for the gate, which was better than having to wait around in plain view, Matt thought, as he raced through the airport. What must the woman at the BA desk have thought – three dishevelled passengers with no luggage, wanting to go to London, but not on a direct flight? It was only by luck that Katherine even had her passport with her.

Matt was tired, but he was unable to get settled on the plane to Amsterdam. He wanted to talk to Robin – not least to ask her where she'd learned to fly helicopters. But irritatingly she slept the whole way. She didn't seem at all worried that her father was left behind in the middle of the rainforest with Harper. But Matt guessed inside she was as anxious and frightened as he was. Probably. He still didn't feel he really knew her, despite all they had been through together.

Amsterdam airport – Schiphol, as the signs proclaimed it – was pretty much like all the other airports they'd been in. They did not hang around. Katherine immediately changed their London tickets for a flight to Birmingham – which was closer to Venture's house. Plus, if Harper had managed to trace them, he might have people waiting at Heathrow.

Matt managed to talk to Robin while Katherine was off sorting out their tickets. He had seen the way Robin glared after Katherine as she left them in the executive lounge. 'She's trying to help,' Matt said. 'Give her a chance. It's all a bit much for her to take in.'

'I suppose,' Robin said.

'Try to see it from her point of view. Her great employer turns out to be some sort of elemental magician who wants to . . . I dunno – take over the world or something.' He smiled. 'Bound to be a bit of a shock to her. It's a bit of a shock to me.'

'Yes, all right,' Robin conceded. 'Only . . .'

'Only what?'

She looked away for a moment. When she looked back at Matt she was smiling sadly. 'Only I just don't like her much. That's all.'

'I didn't like you much when I first met you,' he said. 'So there.'

Robin's mouth twitched, as if she was trying not to smile back at him. 'Liar,' she said.

✝

They'd talked on the flight before Robin slept about what to do when they got back to England, and Venture's house was as good a base to start from as any, although it probably wouldn't take Harper long to guess where they had gone. Balanced against that were the library and other resources that Venture had at his disposal.

There was just one minor detour that Matt wanted to make, though. As the plane began its descent into Birmingham airport, he told Katherine and Robin, 'I want to go to Dad's place first.'

'Why?' Robin asked. 'Homesick?'

'Yeah, right. No, actually – there's something there we need.'

'What's that?' Katherine asked.

'I'll show you when we get there.' Matt wasn't sure he was right and he didn't want to seem stupid. He was pretty sure Robin thought he was an idiot anyway, and after her skill at flying the helicopter he was even less keen to give her any excuse to think the worst of him. 'Just a hunch, at the moment. But the way to stop Harper must be to decipher that disc before he does.'

'But we don't have the disc,' Katherine said.

'That's right.' Matt smiled.

He felt tired and drained by the time they landed. Katherine went to hire a car and Robin to find a pay-phone to call Mephistopheles Smith. She had called from Amsterdam and left a message for him.

'Still not available,' she told Matt when she returned. 'I asked them to have him call me at home as soon as he can.'

'I bet Katherine has her mobile with her,' Matt said. 'Try him on that, or leave them the number.'

Robin didn't reply, and before Matt could ask her why this was a problem Katherine herself was back, so he let it go. But he borrowed Katherine's mobile himself to call Aunt Jane and tell her they'd be back in a few hours.

'There's a lot to tell you,' he said. 'But not over the phone,' and he left it at that.

✝

The car was fast and red and got them to Dad's house in less than two hours despite the slow-moving traffic on the motorway. Matt and Robin sat together in the back, and Katherine drove with an urgency and speed that set Matt's teeth on edge. She overtook when it looked like there wasn't room and took corners so fast the whole car tilted and threw Matt and Robin against each other.

'Why don't you offer to drive?' Matt said to Robin.

'Don't have a licence,' she told him, and they laughed.

'So where did you learn to fly helicopters?' Katherine asked.

'My father's got a couple,' Robin said, as if this was perfectly normal.

It was dark by the time they arrived outside Dad's house and Matt saw the curtains of the house opposite twitching. He waved and the curtains stopped. He smiled as he imagined what Mrs Dorridge must be thinking as she saw him and Robin and Katherine getting out of the sleek new car.

'Bit of a tip, isn't it?' Robin said as soon as Matt turned on the lights.

'Yeah,' Matt admitted. 'Well, it's even worse than usual since Dad was abducted by the mud men.' He kicked at the trail of dirt across the hall floor.

'So why are we here?' Katherine said.

Matt led them into the study and they negotiated a path to the desk. He hunted round for where he had left what he wanted and eventually remembered putting it in a drawer, together with the books and papers that had been with it.

'What is that?' Katherine said.

But Robin could tell immediately what it was and laughed out loud. 'That's incredible. How did it get here?'

'I was wrong about Dad's planned trip to the island,' Matt said. 'There's his itinerary here somewhere. I assumed he hadn't been there yet. But he had. He'd already gone to Valdeholm.' He held the clay disc out carefully on the palm of his hand so they could all see it. The symbols embossed on it were difficult to see as there was no variation in the texture or colour of the material. But it was obviously the same as the disc Harper now had, the disc they had found on the island.

'He went there and he found the treasure,' Robin realized. 'Before Harper had him kidnapped. When they came and took him, they weren't looking for this. And later, they just came back for his notes.' She gave a short laugh. 'And here it was, right under their noses all the time!'

'I bet he worked it out while working for Harper and went there as soon as he could, without telling anyone. I saw where he got in through the tunnel roof, though I didn't realize it. Dad took a cast of the disc and then he put it back – preserving the site for future discovery, he'd do that. Then he came back here. And that's probably when Harper's creatures nabbed him.'

'So why didn't he tell Harper?' Katherine said. 'May I?' She took the disc carefully from Matt and examined it. 'You're right, it's identical.'

'He knew Harper mustn't have the disc,' Robin said. 'But he made a copy to decipher for himself, I suppose.'

'And this is what you wanted to tell your dad?' Katherine asked. 'That you knew he'd already got a copy of the disc?'

Matt shook his head. 'I hadn't realized that. And anyway, till I looked at it again just now I wasn't sure it was the same disc. It might have been something completely different. Then I'd have looked pretty stupid.'

'But it is the same disc,' Robin said. 'You were right, and now we have a copy we're back in the race. We can decipher it before Harper and find out exactly what he's up to, with luck.' She grabbed Matt in an unexpected hug. 'You're a genius.' And kissed him.

✠

It was only a quick kiss on the cheek, but Matt could still feel it all the way to Robin's house.

'We thought it was odd that your dad followed up some leads but not others,' Robin said as they tore along country lanes and frightened cattle in the nearby fields. 'I guess he knew already where the treasure was. He'd already done some work on it and was stalling for time.'

'Or he didn't share all his work with Harper,' Matt agreed. 'If he'd had more time he might have laid a completely false trail and led Harper – and us – to completely the wrong location.'

✠

Aunt Jane was waiting for them outside the main house, standing in a pool of light that spilled out from the porch. She looked pale and close to tears. She had her arms folded tight across her body and was shivering despite the warmth of the night.

Matt ran to her as soon as he was out of the car.

'We're all right,' he said. 'Really we are. And we found Dad. He's OK. We had to leave him, but we'll get him back. I promise.'

Aunt Jane hugged him tight, just for a moment. Matt felt her trembling. He could not remember seeing her like this before. She was more than just upset, more than tearful and worried. She was *frightened*. When she spoke her voice was also shaking. 'There's a . . . visitor,' she said. 'Waiting inside.'

She turned towards the door, and Matt could see the trail of soil and gravel that led through the porch and into the house.

The creature was standing in the hallway – a large approximation of a man, fashioned out of dirt and earth and sand and gravel from the drive. Like some ghastly sculpture that lacked detail or finesse. What might have been a face turned to regard Matt and the others as they entered. It was blotchy and textured, gritty and mottled. A few blades of grass poked out from one side and small stones peppered the face like acne. Thin, pale roots ran through it like veins. An arm moved, detaching itself from the side of the creature, pointing to Matt and the others.

The arm moved in an arc as the thing turned slowly. It stooped down, though it seemed to flow into the new position as if moulded by some giant, invisible hand rather than actually changing position. The stubby fingers touched the floor, leaving a dirty trail across the polished boards as the ends flaked off.

'It's writing,' Aunt Jane said in a hushed voice.

'Giving us a message,' Matt realized.

The whole hand was gone now, the arm following – disappearing into the floor as it rubbed away to leave the letters, like graphite rubbing off a pencil lead. The creature was shrinking down as the dirt and gravel it was made from flowed out of it like ink from a pen . . .

Crude, childish capital letters across the floor. An ultimatum:

DO NOT INTERFERE AND THEY WILL
BE SAFE

By the end of the last letter, the creature was thin and depleted. It hesitated a moment, as if checking it had nothing further to add. Then suddenly it fell – collapsing in on itself so that all hint of humanity was lost and there was just a pile of earth and mud and stones in the middle of the hallway.

'No prizes for guessing who it means,' Robin said. 'Your dad and mine.'

'I guess punctuation and grammar come later,' Matt said. 'I'll see you in the library in a minute.'

'Where are you going?' Aunt Jane asked.

'To get something,' he said grimly. 'I won't be long.'

☩

If Katherine was impressed with Venture's library, she had already said so before Matt rejoined them. Aunt Jane, Katherine and Robin were sitting at the large round table under the domed roof when he arrived.

'Robin and Miss Feather have told me what's going on and we all agree that we can't let Harper intimidate us,' Aunt Jane announced. 'What have you got there?' she added with a wariness that Matt had not expected.

Matt was carrying a small wooden box. He set it down on the table. 'I found it when I was looking for something for Mr Venture. I think it might be useful. I'm surprised you're not more surprised, Aunt Jane.' In fact, she was still looking pale, and Matt wondered how much of their story Aunt Jane believed.

'Very little surprises me any more,' she replied. 'And I saw that thing in the hall with my own eyes. What is that?' Aunt Jane asked again. She was sounding hesitant, as if she didn't really want an answer. Or she already knew. She glanced at Robin and the girl looked back at her, also worried.

Matt didn't wait for them to tell him what the problem was. He opened the box and showed them the disc inside – a disc very similar to the one Harper now had, but made of metal. He took it out and placed it on the table beside the clay copy they had got from Dad's study.

'You see? I don't know where Julius Venture got this or if he realizes its significance. I only discovered it by accident. But it's the same as the disc we found.'

'Similar,' Robin conceded. 'So what?'

'So what?' he echoed. 'So if we have another disc, maybe that can help us work out what they mean, what they're *for*.' He looked into her deep blue eyes. 'Unless you or your dad already know what they are for?' he said quietly.

'They're not *for* anything,' Robin replied sharply. 'They're just . . . old discs. That's all. With patterns on them.'

'Then why is Harper so keen to decipher the patterns?' Katherine asked. 'He thinks it's some sort of ancient language or hieroglyphs or something. Matt's right, having another to work from should help, shouldn't it? Where did this come from anyway? How come it's here in this house?'

'Dad collects all sorts of things,' Robin said.

'You are assuming there is a connection between them,' Aunt Jane said, examining the disc. 'It actually looks very different to me.'

'How do you mean?' Matt asked. 'They're the same size and everything.'

'But look at it.' She pointed to the metal disc from the box. 'This has a series of symbols, a pattern, spiralling into the middle. Whereas this one . . .' She pointed to the clay disc beside it. 'This has a ring of symbols round the edge and then a large pictogram or motif or whatever it is in the middle.'

'They could be from completely different sources and periods,' Robin agreed.

Matt thought she sounded relieved, but if that was the case surely it was a big setback.

'That just means the picture in the middle is really significant,' he said. But he could see what they meant. Superficially the discs were the same, but the details were very different.

'So what is this picture in the middle, then?' Katherine asked. She carefully picked up the clay disc and angled it so the impression caught the light and she could see it better. 'Three irregular shapes. Looks like it might be a single shape that's been split up. Like jigsaw pieces pulled apart or crazy-paving. The edges seem to match up, so you could push them back together. Your father didn't give you any idea what he thought it might be, did he?' She looked from Matt to Robin. 'Either of your fathers?'

Robin shook her head. 'I do think I've seen it somewhere before, though,' she admitted.

It seemed familiar to Matt as well, but that was probably just because he had seen the clay disc before. 'Dad never mentioned it to me,' he said. 'It was on his desk, with some notes and books and stuff.'

'Notes?' Aunt Jane said. 'About the disc?'

He shook his head. 'No, they were notes on some book he'd been reading. Load of old maps, I think.'

'I suppose it could actually *be* a map,' Katherine said slowly. 'Just possibly. Three islands that were once a single landmass maybe.'

Robin was staring at Matt. 'Old maps? Hapgood?'

'What?'

'The book – was it by Charles Hapgood?'

Matt shrugged. 'Might have been. Who knows? Why?'

Robin got up and hurried to one of the bookcases across the room. 'Hapgood published a book of many of the old maps. He thought they derived from even older sources. It's here somewhere . . .' She pulled out an old book, glanced at the cover, then pushed it back again and continued her search. 'Piri Reis, Mercator, all sorts . . .'

'Dad's notes mentioned Mercator. I think. I don't know, maybe . . .' He was struggling to remember.

Robin had found the book she wanted and brought it back to the table. She set it down and started leafing through for the page she wanted. 'Here we are. Mercator's map dates back to the sixteenth century. Bauche is a couple of hundred years later.'

She turned another page and smoothed it down. Matt could see the map on the page, the distinctive three islands that looked like they had once been a single landmass.

'That's it! You've found it. Where is it?'

'It's a map of Antarctica,' Robin said. 'Or rather, of the landmass now buried under the Antarctic ice.

This is Antarctica as it was before the glaciation. As it was 15,000 years ago.'

'That's incredible,' Katherine said. 'I didn't realize they knew what Antarctica looked like so long ago.'

'They didn't,' Aunt Jane said quietly. 'Back then, they didn't know Antarctica even existed.'

'Then – how . . . ?'

'Antarctica wasn't discovered until the early nineteenth century,' she went on. 'And the landmass wasn't mapped until much later.'

'1958,' Robin said. 'As I remember . . .' She was staring into the distance. Suddenly she focused her piercing blue eyes on Matt. 'These maps are old,' she said, 'and they are based on even older maps. Maps that it is thought were taken by the Venetians from Constantinople in the thirteenth century.'

'Constantinople,' Matt said, 'but that's where the Treasure of St John came from.'

'And this disc came from Constantinople with it,' Robin agreed. '*This* is the Treasure of St John – this disc. This, or rather the real disc, is what Harper wanted all along. He thinks the symbols on the disc will give him the knowledge he is after. But actually it looks as if the disc is a map showing him where that knowledge is. Where he will find the knowledge he's after.'

'In the Antarctic?' Katherine said. 'But what can he possibly think is there? Some sort of ancient library or something? And how did it get there?'

Robin was looking at Aunt Jane now. Jane opened her mouth, as if to say something. Then she seemed to change her mind. She pushed back her chair and stood up, turning away from them so that Matt could not see her expression.

'He's searching for the greatest store of ancient knowledge you can imagine and now we have what appears to be a map showing where it is. Harper is looking,' Robin said, 'for the knowledge of Atlantis.'

15

There was silence for a few moments, then both Matt and Katherine were talking loudly at the same time – both incredulous and astonished.

'Oh, please do treat this seriously,' Katherine said.

'Don't be so ridiculous,' Matt was telling Robin. 'OK, so we've had talk about ancient civilizations and all that stuff, but Atlantis is a fairy tale. It's a myth, a legend. No one seriously believes it.'

'That's right,' Katherine agreed. 'I'm no archaeologist and even I know that. It's just some Greek guy's story, isn't it?'

'If Harper found Atlantis, it would be the greatest archaeological discovery ever,' Aunt Jane said, turning back to face them.

'Though that isn't actually what he is looking for,' Robin told them. 'He's after their knowledge. And while Atlantis may be a myth, a legend, those myths and legends are actually based on fact. There is an underlying truth to the stories. Plato didn't just make it up, you know. He got the story from another Greek, who in turn had heard it from an Egyptian priest.'

'It doesn't matter *who* made it up,' Matt said. 'The point is that there is no Atlantis to discover. Harper may think there are untold riches and goodness knows what treasure and relics and forbidden knowledge waiting under Antarctica or even under Cheltenham for all I care. It isn't there. Atlantis never existed. It was really the island of Thira, or Akrotiri, or the Minoan civilization or whatever. I know. Dad's told me all about it.'

'Your father should know better,' Aunt Jane said quietly.

'He does. That's what I'm saying,' Matt told her.

'Look,' Robin insisted, 'it really isn't important whether we think Atlantis is buried under the Antarctic. It doesn't matter what you or I or any of us believe. The point is, what does *Harper* believe? And what does the disc tell him? In fact . . .' She stopped, sighed and leaned forward across the table, her eyes imploring Matt to listen. 'Harper doesn't care about the Antarctic or where Atlantis may really have been. He is only after the ancient knowledge. Control and power. We know that – we've seen what it can do already. It might seem incredible, but it's happening. He's already found some of the ancient knowledge, unravelled some of the mysteries. Whatever he's after now, we have to get there first.'

'So how do we do that?' Aunt Jane demanded. 'How do we get there first? Are you suggesting we go to the Antarctic?'

'Assuming that the disc shows a map of Atlantis,' Robin said, 'that is by no means all that's on it. What Harper is after – the specific knowledge he needs to refine and complete what he already knows – may well be in the other symbols on the disc. There's no point going anywhere until we know what we're doing and what we have.'

'So we need to decipher the disc,' Katherine said. 'And quickly.'

'And we need help,' Robin said. 'I'm surprised Mephistopheles Smith hasn't got back to us yet. If there's one person who can take on Harper, it's him.'

'Really?' Katherine looked surprised. 'He must be quite a guy.'

'He would be if he returned my calls,' Robin said.

'I'll call him again,' Aunt Jane told them. 'If he isn't at home or on his mobile, I'll try his office. Though there's probably no one there at this time of night and anyway you have to hold for hours to get anywhere in Whitehall these days. I'll keep at it till I get him.'

'I can do that,' Katherine told her. 'I feel like a spare part just sitting here. You know where everything is and can help. Let me work the phones. It's the least I can do. And I do have some experience, you know.'

Aunt Jane led Katherine to the door. 'You can use my office. I'll show you where it is.'

'Now we know what the disc actually shows, we're off to a good start,' Robin said. 'I wish my dad was here. If he knew what we have realized, he'd have it cracked in no time at all, I'm sure.'

'He'll be all right,' Matt assured Robin when Katherine and Aunt Jane had gone. He reached across the table and took Robin's hands. 'We'll work it out, and your friend Smith will deal with Harper. It'll all be OK.'

'Thanks,' she said. She blinked away the moisture in her eyes and stood up. 'Let's get started.'

Robin began by looking out books she thought might be useful – books of hieroglyphs and ancient languages from every part of the world. Soon the table was almost covered and there were stacks of books on the floor round it as well. Matt was copying the symbols from the disc. They were difficult to see against the clay and he had to angle the disc to catch the light.

'Once we have a set of symbols we can work from,' Robin told him, 'we can start looking for matches.'

'In these books?'

'And others. And on the disc you found upstairs.'

By the time Aunt Jane returned, Matt had copied almost the whole of one side of the disc, carefully making sure he got not just the shape but the measurements right for each symbol. They looked relatively simple, but it was harder than he had expected to get them accurate. And as he worked, he realized how tired he was – with little or no sleep for what seemed like days and the effects of jet lag as well, he could barely focus.

So it was a relief when Aunt Jane said, 'You know, it's well after midnight. We've all had rather a long day. I think we'd do better to get some sleep and carry on in the morning, when we're more awake and with it.'

'I think you're right,' Matt agreed.

'I'm sure I am. I've shown Katherine where she can sleep, and she tells me she got a message to Mr Smith. He'll be here in the morning. So that's another reason why we all need to be on our toes.'

'I'll carry on for a bit,' Robin said.

Matt thought his aunt would insist. But, as so often before, she let Robin have her own way. The girl might be the daughter of Aunt Jane's employer, but Matt was surprised. Adults were usually pretty insistent about children's bedtimes. Except Dad – who never seemed to notice the time. His mind was wandering, he realized, which was another sign he was tired.

'Matt?' Aunt Jane was saying.

'You're right. But I'd like to finish this side of the disc,' he told her. 'There's only one symbol left after this one. You go ahead – I'll see you back at the cottage in a bit.'

She gave him one of those 'I don't agree but I'm not going to bother to argue' looks and sighed. 'Don't be too long.'

'Ten minutes,' he promised. 'I'll be back in half

an hour at the most. Really.'

He was on the final symbol when he realized Robin was standing next to him. 'You're doing well,' she said.

'Thanks. Nearly finished.'

'Before you came through the telly in our room at Harper's pyramid, Dad mentioned he'd made some notes that might be useful. He didn't want to take them to Harper's – I don't think he trusted the man even before we left. So I'm going to see if I can find them. You all right, or do you want me to wait for you?'

'Almost done. I'll let myself out and see you in the morning.'

She put her hand on his shoulder. 'Goodnight, then. I'll see you soon.'

'Don't stay up too late,' he told her. He watched her all the way to the door, before returning his attention to the final symbol.

✠

Matt's pillow was hard and unyielding. And someone had turned the light on. Was it morning already? And why was he sitting down?

He sat up abruptly, wide awake now. He was still

in the library, one hand resting over the clay disc – he was lucky he hadn't squashed it flat. The paper he had been copying the symbols on to was in front of him, but now a squiggly line led from the last symbol he had been drawing across the paper. He'd fallen asleep while drawing. How stupid was that?

His watch told him it was nearly half past one. He'd been asleep for over an hour – and Aunt Jane would be livid. Actually, he thought, as he stretched and stood up, she was probably already asleep and hadn't realized he wasn't back yet. Robin too, as she'd obviously not returned to the library.

There was a noise. A loud throbbing, like an engine. Probably that was what had woken him up. It was a sound he knew – a helicopter. Was Smith on his way already? But it was receding into the distance. It certainly wasn't coming to the house. Soon it had faded and gone.

Matt rubbed out the rogue line across the paper with the eraser on the end of the pencil. He picked up the disc to take it with him, but then changed his mind and put it down again. He might sleep for hours and someone else could be working on it in the meantime. He left the disc in plain sight on the table and made his bleary way to the door.

The main lights were out in the corridor, but the lamps over the pictures were still lit. Sepia-toned faces stared out at him from old photographs. He smiled and nodded at them as he went past Robin's ancestors – girls with the same distinctive dark hair and facial features. All of them beautiful, he thought. But all of them had grown old and wrinkled and grey. He spared a little wave for the portrait on the table halfway down the corridor – the fair-haired lady with green eyes. Elizabeth Venture, he remembered the name plate said, though there wasn't enough light to read it now.

The hallway was almost in darkness. The only light was coming from somewhere upstairs. It was a strange light – more of a glow. But flickering, like a bulb was about to go. And, Matt thought as he reached the front door, there was a strange smell. He hadn't noticed that before. Someone cooking?

Well, if someone wanted a midnight snack that was nothing to do with him. Though now he came to think about it, Matt was feeling a bit hungry. Best to get back to Aunt Jane's cottage and find some-thing to eat there. It was strange, but it didn't really smell like food. Burnt toast, maybe.

Burnt.

And as Matt turned slowly back towards the flickering light upstairs, the phone began to ring.

'Hello?' he said cautiously. This time of night it must be important. Perhaps it was the elusive Mephistopheles Smith.

'Matt – is that you? Thank God!' It was Aunt Jane.

'I'm sorry,' Matt said quickly. 'I dozed off. I –'

She wasn't listening. She was talking over him – urgent and loud – and it took a moment for him to decipher what she'd said: 'What's going on there? I can see flames. It looks like the whole house is on fire.'

He almost dropped the phone. 'I think the whole house *is* on fire.' His mouth was suddenly dry. The flickering upstairs was growing more intense by the second. 'I'll get Robin and Katherine. You call 999.' He hung up and ran for the stairs, taking them two at a time and shouting at the top of his voice.

The reply came from behind him: 'What's all the noise? Who was on the phone?'

Robin was standing in the doorway to her father's study, looking up at Matt in surprise.

'The house is on fire,' Matt told her. 'Hadn't you noticed?'

'You obviously hadn't,' she told him. 'There are

alarms, sprinklers. Why aren't they working?'

He ran back down the stairs. 'Who cares? Aunt Jane's calling the fire brigade. Let's get out of here.'

Robin hesitated. 'Just a minute.'

'What?'

'Something I want,' she shouted as she ran to the corridor leading to the library.

'Don't be stupid.'

She was already running back along the corridor when Matt got to the front door. 'Where's Katherine?'

Matt stopped dead. Smoke was rolling down the stairs behind him. He could hear the crackle of the fire upstairs. 'We have to find her,' he said. 'Which room's she in?'

'How should I know?'

'It's *your* house. Where are the bedrooms?'

Robin took a deep breath. 'You get out. I'll find her.'

'No way.' Matt grabbed her hand. 'Come on.' And together they plunged into the smoke.

It was clearer at the top of the stairs. The first room they tried was empty, the bed unmade. When they came out, the far end of the corridor was full of flames.

'If she's the other side of that, we'll never get to

her,' Matt said. 'Katherine!' he yelled. 'Fire! Get out now!'

The next room Robin tried was also empty. They could feel the heat of the flames when they came out again.

'We'll have to go back,' Robin said.

Matt couldn't disagree. His face was uncomfortably hot. In the distance he could hear sirens. Leave it to the professionals – there was nothing else they could do. They ran back to the stairs.

But before they got there, a raging ball of flame erupted from a doorway and blasted across in front of them. The carpet caught fire immediately – a wall of red and orange.

'Now what?' Matt yelled.

There was fire both sides of them. He clutched at Robin, who was staring into the flames, and held her tight.

'Look,' she said.

The flames were moving. Not just flickering and burning randomly like a fire. *Moving*. As Matt watched, a whole section seemed to gather itself together, concentrated into a single red and orange shape. A figure stepping out of the flames. Like a man on fire.

Burning feet sent sparks flying from the carpet, left a trail of flame behind them, as the figure lurched down the corridor. Arms reached out, smoke rising from clutching fingers of flame. The head and body were a mass of fire. And behind it, another figure was struggling into life. And another.

Matt turned and found the same thing happening behind them. Figures of flame detaching themselves from the fire and stalking towards Matt and Robin. The walls blackened as they came.

'In here!' Robin dragged Matt through a door, slamming it behind them.

'Like that'll help,' he said. 'Where now?' There were no windows. Only what looked like a built-in wardrobe. 'You think we can hide from them?'

But it wasn't a wardrobe. The door led out on to the upper gallery of the library. Behind them, they could hear the roar of the fire as it engulfed the door from the corridor. They raced across the gallery and clattered down the spiral staircase.

A mass of flame crashed out across the gallery above them, ripping into the bookcases and setting them ablaze.

Down the corridor again. The lights over the pictures were still on, but everything was misty from the smoke. They charged along, Robin leading the way, Matt barely registering that the portrait was gone from the side table.

And out into the hall again. The stairs were on fire. A trail of flame led down and across the hall to the front door. As they watched, the door blistered and smoked. A curl of flame from the wood panelling. Then suddenly the whole door was a raging mass of orange and yellow. A section of the fire seemed to coalesce and an orange-red figure stepped out of the inferno and into the hallway in front of them, as if it was stepping through the door from outside. But it was made of fire – a blazing, raging mass of flame in roughly the shape of a man.

After it came another. The door was almost gone already and Matt could see the darkness beyond. Blue flashing lights. Faint shapes of figures running forward.

More fire demons coming down the stairs.

Matt and Robin huddled together in the middle of the hall as walking walls of flames closed in around them.

Then suddenly Matt was cold – freezing cold. And wet. He staggered back as the water from the firemen's hoses outside ripped through the burning door and splashed over him and Robin. He was laughing, yelling with delight as the water scythed through the fire creatures by the door. The figures collapsed into pools of fire, dwindling and dying as the water splashed over them.

The creatures on the stairs hesitated. Water from the hoses was running across the hall floor. A jet of water dowsed the bottom of the staircase, sending up steam instead of smoke. Matt was almost jumping for joy.

But Robin wasn't. She held Matt's arm tight, pulling him back. 'We need to get to the main circuit boards and stuff for the fire alarms – through there.' She was pointing to a door on the other side of the hall.

'Why?' They could get out now. 'Let's get out of here!'

'Water,' she said.

Matt didn't need to ask her what she meant. He could see it now. The water from the hoses was running across the hall floor. Pooling at the foot of the stairs, rising up into the shape of a figure. In the doorway in front of them, the jets from the hoses seemed to stop. Water was still pouring in, but now it seemed to be filling huge, crudely shaped moulds, building massive figures of water that sloshed across the floor towards Matt and Robin.

'At least they can't burn us,' Matt said.

'They don't need to,' Robin told him.

Wet figures reached out for them from all directions. A hand closed on Matt's face and it was as if his head had been stuck in a bucket of water. He choked and coughed. His vision blurred. He felt himself sinking deep, deep into the water . . .

Drowning.

16

Robin's shoulder crashed into Matt's chest, sending him staggering. His head emerged from the bubble of water, breaking out. He was gasping and retching. Behind him, water splashed to the floor, the surface tension broken.

'Can't you swim?' Robin yelled. 'It's water, not fire. We can get through!' She was thrashing out at the creature that was trying to hold her. It was like she was fighting a mirror – Matt could see Robin's face reflected in the drops and drips and curves of the thing as it fought back. Her arm was encased in water, her whole body being sucked in.

Matt grabbed the nearest thing – the small table with the phone on it. The phone clattered to the floor. He slammed the table into the side of the creature holding Robin. The creature exploded into a million droplets, raining down. Robin flicked her wet hair out of her eyes.

Together they ran at the water creatures between them and the door into the main part of the house. Shoulders down, they smacked into the wet wall – like diving into the swimming pool. One of the creatures shattered like wet glass. The other managed to stay intact, but Robin and Matt were through it, landing in a soaking tumble on the floor.

Robin was up at once, heaving the door open, racing through. Her feet slapped on the floor. Matt was close behind.

The main electrical board was in a cupboard in a small storeroom off the corridor beyond. Matt could see at once that something was wrong – the cover was cracked open and wires had been pulled out.

'This was deliberate,' he said.

'Thank you, Einstein.' Robin's fingers were a blur as she sorted through the mess, pulling at wires and twisting their ends together.

'You know what you're doing?'

'I understand simple electronics, thanks.'

'And helicopters,' he said. 'I heard a helicopter, just before . . . Someone started the fire, then escaped in a helicopter.'

Matt could smell burning again. Smoke was drifting between them. 'I don't know what good you think this will do, but you might want to hurry,' he told her. He ran to the door and looked out.

A figure was lurching along the corridor. A figure made of fire. It crackled and hissed angrily, black smoke wreathing the red flames. A high-pitched wail echoed down the corridor after it – the alarms were working again.

'I'm reconnecting the sprinklers now,' Robin said.

'So we swap fire demons for water-spray monsters. Great.'

'Not quite.' She was working furiously, fumbling for the next wire, pulling it over to reconnect. 'How long have we got?'

Fire spilled into the room. The creature seemed to gather itself and Matt saw with horror that it was going to leap at them.

'Not long,' he said, and his voice was shrill and shaking.

Robin grabbed another wire.

The fire filled the doorway. It surged forward, as if catapulted across the room. Sparks flew through the air and bit at Matt's face. There was a sudden hiss like angry snakes, as his whole vision became one of flames and smoke.

'That's it,' he heard Robin say through the fireball.

And then the wailing and hissing seemed to combine into a cry of anguish and fury. And the fire was gone.

'What happened – where's the water?' Matt said.

The wailing faded in response to a press of a button and Robin closed up the cupboard doors. 'There's no water,' she said. 'That would ruin everything. As bad as fire.'

'Then what?'

'Can't you hear it?'

There was still the hissing sound, even though Robin had shut off the alarms. 'Gas?' He was finding it hard to breathe.

'Inert gas. Starves the fire of oxygen. Us too, if we aren't careful. We should get out and stop the firemen using their hoses.'

'Yeah – they'll just make more water creatures.'

Robin sighed, as if he was missing the point. 'They'll ruin Dad's books.'

☩

They picked their way through the mess and debris in the gathering morning light. The last fire engines had gone, the experts having declared that the house was structurally intact. They implied that, after the fire, it didn't deserve to be.

'It wasn't the house the fire was trying to burn,' Robin told them.

Several of the upstairs rooms were burnt out and the whole place stank of smoke. The carpet down the main stairs was a damp, charred mess. The corridors were blackened and discoloured.

Katherine was gone. Her room was a blackened ruin, but there was no sign of a body.

'Do you think she managed to escape?' Aunt Jane asked.

'I'm sure she did,' Robin replied shortly. 'In Dad's helicopter.'

'But she can't –' Matt broke off. 'Oh, right. She started the fire. She was playing along with us.'

'She thought you knew something useful about the disc,' Robin reminded him. 'She wanted to know what it was. And then last night I said I thought Dad would be able to decipher the symbols on the disc easily. She didn't need us any more. Simple as that.'

'Bitch,' Aunt Jane said. They both looked at her. 'Forget I said that,' she told them. Then she put her hand to her mouth. 'She probably never called Mr Smith. I left her to it. She said she'd spoken to him. That . . . woman.'

Something had occurred to Matt too. 'I bet she's taken the other disc,' he said. 'It was in the library, on the table. While I was asleep, I bet she took it.' He ran to check.

The wood panelling lining the passageway from the hall to the library had warped in the heat. The glass on several of the pictures was cracked and discoloured. One of the paintings had burnt almost away, leaving just the heads of two girls staring out from history – one dark-haired and blue-eyed like Robin, the other fair-haired with smudged green eyes.

The library was in surprisingly good shape. The water hadn't reached it, but several bookcases on the gallery were a charred mass. A ragged black line ran down the stairs and across to the door. But the fire had followed Matt and Robin and hadn't stopped to burn the books.

The table was as Matt had left it. His drawing of the symbols from the disc had curled in the heat, but it was intact. The books were where Robin had left them. And, as Matt had expected, the wooden box containing the metal disc was gone. Only Dad's clay copy of the disc from Valdeholm was still there. Katherine Feather had not wanted to risk disturbing him by taking it from under his hand, Matt guessed.

Matt found Robin and Aunt Jane in the passage. Robin was holding the blistered remains of the burnt canvas. She had been crying – smears running down through the dark grime on her cheeks. Aunt Jane was comforting her – hand on the girl's shoulder.

'There are others,' Aunt Jane was saying.

'Poor Lisa,' Robin murmured. Then she saw Matt and she forced a smile. 'The picture got burnt,' she said.

'Tell him,' Aunt Jane said to Robin. 'You should tell him.'

But Robin did not answer. She took the burnt fragment of canvas and walked slowly into the library. The picture, the portrait of the fair-haired woman, was back on the side table.

✠

Even the little room off the library where Matt had used the computer smelled of smoke, though it was otherwise undamaged. It was in here he had first properly met Julius Venture, Matt thought – it seemed such a long time ago, but it was only a few days.

Robin had her father's notes – a sheaf of papers covered with small, neat handwriting and what looked like mind maps. Matt had done some mind maps at school – boxes of ideas linked together with a web of lines showing connections between them. She set the notes down on the table and switched on the computer.

'Let's take stock,' Aunt Jane said. 'We still have Arnold's copy of the disc, but we've lost the other one. We know that *this* one shows a map of some sort, probably Antarctica, and possibly it gives the location of Atlantis. But with Katherine gone, we know nothing that Harper won't now know.'

'Not true,' Robin said without looking up from the screen as the system loaded. 'At least, we know more than Harper thinks we do. Dad's notes and what we've seen for ourselves confirm it.'

'What do you mean?' Matt asked.

'I mean that we know what he's up to. Look.' She gestured to the screen and Matt and Aunt Jane came round the table to see.

It showed a map of the world, a simple outline of the continents and landmasses. But overlaid on it was a series of dots. As Matt watched, the dots were joined by thin lines arcing down and across the map.

'Looks like what Harper had in his computer system. Showing ancient sites,' he said.

'I was afraid you'd say that. This is something Dad worked out ages ago.'

'And what are the lines?' Aunt Jane asked. 'Flight paths or something?'

'They are significant lines of longitude and latitude round the earth's surface,' Robin said. 'Now watch.'

She worked the mouse and more lines appeared. The new lines were not as regular. Some were straight, while others ran in gentle curves. But all of them went through several or more of the dots.

'Ley lines and lines of magnetic force,' Robin said.

'Ley lines? You mean that people claim to find by dowsing and stuff?' Matt said, remembering.

'Tracks or paths connecting ancient sites,' Aunt Jane said. 'That's right. Ancient connections.'

'And what does this tell us?' Matt wondered.

'These are all sites that adhere to the blueprint we talked about,' Robin said. 'They are all interconnected. You can see, they're all linked in a vast web. They are all in significant locations. And they are all on Harper's model.'

'You think.'

'I know. I saw it. I remember.'

'You've got a better sort of memory than me, then,' Matt told her.

'I've got a different sort of memory from you,' Robin shot back. 'But there's another thing too. All these sites are themselves models of the real world in some way. And that's what Dad's notes told me. That's what he was afraid Harper was up to. He's defining the linkages between the sites, he's putting the overall *model* back together. Each of these sites is just a small part of the whole. Harper's been researching them for years, remember – looking for more and more of these significant ancient sites. Put them all together and it gives you a single, unified, over-arching model.'

'You mean like a computer model? Some sort of simulation?' Aunt Jane said.

'Like his model of the pyramid and the amphitheatre?' Matt asked. 'Like the way we think he controls these elemental creatures of his?'

'Exactly like that. They're all tiny parts of the overall blueprint we talked about. Bits of what he's up to. Pieces of information he needs to complete his overall plan.'

'Which is what?'

Robin stood up. She walked across the room, head down in thought. Then she turned to look at them. 'Don't interrupt till I've finished,' she said. 'Then you can ask me questions about it, but hear me out first, all right?' She seemed suddenly older, more serious than Matt had seen her before. Like a concentrated version of herself.

'All right,' he said. 'Go on.'

'The ancient sites that Harper has marked, the sites on *his* blueprint, if you like, form a network, as you can see. Each of them in some way mirrors the world and the heavens – time and space. You know that the pyramids and their relationship to the Nile mirror the major stars and the Milky Way. We talked about the Nazca Lines in southern Peru too. Well, each of these ancient sites has some property or aspect that mirrors the real world. Its size, or shape, or alignment – whatever. So, for example, Stonehenge is a giant clock that calculates and echoes how the sun moves. The Great Pyramid at Giza has dimensions that are based on the size of the earth itself and actually models the northern hemisphere. The temple of Angkor Wat in Cambodia is an even more accurate definition of time. Have you ever been there?'

Matt shook his head. He looked at Aunt Jane and saw that she was watching him.

'This is important,' she said quietly. 'Robina knows what she's talking about.

'Robina?'

'Please,' Robin insisted. 'Questions later. Even questions about my name. OK?'

'OK. Sorry.'

'I'm sorry too. Of course you've never been to Angkor. But I have. It's magnificent. And its whole construction echoes and defines the passage of time – right down to taking precession into account. The wobble of the earth on its axis, remember?'

'One degree every seventy-two years, wasn't it?' Matt said. 'I remember.'

'That's right. Which is, incidentally – or rather, not incidentally at all because it's quite deliberate – a component of the ratio between the dimensions of the Great Pyramid and the earth. You see, *everything* interconnects. It's all part of a whole. These aren't isolated, coincidental sites, they're all part of an overall model – like a blueprint of the world.

Angkor Wat, for example, is incredibly impressive. It's made up of seventy-two small temples brought together in a single structure. And, like the pyramids, it mirrors a constellation – in this case the northern constellation of Draco. But because of precession the earth moves in relation to the constellations as it wobbles. Angkor was built some time between AD 800 and 1200, but it maps the constellation exactly as it appeared in 10,500 BC. At the point in history that the ancient Egyptians call "The First Time"'.

'In fact,' Robin went on, '*all* the models are correct as at 10,500 BC – that's the date when each of them is perfectly aligned, or would have been if they were there. It's like a baseline date. To give you just one example, in 10,500 BC the Great Sphinx would have been looking directly at the constellation of Leo at the spring equinox. All of the ancient sites are exactly aligned as they should be 12,500 years ago. Because each was built to a design created in 10,500 BC, even though many – most – of them were actually constructed long after the original purpose had been forgotten. But they were built to plans and using techniques that were remembered and passed on. Passed on by the last few survivors of an ancient civilization.'

Robin paused. She glanced at Aunt Jane, then said, 'The last few survivors of Atlantis.'

Matt couldn't stop himself. 'According to some theory or other,' he blurted out. 'I mean, yes, you've got some impressive facts and figures and an incredible memory for the detail. But I keep telling you, Atlantis is just a myth. It was never *real*.'

He was surprised at the vehemence behind her reply. 'It's not just a myth,' she shouted at him. 'How many times? You think I'm making all this up? Do you? It isn't theory, it's fact.'

Robin paused, breathing heavily. Matt didn't dare say anything. He waited until she had calmed down enough to continue, albeit in a rather more terse and abrupt tone.

'The whole ancient system is a giant simulation of the world,' Robin said. 'I assume that you can understand *that* much. You said yourself, it's like a computer model. A representation of time and space. An attempt to map out the chaos of the world. And with his knowledge of how to manipulate the elements – like the golems from the earth and fire demons and water creatures – Harper can use the model of the world not only to predict events but to manipulate them. All he needs is the key – the knowledge of how to control that model rather than just read it. Like the difference between looking at data in a spreadsheet and being able to change it – to recalculate the spreadsheet with his own numbers, or rewrite a document so it says what he wants it to say. And Harper's document is the whole world.'

'That's crazy,' Matt said.

'You think so? He can already make small changes. Insignificant in global terms, but you've seen it.'

'Well, yes. A bit of it. But are you saying he can predict what we're going to do, or who's going to win the FA Cup, or what the winning numbers are in next week's lottery? Or even pick a winner he chooses at random and then make that prediction come true?'

'No, not yet. But,' Robin said, 'that *is* what he is after. That's the level of control he thinks he can achieve when he knows what is written on that disc. It will tell him, or it will guide him to something else that will. Unless we can stop him.'

'So, is that what the people of Atlantis were aiming for?' Aunt Jane asked. Matt was surprised she was accepting it all so easily, despite what she had seen the night before. 'They were striving for a world over which they had total influence and control?'

'That's right,' Robin said. 'Control even over nature. How perfect would that be? But they allowed their ambition and greed to take over from their earlier peaceful, altruistic notions as their empire and their influence grew. They had mastery over their environment. They understood the deeper mysteries of the universe. They knew things that people are only just rediscovering today. The important thing for us now is that they had a different way of thinking, a different way of reasoning.'

'And they could predict the future?' Matt said. 'Is that what you're telling us – they actually foresaw future events? Like some sort of fortune-telling?'

Robin sighed. 'I'm saying they were getting there. That was their aim. That was a skill they wanted to add to their repertoire, if you like. And they were close, so very close, when the catastrophe came. It was the remnants of those predictive skills that saved the people of Akrotiri when Thira was destroyed by the eruptions. That's why no bodies have ever been found in the ruins. Not like Pompeii, for example, where no one warned them what was about to happen. But thousands of years before that, in 10,500 BC, the Atlanteans could not save themselves . . .' She gave a short laugh. 'Some said it was nature's revenge.'

She stood in silence, staring at the table, suddenly lost in her thoughts. Matt glanced round and saw the surviving piece of the burnt painting lying by the computer.

'The other thing you need to know about,' Aunt Jane said slowly, as if she was not sure she should tell him, 'is their longevity. That the people of Atlantis lived incredibly long lives.' She picked up the piece of canvas, holding it so Matt could see the faces of the two girls looking back at him. 'Do you understand what I'm saying?'

Matt just stared. He felt cold inside, out of breath. Not sure of anything any more. Just staring at the blue-eyed, black-haired girl in the old painting. 'That's you?' he said at last, turning to look at Robin on the other side of the room. 'It can't be you. Can it?'

'With my sister, Lisa,' she said, her voice completely level. No tone, no emotion. 'Poor Lisa. I inherited the curse, but she didn't.'

'What curse?' Matt said, hardly daring to think what she might mean.

'Longevity.'

Matt's head was reeling and it felt as if the room was spinning round him. 'But then – just how old *are* you?' he managed to ask.

Her mouth twitched as she suppressed a smile. 'Oh, compared to Dad I'm a youngster. Robina Jane Venture, born 12 August 1835.'

17

It was a joke. They were having him on. But it wasn't like Aunt Jane to joke, and Robin looked so sad. She was fourteen, Matt told himself. Fifteen at the most. Had to be.

'I tried to warn you,' Aunt Jane was saying. She sighed, like she was upset with *him*. 'You are so like your father, though. You just won't be told.'

'Told what?' Matt demanded. He was angry now. He didn't know why or who with. He just was. 'Don't hang out with her, she's old enough to be your great-great-great-great-grandmother several times over? What? Didn't stop you and Dad, did it? I saw your pictures. *You* can have fun, but I should keep well away – is that it?'

Aunt Jane shook her head. 'No, that isn't what I meant. Just . . .' She sighed again and turned away.

'It's true,' she said, more quietly, more sadly. 'Just that. Just believe it.'

'I don't even know what you're asking me to believe. I don't know if you're lying to me now or if you've been lying to me all along.'

'I never wanted to deceive you,' Robin said gently. 'I didn't know what was going to happen. I didn't know we . . .' She stopped, closed her eyes for a moment, then went on, 'I can't just tell everyone I meet that I'm getting on for 200 years old, can I? They'd either lock me up or cut me open. Maybe both.'

'That picture you went back for?' Matt said. His mouth was dry and his tongue felt like it didn't fit. 'Elizabeth Venture, in 1833.'

'My mother. Dad loved her so much. There was never anyone else, not before and not since. But she grew old and died. And so did my sister, Lisa. You've seen her in the pictures. With me.' She swallowed a sob and blinked away a tear.

Matt remembered the old woman he had thought was a grandmother, with the dark-haired girl he had thought was an ancestor of Robin's. He thought of the pictures in Aunt Jane's scrapbook – the children playing. The man who looked like

Julius Venture. The girl who looked like Robin.

'I don't get old,' Robin said. 'At least, not quickly. Another hundred years and I'll look like I'm all grown up, and then I'll stay like that for centuries. Getting older, but oh so slowly, like Dad. Not like everyone else. Everyone gets old. Everyone except Dad and me. Yes, it's us in the pictures and portraits. There are so many of Dad, so many things he's collected down the years. The lonely, boring years. Like the metal disc.' She fixed her startling blue eyes on Matt. 'He was there,' she said. 'He saw it happen. The eruptions and the floods. The end of Atlantis.'

'And you're really over 170 years old?'

Robin smiled. It was a thin, sad smile, but there was some warmth in it. Some friendship. 'I was flying helicopters before you were born,' she said. 'I played with Jane and your dad when they were children. I've watched them grow up. But I stay the same. It's difficult to understand, I know.'

'Your father never understood,' Aunt Jane said. 'Not really. But then . . .' She suddenly turned to Robin, like a small girl might turn to her older sister for comfort.

Robin held her close as she cried quietly, finishing the sentence for her: 'But then, he was in love. And he did try. He tried so hard to understand, to work it all out. That's why he got interested in archaeology.'

'Dad?' That sounded harder to believe than anything else. Matt couldn't imagine Dad loving anyone. Except Mum. And that was all over and done with. Dad was a loner; he didn't *do* relationships. 'He couldn't have been at your christening,' Matt realized, his mind setting off at a tangent rather than follow the thoughts through.

'He was giving us a clue,' Robin agreed.

'Telling us that Harper wasn't to be trusted.'

'That too.'

Aunt Jane had pulled away from Robin and was dabbing her eyes with a tissue from her sleeve. 'What else?' she asked. And Matt realized what was odd about the way Aunt Jane was with Robin – she treated her not as a child, not even as an equal, but more like an older, wiser friend.

'What happens at a christening?' Robin asked.

'You get your Christian name,' Matt said.

'What else?' Robin prompted.

'Well, water. The . . .' He hesitated. Had she seen that back then? Was this how her father had worked out the truth about the churches of Valdeholm? 'The sign of the cross,' he said.

'That's right. Arnold wanted us to find the Treasure of St John. And he wanted to warn us about Harper. He knew we'd work it out from his clue, just as he left clues for you on that website.'

'My clues were a bit easier.'

'Different, maybe,' she corrected him. 'You have a way of looking at the world, of analysing it and working things out. Dad and me . . .' She shrugged. 'We just know. Our minds make different connections, see different patterns in things. That's all.'

'We used to hunt for treasure when we were kids,' Aunt Jane said. She had recovered most of her composure now and was leaning against the side of the table. 'Your father loved it. We'd leave clues for each other to work out. It was so funny how Robin would work out some things just like that.' She clicked her fingers. 'But others, which I thought were so easy, she couldn't get at all. I imagine she thought the same about us.'

Robin nodded. 'Let's Find Treasure,' she said. 'You said that, Matt. I assume you and Arnie did the same.'

Matt nodded. 'He's still hunting for treasure now. Poor Dad. He never grew up either. Just grew old.'

'Not *that* old,' Aunt Jane said sternly. Then she

smiled. 'And we have treasure to find too, don't forget.'

'Yes,' Robin agreed. 'Time to get back to work.'

✝

It was difficult to concentrate. Matt was copying the symbols from the other side of the clay disc, while Robin and Jane went through books and papers and manuscripts, comparing old scripts with the symbols Matt had already copied.

His mind kept wandering. He thought of what Robin must have seen, what she must have done. Had she really lived through two world wars? He remembered her describing the Russians tipping their gold into a deep lake – how she'd sounded like she'd been there and seen it. He felt somehow cheated that she could be so much older than him. He'd thought she was a friend.

She was still a friend, he decided. Nothing would change that. He liked her. He liked her a lot. Only . . . And it was a big 'only' and it made him think of Dad.

Even so, he almost missed it. He actually copied the symbol – mechanically, without really looking at it. Just letting his hand do the work. Only as he paused and checked back over what he'd done did Matt see it.

The shape was different from the others because it looked more like a letter than an abstract symbol. Like a capital E, but with a line across the top. He hesitated, wondering why it looked familiar. Was there a similar symbol on the other side of the disc? Or had he seen it in one of the books that Robin had hunted out?

The answer came like Robin had said. Like a pattern – like a jigsaw slotting suddenly into place to give a bigger picture that the individual pieces didn't show. Matt felt the blood draining from his face. He shivered.

'I think we've got a problem,' he said, and explained what had just occurred to him.

Robin and Jane each examined the clay disc closely.

'Could be a coincidence,' Jane said. But she didn't sound convinced.

'What do you think, Matt?' Robin asked.

'It's LFT,' he told them. 'Has to be, doesn't it? It's Dad's shorthand symbol for "Let's Find Treasure", the capital letters all laid over each other.'

'Go on,' Robin said. She was watching him closely and Matt guessed that she had known in an instant what that meant, though he had to work it out.

'So this isn't a clay copy of the disc that we found.

I think *this* is the original disc.' He held it up.

'But that isn't thousands of years old,' Aunt Jane pointed out.

'No, it isn't. And since it has Dad's own shorthand on it, his mark, he must have made it.'

'Why?'

'I was wondering that too. It didn't strike me before and it should have. Why did Dad have a clay copy of the disc rather than an impression? Or a plaster copy taken from a mould he'd made? I mean, how would he copy the disc in clay?'

'Go on,' Aunt Jane prompted.

'The answer is that I don't think he did,' Matt said. He was still working it all out himself, talking through it as his mind followed the train of thought. 'What he did was he *made* a clay disc and from that he took a mould. It's probably in his study somewhere, buried under a heap of junk. Anyway, wherever it is, he used that mould to make another disc. The disc we found on Valdeholm. So what Harper has got isn't an ancient key to Atlantis that is going to unlock the final secrets of the ancients for him so he can complete his model, or whatever it is.'

Matt was grinning now, proud of his reasoning and also proud of his dad. 'Harper's got a fake, a made-up disc that Dad planted and led us to find. He'd already been to Valdeholm, like we thought. He found the treasure, took the real disc – if there ever was one – and replaced it with a *fake* for Harper to find. To throw him off the scent, lay a false trail. We can't decipher these symbols and neither can Harper, because they're just made up by Dad. It's gibberish.'

'Which is fine,' Aunt Jane said. 'Until Harper realizes he's been tricked.'

'Then he'll be after the real disc,' Robin agreed.

'If there is one,' Matt reminded them.

'Oh, there is one,' Robin said. 'We can be sure of that.'

Matt looked at her closely, staring deep into her dark, blue eyes. 'What haven't you told us?' he asked.

But before Robin could answer, the doorbell rang.

✠

Once again they met in Venture's study. It reminded Matt of the first meeting with Harper, except that instead they were joined by the rather more rotund form of Mephistopheles Smith. And Robin's dad was absent. She had taken his place behind the desk, Smith sitting where Harper had been on the other side of it. Matt could tell they were firm friends.

Smith listened and nodded and did not interrupt as Robin told him what had happened. Matt waited for him to leap to his feet and declare it was impossible, or stupid, or the imaginings of a teenage girl. But he never did. It slowly dawned on him that Smith knew the truth about Robin and her father. He was an old friend of the family – why wouldn't he? Everyone knew. Aunt Jane, Matt's dad, Mephistopheles Smith.

Everyone except Matt.

'Robin thinks there is a real disc that Harper will want when he finds he's been duped,' Matt said as soon as Robin had finished.

Smith nodded, though his expression was hard to read behind his dark glasses. Matt wondered if he ever took them off. 'It seems reasonable,' the man said. 'After all, for whatever reason, Harper was expecting to find such a disc.'

'And it's another reason to plant the fake,' Robin said. 'Give him what he was expecting anyway. Less suspicious. He must have found references to the disc in some other source and realized it could lead him to the knowledge he needs. Besides . . .' She hesitated, and again Matt was sure she knew more than she had told them.

'Besides?' he prompted.

'We have Dad's notes,' she said, 'though you have to realize he was working it out still, guessing at some things and filling in the blanks in what he knew. Trying to discover what Harper was really up to. But from what Dad *did* manage to work out, the way it works is this. They didn't have computers back in the old times. So their model wasn't bits and bytes, it was a physical thing, created from the elements. Principally made from the earth itself. A miniature recreation – a universe in little. A copy of the earth and the heavens in the architecture and the locations of the ancient sites, with the discs as a vital component. That's what Harper is trying to recreate inside his computer. He wants a computer model of the world as accurate and as powerful as the physical model the ancients were building.'

'So?' Aunt Jane said.

'So how do you think they planned to use that model?' Robin asked.

'All right,' Matt said. 'Tell us how.'

'Remember they were trying to predict things,

but they were also trying to manipulate events – people, places, things. To do that they needed to focus the model, to define exactly what they wanted to manipulate.'

'Like hair for a voodoo doll,' Matt remembered. 'So that the doll is tied, linked in some way, to the specific person you want to affect.'

'Exactly. You have to sort of aim the model – target it at the part of the world you're trying to change. Now, there are two ways of doing it. By a direct link of some kind, like with the voodoo doll and a lock of hair. Entanglement. That's how Harper creates and controls his elementals, the creatures he set on us. They are linked to his computer models and he gives them instructions from his laptop. Like playing a computer game.'

'Avatars,' Matt said. 'Creatures you give instructions to or move round with your mouse or whatever. He sets them off to complete some task and leaves them to it, like the little people in *Sim City* or whatever.'

'And the other way of specifying what you want to affect,' Smith said, 'would be by giving the location. Defining exactly where the events are to take place.'

'Like map coordinates?' Matt said.

'That would give the place. You also need to give the time,' Robin said. 'You need to specify the moment when you want the effect to take place. Like setting a timer. And that, Harper cannot do – not yet. He can only affect the things he has fully modelled in his computer code.'

'So, how did the ancients do it?'

'With the discs. I told you they were vital to the whole thing. And the reason is that the metal disc we had here was used to define the exact time of events that you want to change. It's like playing back a recording, except it could be future events that are played back. You can choose any time you want using that disc to set the exact year, month, day. Right down to the hours, minutes, seconds . . . But Katherine Feather took it. So Harper has it now.'

'And what about location?' Smith said.

'That requires another, different disc, which specifies geographical coordinates. One vitally important disc that has been lost for millennia. Or so my father reckons.'

'The disc that Harper is now after,' Matt said.

'But what can he do with it if he gets it?' Aunt Jane asked.

'Assuming he realizes how the discs work and what they are for, then he can manipulate, control, predict *anything*,' Robin said. 'If Harper knows what he is doing, he can recreate the discs inside his computer model – make his own versions of them, just as he has been modelling the ancient sites themselves. If he does that . . .' She pursed her lips for a moment before saying, 'Well, then he can probably predict what we're doing right now.'

'Even without this second geography disc?' Jane asked.

'We have to assume so,' Smith told them. 'If he has the rest of it worked out, he may be clever enough to solve the missing pieces himself rather than rely on copying what has already been done. It's like a code and he is dangerously close to cracking it – to discovering how to control and harness the chaos that is our world. The secret is, I suppose, to be *un*predictable.'

'And find the other disc, the *real* last disc, before he does,' Robin said.

'Dad knows where it is,' Matt said. 'That's why he created the fake. Has to be. Remember all those times we thought he'd jumped to conclusions or made a lucky guess?' He shook his head. 'Wasn't luck at all, was it? He already knew where the real disc was and he was leading us – or rather Harper – away from it. Things, clues, he ignored. It was because he didn't want to draw attention to them.'

'You could be right,' Robin agreed.

'Does that mean we can work out where the disc is?' Aunt Jane asked. 'If so, we can still get to it before Harper.'

Robin was already working at the computer. 'There was a point,' she said, 'where the Hospitallers split up. There was a lead that Arnie ignored, remember? An entry in a journal. A sighting. It's here somewhere . . . The possible locations . . . He discounted Rosslyn in Scotland, which is probably right. But there was also the possibility of the disc ending up in Pomponini in Italy, or Pont St Jean in the south of France.'

'I'll have them both checked,' Smith said. 'But I suspect we are too late.' He went to the door and spoke quickly and quietly to the large man in sunglasses standing outside.

'What makes you think we're too late?' Matt asked when he had finished.

'At some point,' Smith said, 'Harper must realize the disc is not the one he is after and that he has been tricked. At that point, he will be as able to trace back the clues as we are. Your father knows that.'

'Which just means we have to hurry, to get there first.'

Smith held up a pudgy finger. 'Another thing. To create an authentic-seeming disc, your father must have had some idea what he was making a copy of. You can't expect a forger to create a fake painting if he's never seen the artist's original work.'

'You're saying that Arnold must have seen the original disc,' Aunt Jane said. 'So that he knew what Harper was expecting to find.'

'It seems likely. He must have had a good idea of what the real one looked like so he could make a convincing fake with useless symbols on. That and his determination that Harper should not find the original would both suggest that Dr Stribling did indeed discover the disc himself. It doesn't matter where, because he didn't leave it where he found it.'

'So where is it?' Robin asked. 'Did he hide it somewhere else? Or destroy it, even?'

'It's a relic. It's old,' Matt said. 'He'd want to look after it, keep it safe.'

'And he wouldn't leave it at his house,' Robin agreed. 'He was expecting Harper to come for him.'

The realization came to them all at the same moment. Aunt Jane was the first to speak.

'Oh, the silly old fool,' she said.

'Typical,' Robin agreed.

Matt shook his head in disbelief. 'He hasn't hidden it anywhere, has he?' Matt said. 'Dad's still got it with him. At the pyramid. With Harper.'

18

Having had practically no sleep the night before, Matt had been functioning on adrenaline. Aunt Jane was the same, judging by how easily he managed to persuade her that he was going with Robin.

By the time Smith's limousine got the two of them to RAF Cosworth, Matt could barely keep his eyes open. He was asleep almost as soon as the huge transport plane was in the sky. And despite the discomfort of flying in the back of a military aircraft designed to move soldiers and their equipment, he didn't wake until Robin gently nudged his arm and told him they had to disembark.

Word had come back quickly from Smith's enquiries and, as they suspected, the curator of the local museum in Pont St Jean was pleased to report that a recent excavation had provided his establishment with some interesting old documents and relics. There wasn't a metal disc among them, but now it was mentioned the Englishman had taken some things away to be dated by the British Museum. He was fairly sure there had been such a disc among those artefacts.

'Typical Arnie,' Robin had remarked. 'Not content with finding one hoard of treasure, he has to go and find himself another one as well.'

'You think the Valdeholm stuff was genuine?' Matt had asked.

'Oh yes. He just added the fake disc to it.' She shook her head in renewed disbelief. 'He's so brilliant, but so daft. How's he manage that?'

'Perhaps it's hereditary,' Matt joked, coaxing a smile from her.

Now, refreshed but anxious, Matt watched the helicopter that had brought them on their final stage of the journey turning in the sky and heading back towards Rio. Leaving him and Robin standing in a small clearing in the rainforest, as close to the Waterfall Pyramid as they could get without fear of being detected. Alone.

'So what's the plan?' he asked. 'Your mate Mr Smith said we just have to make sure Harper doesn't do anything till his people get here. Whenever that is.'

'It won't be long,' Robin reassured him.

'Good.' Matt slapped at his neck where he could feel something crawling over his skin. Or was it his imagination? Probably sweat, he decided – it was so hot and humid. Away in the distance, poking up from the canopy of the forest, they could see the blunted shape of the mountain where Harper's pyramid was. 'That way, I guess.'

They walked for hours, keeping to the shade. It wasn't difficult, as the tops of the trees formed an almost unbroken canopy. The disadvantage was that this canopy trapped the heat so that the air was warm and humid and clammy. They each had a small backpack with water and some food. Robin also had a torch. The closer they got to the mountain, the less they could see of it. Eventually only the flattened top was visible above the tall tress that surrounded them. They forced their way through the dense vegetation – pushing aside creepers and stepping over the rotting remains of fallen trees and branches. The ground was soft and seemed to sap the strength from Matt's feet as he walked. The air was so damp it seemed to cling to his skin. The whole place smelled like a hot, dank greenhouse.

They talked hardly at all. In fact, they had barely spoken except when they had to since Robin had explained about the discs and what Harper was up to. At last Matt summoned up the courage to ask if they could stop for another break. He gulped thirstily from his water bottle.

'You don't need permission. You don't have to act like I'm a grown-up and you're a child,' Robin told him sternly.

'I'm not,' Matt protested.

'Course not.'

'Anyway, listen to you – telling me how to behave suddenly.'

'I've always done that,' she said, looking away. When she looked back at him, her face was set and stern. 'Look, I know you're not happy, but there's nothing I can do.'

'I'm not asking you to.'

'It's still me, you know. Nothing's changed. Except your perceptions, all right?' She checked her compass, avoiding his stare.

Matt shrugged. 'If you say so.'

'I'm still Robin. Still the same . . . girl you met a few days ago.' She tilted her head to one side. Her hair was tied back in a ponytail which swung behind her head. 'Nothing's changed.' She hesitated a moment, then added, 'We're still friends, you know.'

'Are we?'

'Aren't we?'

'I guess,' he admitted.

She punched him gently on the shoulder. 'Good. Come on, then. Friends.'

'Friends,' he agreed. And just saying it made him feel better than he had all day.

'One thing,' she called back over her shoulder as she forced her way through the forest. 'Just friends, all right? Don't get to like me too much.'

'As if,' he muttered.

☩

Smith had given Robin a satellite photograph of the area. Matt was surprised at how detailed it was, how close-up. It looked as if it had been taken from a low-flying plane, not from space. It showed the mountain, and from above you could see that the top was hollow, covered with a mesh of vegetation but with water glinting beneath. The waterfall was a white smudge on the side of the mountain. Further round, a small dark area had been circled in white. According to Smith, it had taken a trained expert with a magnifying glass to spot it on an even sharper and closer printout than he was allowed to give them.

They hoped it was where the underground river that ran through the amphitheatre emerged from beneath the mountain. A pale line, as thin as a hair, could – just possibly – be the river itself, weaving through the forest on its meandering path to join the lake under the waterfall.

As they got closer, they could hear the crash of the waterfall. Then, suddenly, there was the river. They broke through a mass of creepers and branches hanging low in front of them and found themselves standing on the bank. Or rather ten metres above the river which roared past them in the gorge below. Even so, the sound of it was almost drowned out by the massive waterfall further round the mountain. Matt could see the spray from it like a haze against the bright blue sky. As blue, he thought, as Robin's eyes.

'Look.' She had to shout above the sound of the water. Robin was pointing along the river. 'See where it comes out.'

Matt looked where she was pointing and saw the small, dark shape of the opening into the mountain. Was there a way in? Did the ledge below continue all the way along the side of the river and into the mountain? It was hard to see from so far away.

'How do we get there?' he shouted back. 'We can't swim against the current.'

'We need to get closer and find a way to climb down.'

They made their way carefully along the top of the gorge, keeping back from the edge as far as they dared. Too far and the river was lost to sight behind the vegetation and they might be heading away from it and never know. But too close and they risked losing their footing on the slippery ground and plummeting into the gorge.

After what seemed like hours, they arrived at the side of the mountain. It thrust up out of the jungle like some gigantic tree. The steep slope was encrusted with creepers and branches and roots and leaves. Ten metres below them, Matt and Robin could see the dark opening with the white water crashing out.

'Let's hope it's the right river,' Matt said.

'Let's hope we can get down there,' Robin said.

'And how do we do that? Climb?'

'Not a bad idea,' she told him. She crouched down and started examining the creepers. 'We need a strong one that runs all the way to the bottom. Then we can abseil.'

'Oh, we can abseil, can we?'

'You *can* abseil?'

'Well, I've never tried, so we'll find out.'

Robin took a deep breath. 'I don't know what they teach kids these days,' she said.

The most promising of the creepers looked dangerously thin and suspiciously fragile to Matt. But Robin assured him it would do the job, and he assured her that he was not a wimp and would follow her down.

'Just don't fall on top of me,' she said. She swung herself expertly out from the side, holding the creeper between her hands and with her feet planted flat against the almost sheer side of the cliff.

'Aren't you supposed to have a safety line or something, then just slide down?' Matt asked.

'And you brought a safety line with you?'

'Well, no.'

'Then we'll have to do it my way, won't we?'

'You're enjoying this,' he accused her. 'You're actually having fun.'

'Something to do,' she replied casually. 'Here goes.'

She made it look incredibly easy. Like walking down the cliff face, holding on to the creeper like a rope as she lowered herself hand over hand, one step down the vertical side after another. All too soon she had reached the ledge beside the river and it was Matt's turn.

'Coming, ready or not,' he shouted, trying to sound as unconcerned as Robin seemed.

'Just be careful,' she told him. 'It isn't as easy as it looks.'

'Now you tell me!' He was over the edge by this time – dangling from a slippery creeper, with his feet flailing at the rock face. He tried to place them, as Robin had, solidly against the side. But he only succeeded in pushing himself away, and starting to spin. He could feel the creeper slipping through his hands and tightened his grip.

There was a jolt as he stopped sliding down. Another jolt, as the creeper moved. Matt looked up and could see the makeshift rope was tearing – strand after strand of slippery green creeper snapping and breaking above him. He loosened his grip and started to slide again, hoping he could stop before he hit the water.

Then the creeper broke.

He slammed down, into the rock ledge, the creeper falling with him – tangling in his feet and dragging him to the brink. Robin had an arm round his waist, trying to pull him upright. But then his feet were whipped from under him and Matt was falling again. He twisted desperately, arms thrashing as he tried to regain his balance. Falling, he smacked into something, and felt it move.

It was Robin. His shoulder caught her in the stomach and sent her reeling. To the edge. She stood frozen for a moment, back arced as she tried to heave herself upright again.

Then she was falling backwards over the ledge and towards the raging torrent below.

Matt lashed out. His hand slapped against something – Robin's hand. She grabbed him and suddenly he had her entire weight pulling him to the edge too. He managed to brace his feet against the rock and looked down – into the river, into Robin's face as she looked back up at him. She was hanging from his hand, over the sheer drop to the water below. Matt's hand was still slick from the creeper and he could feel her slipping away. Falling. Her backpack slipped from her shoulder, crashing into the river below – ripped to shreds. Matt saw the torch explode into pieces as it hit a jagged rock poking up from the swirling torrent of water.

Without the weight and awkwardness of the backpack, somehow Robin managed to hold on. And somehow Matt managed to drag her back up towards the ledge. When she was close enough, she reached out with her free hand and clamped it over the edge. She let go of Matt and hauled herself back up.

'Sorry,' he said, embarrassed now that she was safe. 'The creeper . . .'

'I saw. Wasn't your fault. I picked the wrong creeper.'

'Like we had much choice,' he told her.

'Forget it,' she said. 'But – you know, thanks.'

'Pleasure.'

Robin turned to stare into the dark opening, into the tunnel where the water emerged. The ledge they were standing on seemed to continue into the mountain. 'Shall we?' she asked, taking Matt's hand. 'This is where it really gets dangerous.'

Together they walked into the darkness.

✠

Matt could barely make out Robin's shape in front of him and he could hardly hear himself think.

They walked with their hands on the wall on one side, the river surging noisily but invisibly past on the other, hoping they would not reach the end of the ledge. Or that if they did, they would notice before they fell. When the going was tricky, Robin slowed down – sometimes so much that Matt walked into her and she yelled at him above the noise of the water to be careful, and he yelled at her that he was sorry, and they both yelled at each other, 'What did you say?'

In several places the ledge was so narrow they had to shuffle along with their backs pressed hard against the damp rock wall. Always the spray and spit of the river was soaking into them. At first, Matt found it invigorating. He liked the sting of the cold water after the close heat of the jungle. It seemed to cleanse and sharpen him. But after a while he was just feeling wet and cold and bedraggled.

'I wish you hadn't dropped the torch,' he shouted to Robin. But he knew she couldn't hear him above the rage of the river.

Finally, light. A tiny dot in the distance at first, but growing gradually larger with every step they took. Before long, it was enough to illuminate Robin's face as she looked back at Matt, her eyes gleaming.

'Nearly there,' she mouthed.

The ledge widened slightly where it emerged into the light. They paused, standing together, and peered cautiously into the huge amphitheatre beyond. It seemed even bigger after the cramped, dark confines of the tunnel. Another difference was that it was busy – Matt could see several of Harper's guards in their distinctive khaki camouflage uniforms erecting more lights and clearing away some of the rubble.

'Looks like he's giving up on archaeology,' Matt said quietly. Outside the echoing tunnel, the river was not so noisy.

'Looks like he's getting ready for something,' Robin agreed. 'Not good.'

Even with extra lights, the edges of the huge cavern were still in darkness. It was relatively easy to keep to the shadows and work their way carefully up towards the top of the amphitheatre.

'The way into the pyramid will probably be guarded,' Matt said quietly.

Robin nodded, a vague silhouette in the gloom. 'But we're not going to the pyramid.'

They froze as two of the guards walked past them, just several metres away. Then Robin was moving again, Matt following as quietly and as closely as he could.

There was even more activity in the office area where Matt had found his father. Matt and Robin got as close as they dared and watched from an area in the shadows behind several fallen pillars. Guards were setting up computers and other equipment. A huge plasma screen, like the ones in the guest rooms and on Harper's jet, was being installed and connected to the systems.

Robin nudged Matt's arm, pointing. He had already seen – Dad and Julius Venture were standing a little way back from the main activity, talking.

'We have to get their attention,' Matt whispered. 'We can't get to them, but they might be able to come closer to us.'

'What are you going to do? Jump up and down and wave?'

Matt shook his head. 'I thought I'd bung a rock at them,' he said.

He found a pebble that wasn't too big to attract unwanted attention and lobbed it towards where Dad and Venture were standing. He was way off and the stone bounced on the floor several metres away. It ricocheted back up and landed on one of the tables. Matt could hear it clattering across the table top and ducked down quickly into the shadows.

'Good shot,' Robin told him.

'You want to try?'

'OK.'

Robin's attempt was rather more successful. She skimmed her stone close to the ground, just above the fallen pillars and other debris, but low enough to go under the table that Matt's pebble had hit. It bounced close to her father's feet before clattering off into the shadows beyond.

Venture looked up immediately. His eyes connected with Robin's and he gave the slightest hint of a nod before turning to talk to one of the guards. Maybe he was apologizing for having kicked a stone across the floor. Maybe he was saying he was going for a short walk to stretch his legs. Whatever he said, Venture and Matt's dad were moving.

They looked casual, like they were just wandering, talking quietly together. Venture nodded to one of the guards as they passed.

'Where do you think you're going?' another guard shouted as the two men reached almost to the edge of the light.

'Just getting out of the way,' Venture called back.

'If that's OK?'

'No further than that,' the guard warned. He had a gun slung over his shoulder and he pulled at the strap to make the point.

'Wouldn't dream of it,' Venture said pleasantly. He leaned back against a fallen pillar. The fallen pillar that Robin and Matt were crouched behind. 'Were my notes useful?' he asked, in the same relaxed tone of voice. But he spoke more quietly now, looking at Matt's dad but addressing the question to Robin.

'They were,' she replied. 'Smith's on his way, but it'll take him a while to get people ready. He called it "getting his ducks in a row".'

'He would,' Venture said. 'Sounds impressive, means little.'

'Can you trust him?' Matt's dad asked.

'To the ends of the earth,' Venture said. 'And back again. The question is whether he'll have his people here in time to stop Harper.'

'So what's going on?' Matt asked. 'What are all these people doing down here?'

'This is the place,' Venture said. 'Well, one of many places, originally. This amphitheatre, where we are now, this is where the world model could be realized. Where events could be played out – past, present and future. They could manipulate the world like watching a video recording. Rewind to show the past or fast-forward to predict – and change – the future. All played out in miniature on this stage. That's why Harper is here, though I doubt he realized the significance of its point in the web of ancient sites until long after he found it. But now he is too close to the truth and he must be stopped.'

'What do you mean by events being played out like a video?' Matt asked. 'You mean, like on a stage with actors and props and stuff?'

'In a sense,' Venture told them. 'Except that the actors and the props and stuff would be elemental. Like Harper's more limited creations, they were fashioned out of the earth and the air, out of fire and water. Remember I said it was like a video playback? Only it isn't pixels on a screen, it's the raw elements themselves that are used to represent the world. And, using that recreation, Harper can predict and he can manipulate and change . . . everything. When the model is complete, that is, and the time and location are specified . . .' He gave a quiet chuckle. 'All the stage is a world, if you like.'

'It's like he has a whole collection of voodoo dolls. And he can work it all using the discs,' Robin said.

'One of which Harper now has,' Venture pointed out. There was no hint of blame in his voice, but Robin and Matt exchanged guilty glances. 'There is a mechanism,' Venture went on, not noticing as he continued to pretend to talk with Matt's father. 'The discs are slotted into the floor down by the stage, then turned to define the time and the place. Not that Harper knows that.'

'He doesn't have to, though,' Matt's dad said quietly. 'He's copied the data into his computers. He doesn't have the geographical data, but he can work out the format for that easily enough now he knows how the time disc works.'

'So where is the geographical disc?' Matt asked. 'We know you made a fake for Harper to find, one that wouldn't work.'

'Kept him guessing for a bit,' Dad said with evident satisfaction. 'But he's worked it out now, I'm afraid. The original is quite safe.' He glanced down at the shadows where Matt was crouched. 'It's in my pocket,' he said, patting his jacket.

'Didn't they search you?' Robin asked in amazement.

'Only for weapons. Harper wasn't there, would-n't dirty his hands. And he had no reason to tell them to look for a disc. Not that it matters much now.'

'So what's all this stuff for?' Matt asked.

'Harper is preparing to compile and run his model, his code,' Venture said. 'It may be realized within the silicon of the computer rather than the rock and sand of this theatre, but the location is still important. As I said, this place, like several others around the world, was well chosen; its location is critical. That's how Harper found it, of course – because it is on such an obvious gathering of lines of power and influence. Now, he thinks that running his computer code, his model, on systems based here – directly above us at the same longitude and latitude, on the same lines of power – will be advan-tageous.' Venture clicked his tongue. 'Disastrous, more like. We have to stop him.'

'But how?' Robin asked.

'It looks like he's almost ready,' Matt said.

'You need to stop him from compiling his code and creating the model,' Venture told them. 'Once he runs the model, he'll have control of everything – even us. It will be like the whole world is a simulation inside his computer that he can manipulate like a child can a computer game – building, guiding, destroying whatever he likes. Except whatever he does in this game will actually happen. He can find a person and make that person do what he likes. If he sets a monster loose in London, then a monster will indeed run riot through the city.'

'A monster created out of earth, air, fire and water,' Matt realized. 'He can do whatever he wants.'

'And nothing can stop him then,' Venture said. 'You have to destroy the supercomputers in the pyramid. Can you do that?'

'We have no choice,' Robin said.

'If we can get to them,' Matt added.

'You need a diversion,' his dad told him. 'I think Julius and I can probably arrange that for you.'

☩

When the lights went out, Matt and Robin were ready. The guards had been grateful for Julius Venture's enthusiastic help connecting up the computers. They were less impressed when the way he did it overloaded the circuit.

Matt could hear men shouting, Venture apologizing, his father laughing, and the angry cries of people plunged into sudden darkness. In fact, the amphitheatre was not in total darkness – it was only one section of the lighting that had failed. But it was enough.

Matt was grateful for the warmth of Robin's hand holding his as they ran together across the uneven ground and up the steep steps. She seemed to know exactly where she was going. Unlike Matt, she did not trip or catch her feet on the debris scattered across the ruins. Unlike Matt, she didn't seem worried by the guards – vague, dark shapes – running past them to find out what had happened.

Into the short passageway up to the entrance to the pyramid. The lights here were flickering – on and off, then on again. Sending shadows dancing like firelight on the rough walls.

There was a guard at the end of the passage, standing by the open door. Matt hesitated as the guard turned towards them, but Robin pulled him onwards.

'Thank heavens,' she gasped. 'They need you, back there.' She pointed down the passageway.

The guard looked not much older than Matt. He was staring at them open-mouthed, his hand hesitant and nervous on his gun. 'Who are you?' he asked in heavily accented English.

'Never mind *us*, get going now!' Robin said urgently. 'Can't you see the lights are failing. The generator's exploded, there are casualties, people injured. They need you, now.'

The guard frowned. 'Generator?'

'Just go,' Matt told him. 'We'll find Mr Harper. You'd better not still be here when he arrives.'

He didn't wait to see what effect this had. They pushed past the young guard and hurried up the narrow stairs into the Waterfall Pyramid.

'You think they know we're here?' Matt asked as they stepped out from the stairs into the passageway leading to the computer suite.

'I hope not. Probably think it's just Dad trying to cause trouble.'

'Dad*s*,' Matt corrected her. 'My dad can cause trouble too.'

'And you are *so* like him,' Robin said.

'Better believe it.'

The flickering, fake torchlight gave the corridor an eerie feel as they hurried to the door. Robin keyed in the code and the door clicked open.

'So far, so good,' she said quietly.

They stepped carefully into the computer room. It was exactly as Matt remembered it, except that the bank of screens across from the door were not showing the spinning 'H' symbol. They all showed the same picture, but it was the wire-frame model of the pyramid. And sitting at one of the screens was the broad, unmistakable form of Atticus Harper himself.

Matt put his finger to his lips, warning Robin to keep quiet. Harper seemed engrossed in the images on the screen. They would have to sneak past him, down to where the supercomputers were crunching their numbers, creating the model.

The door slammed shut behind them, like a gunshot over the gentle hum of the air conditioning. Matt spun round – to find Klein standing there. He had been behind the door when they came in and he had a machine pistol pointing straight at them.

'Do come in, my young friends,' Harper called, still without looking round. 'I've been waiting for you. Look.'

He pointed to the screen, and Matt and Robin were close enough now to see that there were two tiny figures standing in the pyramid. The image zoomed in on them – a man and woman. Or rather a boy and a girl. Colours and textures filled in as they watched and it was now unmistakably a crude computer rendition of Matt and Robin.

'I have it keyed to you,' Harper said. 'I've been watching you all the way from downstairs. I must say, you took your time. I expected you several minutes ago. But never mind. When my model is complete, I'll be able to predict you precisely. All I need to do is watch the representations of you on my model, my simulation, and wind forward in time to see what you are about to do. Like watching a video. Then I can decide whether to let you do it, or whether to change your actions and make you do something else entirely.'

He swung round in the chair, his face one enormous smile of satisfaction and victory.

'You'll never make it work,' Robin said calmly.

'You don't think so?'

'It'd take a genius to create a computer model like that,' Matt told him. 'I doubt *you* could configure the systems or create the code.'

Harper sighed. 'Yes, you're probably right,' he agreed. 'But I have reverse-engineered the disc you so kindly provided. And from that I've managed to extrapolate the geographical information I need. All that remains now is for the computer to build all the information into the complete model. But, as you say, I needed expert help. I could not have done it all on my own.'

Somewhere at the back of the room, a door banged shut.

'Which is why I employ the very best people,' Harper was saying.

Footsteps across the floor, the click of high heels.

'Plus, of course, it gave me an added advantage when dealing with your father. An extra incentive for him, shall we say?'

A figure stepped out from between the rows of computer drives and storage systems. A woman.

'She's not been with us long, but I think you already know my head of computing,' Harper said.

Matt barely heard him. He was looking in silent astonishment at the woman who was staring back at him, equally amazed.

'What are you doing here, Matt?' his mother asked.

19

The black dots on the horizon resolved themselves into shapes, identifiable by the noise they made before they became properly visible. The massive, throbbing sound of the engines preceded them across the rainforest. Mechanical and alien.

The helicopters swept in low over the canopy of trees. They hovered above the ruins of the city, ropes lowered from their open doors. Dark-suited figures slid down the ropes with well-rehearsed ease and dropped to the ground below. Immediately they were up again, running, guns at the ready.

The helicopters moved away, searching for suitable flat landing spaces in among the ruins further off. They rested heavily on their wheels, rotors slowing to a lazy, drooping halt. A rather portly figure climbed clumsily down from one helicopter and looked up at the huge majesty of the waterfall through small, round, dark glasses.

✟

It was one of the few times – possibly the only time – that Matt had seen his mother lost for words. Her initial surprise had given way to anger and disbelief as Harper told Klein to take the three of them at gunpoint down to the amphitheatre.

'You can establish a link to the servers,' he said to Matt's mum. 'And then we can compile the final code so it is ready to run and the model will be complete.'

'You can do that from here and route the results to the other screens,' she replied irritably. Even with a gun pointing at her, she had to do things properly.

'Mum – don't!' Matt warned. 'Don't help him.'

'Shut up,' Klein told him, swinging his gun at Matt.

Robin stepped forward and blocked the gun with her arm. 'Leave him alone.'

Klein was grinning. 'Or what?' he demanded. But he lowered the gun.

'Do it,' Harper told Matt's mum. 'If you value you son's life. And your husband's too. Oh yes, he is here as well.'

Without comment, Matt's mother pulled a keyboard towards her across the workstation. She typed away for a moment, then clicked on a button with the mouse pointer. She turned to stare sternly at Harper. 'That's *ex*-husband, if you don't mind,' she said.

On every screen that Matt could see, a thin red progress bar appeared. 'Code Compilation in Progress', the text beneath it said. The bar started to stretch slowly across the screen as the computers set to work, putting all the different computer programs that formed Harper's model into a single piece of computer code ready to be run.

'Oh, Mum,' Matt said quietly.

Harper led the way. By the time they reached the lift at the end of the corridor, they could all hear sounds from outside.

'Is that thunder?' Matt's mother wondered.

But even as she spoke, there came the sound of a staccato burst of gunfire.

'That's Mr Smith,' Robin told her.

Klein had his hand to his ear and was talking quietly but urgently into a microphone on his lapel.

'What's going on?' Harper demanded.

'Some sort of raid,' Klein said. 'They're armed

and they know their business. We won't be able to hold them off for long.'

Harper pulled a mobile phone from his pocket. On its screen Matt could see the red thermometer showing the progress of his code. 'You don't have to hold them off for long,' Harper snapped. 'Just a few minutes.'

'That may not be possible. I don't have many men. Not enough to withstand a full-scale assault.'

'Then we'll get you some reinforcements,' Harper said. 'Come on. We'll take the stairs.'

The sound of explosions and gunfire was louder as they hurried down the narrow, winding staircase with Klein waving his gun to encourage them.

'Who are they?' Matt asked Robin.

She shrugged. 'CIA, SAS, whoever he could find and persuade to help.'

'I should have stayed at school,' Matt muttered. But even when they paused at the ground floor and a bullet ripped past his ear, taking a chunk out of the stonework behind him, he knew he didn't mean it.

Klein let loose a burst of machine-gun fire in return and then they were off again – almost falling down the stairs in their enforced haste.

'What is going on, Matthew?' his mother asked.

She sounded like she believed it was all his fault.

'I don't have a clue,' he lied. 'Ask Dad.'

His mother grunted, stumbling down another step in her stiletto heels. 'Might have known he'd be behind the problem,' she said. But to Matt's surprise, she added wistfully, 'I do hope he's all right.'

The young guard that Robin and Matt had bluffed their way past was back at the doorway. He glared at them and Robin winked at him. Klein stopped to give him new orders, then continued to herd Matt, his mother and Robin through into the amphitheatre.

'Well, I never knew this was here,' Matt's mum said as they emerged into the bright artificial light at the end of the passage. 'Probably why your father came,' she confided to Matt, before being prodded forward by Klein's gun. She glared at the skull-faced man. 'I never liked you,' she told him.

'Mum,' Matt said. Despite everything, she was embarrassing him – how did she manage to do that? Even here, even now?

Dad seemed rather more surprised to see his ex-wife than he had been to see Matt. She glared at him, but only for a moment, then they embraced. Matt looked away.

'Just good friends?' Robin asked quietly.

'Oh, they love each other,' he told her. It hadn't occurred to him till then, but now it seemed so obvious. 'They just can't live together, that's all. They get on each other's nerves so much.'

'Can't believe that,' she said, watching as Matt's parents disentangled themselves and his dad introduced his mum quickly to Julius Venture.

Harper ignored them. He clapped his hands together like a pianist about to give his greatest ever concert and seated himself at one of the computers. 'Now then,' he declared.

The huge plasma screen dominated the small area to the side of the amphitheatre. It flickered into life. On it, the progress bar inched its way along. It was almost halfway now. In the background, the rattle of gunfire was getting closer.

'Stop this immediately,' Venture said loudly. His voice was full of authority, but Harper seemed not to hear. Venture stepped closer, but two of the guards pulled him away before he could reach Harper.

Klein was again listening to the reports coming in through his earpiece. 'If you really can get us reinforcements,' he told Harper urgently, 'then we need them now!'

'And you shall have them.' The slowly filling progress bar shrank to a smaller version, in a window at the top corner of the screen. The rest of the screen was now taken up with the familiar wireframe model of the pyramid. 'Though in just a few minutes, when the code is fully compiled so it can be run and the model is complete, I shall be able to call off your assailants.' At the click of a control, figures appeared in the pyramid. 'Your guards, Mr Klein,' Harper said. 'And –' he clicked on another control – 'your attackers.'

More figures appeared – outnumbering the first. The new figures were shown in blue, Klein's men in green. It was like watching an old 'shoot 'em up' computer game as the blue figures slowly forced back their green opponents, moving slowly but steadily through the pyramid. Green bodies were lying on the ground, blue figures stepping over them as they advanced.

'Now then,' Harper said again, 'let's see if we can even up the odds, shall we?' He reached for the mouse and the image moved, panning down to the amphitheatre below the pyramid.

In the window at the top of the screen, the progress bar inched closer and closer to completion.

+

The rock walls at the edge of the cavern – the sides of the huge cave itself – began to bulge and ripple. The solid rock was like the sea. Shapes were forming, just below the surface, pushing themselves out through the walls of the cave as if they were elastic. The cave walls stretched and burst. Figures made of earth and stone – crude, lumpy, misshapen creatures – forced their way out.

The ground burst. An earthen fist punched through the sandy floor. It rose upwards – an arm, then a whole body growing up out of the ground. A forest of arms, followed by more and more of the creatures, rising like divers from a swamp . . .

As one, they turned slowly in the direction of the passageway leading into the main pyramid and started to walk slowly, stiffly, inexorably towards it.

+

The progress bar was two-thirds of the way across the screen now.

'We should be able to start very soon,' Harper said. He seemed to be talking to the screen itself as he watched the red line edge slowly along. 'You

oo 419 oo

know, I call the core code, the main program, my chaos engine. But in fact it is the opposite. It understands chaos, but I shall use that understanding to eliminate the chaos and bring order and method to the world. The weak-minded will be affected first. We don't need to run the whole model to be able to control them. But soon the only mind capable of independent thought will be mine.'

Behind him, Venture struggled desperately with the two guards holding him. Klein was covering Matt's parents with his machine pistol. The other guards were standing with him, all of them glancing nervously towards the line of misshapen figures marching slowly through the upper tiers of the amphitheatre.

'Now or never,' Matt said quietly to Robin. No one seemed to be paying them much attention. Two kids whose parents were already under guard and held hostage.

'The main computers?' Robin murmured.

'The main computers,' he agreed almost under his breath.

Across from them, Venture stopped struggling, just for a moment. He was looking at them and Matt knew that – somehow – he could tell what they were saying. Venture nodded grimly. There was a guard holding each of his arms and suddenly, with an almighty yell, Venture dragged them together.

The guards collided – head to head – with a crack. Both slumped to the ground and Venture leapt at Harper.

Klein turned quickly, bringing up his gun.

Matt's father kicked out at Klein, his foot connecting with the side of the gun and knocking the spray of bullets wild – into a computer and its screen. The screen exploded, sending glass fragments flying. The computer popped and sizzled.

More guards ran to grab Venture, to drag him away from Harper's keyboard even as he reached out for it.

Matt and Robin did not stay to watch what happened. They were already running as fast as they could, desperate to reach the passageway to the pyramid before the earthy elemental creatures that were almost there. If they didn't make it, they'd be trapped in the amphitheatre and then nothing could stop Harper.

But it was like running through treacle. Like a nightmare where your feet don't work. Matt was forcing himself onwards, but his body didn't seem to want to know. Beside him, Robin was slowing too.

'It's Harper's code,' she gasped. 'The model. It's affecting us already. He hasn't . . .' She had almost stopped. 'He hasn't given us orders to move, so we can't.'

'We have to . . . have to keep going . . .' He forced himself onwards.

Black-clad figures rushed through from the passageway ahead, driving a group of Harper's khaki-uniformed guards in front of them. A rattle of gunfire felled one of Harper's guards, sending him careering backwards into the wall.

Matt watched in disbelief through muzzy eyes. The figures were slowing – Harper's guards seemed sluggish. But the attackers, like Matt and Robin, were almost still. Some of them were forcing their way onwards, as if they were battling against a hurricane. Others had stopped dead.

One of the black-clad attackers who had stopped turned slowly around. He was at the front of the group. Matt could see the concentration and fear etched on his face. His gun was coming up. He screamed – a defiant, throaty sound that might have been, 'No!'

Then he was firing the gun. At his own comrades.

Others were turning too.

Some of the attackers at the back seemed to come to their senses and started to retreat, letting off sluggish bursts of machine gun fire as they went.

Bullets smacked into the rock and earth and sand without effect. The rock and earth and sand that were walking into the passageway, pursuing the attackers relentlessly back into the pyramid.

Robin and Matt were frozen, caught in mid-step, almost at the entrance to the passageway. Unable to move.

Meanwhile, behind them, a tall figure made its way easily up the tiers of the amphitheatre towards them.

20

Colour and texture poured into the wire-frame model like liquid into a glass container. Harper watched the detail etch into place, watched the figures fill out and gain features. Figures standing motionless, waiting for orders.

'This facility is complete,' he said quietly. 'The code is running. The rest of the world can follow soon enough. It's a start. From here my control ripples out as the code is completed . . .'

He paused, realizing that no one was listening. Klein stood behind him, staring emptily into space. Harper laughed and clapped his hand together. 'I think perhaps I can trust a few of you with your own free will,' he decided, working the mouse and keyboard.

Klein blinked and took a step backwards. 'What

. . . ? What happened?'

Around him, his guards were also looking bewildered and confused. Only Matt's parents still stood motionless and blank-faced, staring unseeing into the distance. Harper watched them, smiling with satisfaction. Then the smile froze on his face.

'Where is Venture?' he said.

✠

Matt was under water. His vision was misty and blurred, and the voice he could hear was echoing, faint, distorted. He tried to turn his head, but he couldn't. Tried to move his eyes, but couldn't.

The man moved and now Matt could see him – the dark hair and the blue eyes. Julius Venture, speaking urgently to Matt and Robin. He struggled to work out what the man was saying.

'You must concentrate . . .' Venture's words were faint, but Matt could hear them now. 'Harper is trying to control your mind using the model. So far he's only beginning to scratch the surface of what it can do. The effects are localized and he doesn't yet understand it. It even affected his own guards for a while. It's difficult, I know. I can feel it too – reaching into my being, my soul.'

Venture was walking round them, talking to each of them in turn, but his words were meant for them both – Matt and Robin. Matt could see that Robin was moving – turning her head just a fraction. If she could do it, then so could he . . .

'You can resist it,' Venture said again. 'The model is powerful, but it isn't complete. It can't be, can it, Matt? He's modelling the real world on a computer. And we know that can't work, can't be perfect, can never be exact. Don't we? There will be flaws, imperfections, inaccuracies. Enough to invalidate parts of the model.'

His deep blue eyes were staring into Matt's. Matt felt himself blink. He remembered his first meeting with Venture and knew he could do it. Harper hadn't won – not yet.

'Digital.' His voice was a rasp, barely more than a whisper. But Matt had managed it. 'Computer is digital,' he said, stronger and more confident with every word. 'Ones and zeros. The real world isn't like that.'

'You're right,' Venture encouraged him. He took Matt by the shoulders, shaking him gently. 'Think about pi – think about every circle ever drawn, and how no computer can ever understand any of them. How could it?'

'Yes.' It was Robin speaking. She sounded drained and tired, but she was speaking. Moving – lifting her arm and watching her fingers flex. 'Get . . . out . . . of . . . my . . . . mind . . .' she croaked. She closed her eyes. And when she opened them again, she seemed almost herself once more. 'That's better,' she said. 'Thank you.'

Matt struggled to reassert himself within his own mind. He could feel the clouds drifting away – like condensation on a car windscreen slowly clearing to reveal the wintry road beyond. He could see. He could hear. He could move.

'Easy as pi,' he said.

'Well done.' Venture was smiling at them. He nodded as if to tell them he'd known all along they could do it. 'Now, we haven't much time. And there's lots to do. We can't let Harper get control. We can't allow him to use his world model.'

Venture was striding up towards the passageway into the pyramid. Matt and Robin struggled to keep up. Matt's legs felt as if he'd been sitting awkwardly for hours and they were only just getting the feeling back.

'What about Atlantis?' Matt said. 'What about them? They tried the same thing.'

'That wasn't right either,' Venture told him. 'It couldn't be permitted then and we can't let it happen now.'

'But they were trying. They built all this.'

'And remember what happened to them, over 12,000 years ago,' Venture said. 'We can learn a lot from the past.'

The crack of gunfire from Smith's men and Harper's guards outside was still audible. But it was down to the odd few shots now rather than the constant thunder of earlier. Venture paused, just inside the passageway, listening to the distant sounds and waiting for Matt and Robin to catch up.

He was looking back at them. So he did not see the floor of the passageway buckle and heave, the flagstones lifting as if forced upwards by an earthquake. Dark earth and rubble spewed out of the hole in the floor. Matt yelled. Robin was running. Venture turned – to see the huge weight of earth and rock crashing towards him. Without hesitation, he leapt.

Right at the mass of soil and stone and rubble. Shoulder down, through the crashing wave. Black rain engulfed him and he disappeared.

Matt and Robin skidded to a halt. The shapeless

mass was moving, re-forming, coalescing into a huge figure. But, on the other side of it, they could see Venture – his clothes stained and torn, his face grimy and caked in dirt – running.

'The computers!' Matt yelled. 'Shut them down and you stop Harper's model. We'll try to stop him here.'

Venture glanced back, just once, quickly. His face was a mask of grim determination. Then the blackness between them moved, heaved itself down the passageway and blotted out Matt's view.

Matt turned to run back into the main amphitheatre, grabbing Robin's hand.

But another figure stepped into the opening in front of them.

'You're too late,' Katherine Feather said. 'And Mr Harper would like a word.' She had a machine pistol slung over her shoulder and she was aiming it unerringly at them.

✟

A single figure strode purposefully through the mayhem. Smoke drifted from explosions and gunfire. The fighting had almost stopped – only a few of Smith's attackers still able to think and move for themselves. They were chased back through the pyramid – by their enemies, by their former colleagues, by hideous creatures made from the earth itself . . .

But through it all, a single figure.

Venture pushed aside one of Klein's guards, ripping his gun from him and tossing it away. The guard slammed into a wall and fell unconscious. Another figure appeared in the hazy corridor and Venture's elbow smashed into its stomach. His arm swung upwards from the point of impact and his fist cracked into the man's face. Without pausing, Venture started up the steps into the main part of the pyramid.

The steps emerged at ground level and Venture turned immediately to start up the next flight. A rough, earthy paw clamped over his face from behind. He levered it away, turned, kicked. The creature staggered back a pace. Far enough for Venture to take a flying leap. He feet connected with the mass of earth, sent it staggering back still further – to the edge of the stairs leading down. It flailed helplessly for a moment. Venture was on his feet again. Another kick.

The creature fell backwards, crashing down the

stairs, earth and stone flying, scattering behind it as it fell.

Already Venture had turned away and was continuing up the stairs, towards the main computer suite.

✛

'Where is he?' Harper demanded. 'Where *is* he?!' He was talking to the screen.

Matt and Robin watched too, aware of Katherine standing behind them with the machine pistol. Klein was covering Matt's parents with his gun. Matt could see several hand grenades hanging from his belt, heavy and brutal like Klein himself. The picture on the screen was changing rapidly, scrolling through the pyramid and the amphitheatre as Harper hunted what he was looking for.

The image paused. It showed one of the misshapen creatures fashioned from the earth. The creature was flying backwards, towards a stairwell. The image flickered as the software struggled to repaint it quickly enough and the creature plunged downwards.

'That's him,' Harper said.

'There's no one there,' Katherine told him. 'The thing simply fell.'

'No, he's there. We just can't see him.' He slammed his fist down on the table beside the keyboard in frustration. '*Why* can't we see him?'

'Because your model doesn't show what's really happening. It makes predictions. It's calculating what is happening right now,' Robin said, her voice confident and defiant. 'And you can't calculate what Dad will do. He doesn't want to be predictable.'

'Everyone is predictable,' Harper snapped back.

'Oh, you have no idea,' Robin told him.

'Everyone!' Harper snarled.

The image moved again, zooming out and then back in rapidly on a new location – beneath the pyramid. The amphitheatre. The office area. It showed Harper sitting at the screen, Katherine behind him, Klein and Matt's blank-faced parents. And vague, flickering shadows where Robin and Matt should be.

'Then predict us,' Robin said. 'Guess what I'm going to say next, or how Matt feels seeing his mum and dad turned to zombies. You think you're reinventing the power of the ancients?' She laughed. 'You're not even close.'

'Your model's rubbish,' Matt told him, his own confidence growing with Robin's defiance. 'It's digital and the world is analogue. And soon it won't work at all anyway when . . .' He broke off, realizing he had said too much.

'So that's where he's headed,' Harper said. 'Klein – the computer suite. Stop Venture. Hurry!'

'My pleasure,' Klein said. He shouldered his gun and set off at a run.

'You'll never stop him,' Robin said. But there was a hint of doubt in her voice now.

'Then I'd better take precautions,' Harper said. He turned to look at Matt's parents. And his mum slowly walked over to the nearest keyboard and began to type. 'It's always wise to keep a back-up, I believe,' Harper said. 'So she can copy the data for the model to the computers down here. If necessary, I can reboot it from that copy of the data. Start all over again.'

Another of the progress ribbons was starting across the screen where Matt's mum was working. The data was copying down to the computers here. If Venture didn't destroy the servers soon, it would make no difference.

'But it's still flawed,' Matt insisted.

'I don't think so,' Harper said dismissively.

'I know so,' Matt insisted. 'Your system can only

work if it's entirely accurate. And it isn't. You can't model the real world to that level of detail in a mere computer. It's just not possible.'

'Matt!' Robin warned.

Harper was staring at Matt, frowning. 'You know, don't you?' he said. 'You know how this place is supposed to work. Oh, I understand the principle, of course I do. But you actually *know*.' He got to his feet, towering over Matt. 'Show me!'

Matt shook his head. 'Never.'

'Don't be stupid,' Katherine said, poking the gun into Matt's back.

'We'll see who's stupid in a minute,' Robin told her. 'Once Dad sorts out the main computers. All you can do is look at the present and try to predict the future. OK, yes, you can manipulate the model. But so what? What can you learn from it? Does it tell you about the past, about history, about what really happened?'

'And you'll never know,' Matt said. Anything to buy them time. 'I'll never show you. You can kill me first.'

Harper laughed. 'Oh, you'll show me. Or I shall kill *her*.' He pointed at Robin, and he smiled.

'Don't do it, Matt,' Robin said. 'Let him kill us. It doesn't matter.'

'Yes, it does,' Matt said. He looked at her, willing her to understand what he was doing. An idea, just a glimmer of a thought at the back of his mind. But it was rapidly becoming a pattern – a plan.

'I thought you'd see sense,' Harper told him.

'It's not like we could control the thing anyway,' Matt said. 'The most we can hope to do is just get it going. But maybe we can show Mr Harper what happened, in the past. What happened to that explorer – Percy Fawcett. See whether it really is him they found. We could even see what really happened to Atlantis.' He held his breath, wondering if he had said too much. Robin's expression was unreadable, but she didn't argue.

Harper's face was equally impassive. Then, 'You need the disc?' Harper asked.

'Yes,' Matt said.

'Just like a computer. Perhaps a little demonstration, then.' He stood staring at Matt. 'Any hint of a problem and Katherine here will shoot your girlfriend. Understood?'

'Understood,' Katherine said. She sounded like she was looking forward to it.

✠

The entry code was easy to work out. The room was deserted. The lights flickered on as motion detectors picked up that someone had walked into the main computer suite. Row after row of servers and disk drives and storage and networking. Julius Venture walked down the first aisle. He didn't pause; he didn't look to right or left. But as he went he ripped out every cable and connector. He pushed over stacks of equipment and sent monitors hurtling into the wall.

A wave of destruction, rippling along the aisle. Like an elemental force, destroying everything it touched.

Then back up the next aisle. A screen exploded as it hit the floor, sparking and spitting glass. Cables snagged and ripped free. Computer storage disks shattered. He walked slowly, deliberately, the length of the aisle.

Right up to the man waiting for him at the main doors. The man with the face like a grinning skull, grenades hanging from his belt and a gun pointing at Venture's face.

'Stop right there,' Klein said. 'One more step and you're history.'

And for the first time since leaving the amphitheatre, since leaving his daughter, Venture's face betrayed some emotion.

He smiled.

☩

Matt checked the wooden box and found the disc from Venture's house was inside. 'We still need the other disc,' he said.

'That was a fake,' Katherine told him. 'Didn't take us long to work that out. You still thought it was real? You really are so stupid.'

'There is no real disc,' Harper said.

'Yes, there is,' Matt said. 'It's in Dad's pocket.' He turned to stare at Katherine. 'You really are so stupid.'

Her eyes widened dangerously and he thought she was going to hit him. Or shoot him. But she settled for prodding him sharply with her gun, pushing him towards his father. 'Get it,' she snarled.

Matt walked slowly over and made a play of fumbling in his Dad's jacket pockets. 'Dad!' he hissed. 'Dad, can you hear me?'

His father stared ahead blankly.

'If you can hear me, try to help Mum. Try to break Harper's control. You – *we* – have to get out of here. And she has to stop him copying his program code. Dad?!'

But there was still no reaction and Harper was shouting at Matt to hurry up. He sighed and took the disc from Dad's pocket over to Robin. It was made of metal, like the disc in the wooden box, and the patterns on it spiralled into the centre.

'You know the location,' Matt said, handing the disc to Robin. 'You know what to do?'

She nodded. With her dark blue eyes and black hair, she looked very pale. 'And you?'

'Of course.' He tried to smile, to make light of it. 'We're going to get the old technology working. For the first time in thousands of years, we'll make it work for Mr Harper. And we'll show him the past.'

They had to hunt round at the edge of the stage for the slots in the stone floor where the discs fitted. Sand had blown into them, hiding the ancient mechanism. But Matt and Robin brushed and blew it away. A single slot on either side of the stage. Each slot the same size as one of the discs.

Robin took the disc and pushed it into place in the slot. Katherine Feather was watching her closely. Behind her, further up the tiered steps, Harper watched with interest.

'Come on,' he shouted. 'Prove to me that the ancients really knew what they were doing.'

On the other side of the stage, Matt took the disc from the box and pushed it into its slot in the stone slab. He hoped that the way the disc fitted would set the time to a baseline – to a specific time. He knew when it would be – 10,500 BC. 'The First Time' of the ancient Egyptians because they took the era of Atlantis as their starting point. The disc slid smoothly into place and clicked into position.

The sand across the huge stage area trembled and danced. It was moving, slowly shifting, rippling. Like a time-lapsed movie of someone building sand-castles on the beach, the grains were coming together to create a landscape.

'Oh, it's beautiful,' someone said, and Matt realized with surprise that it was Harper. The big man stepped down towards the stage. 'Is that . . .?' He left the question hanging in the air as he gazed awestruck at the stage.

Sand built up into a mountain. In its shadow, buildings rose, intricate structures that might have been made of stone. Water splashed in from the river behind, creating moats round the buildings – circles within circles within circles, islands connected by intricate bridges and walkways. People – tiny, perfectly formed figures of sand – walked across the bridges and between the buildings. *Lived* in them. An entire world in little.

'Atlantis,' Robin said. 'Nearly 11,000 years before Christ.' She looked across at Matt. 'Go forward,' Robin said. 'Turn the disc towards you. Five hundred years . . .'

Harper took another step down. He was standing close to Katherine now. 'With this, we can truly control the world,' he said. 'Down to the last detail. An *analogue* model.'

Katherine's ice-white hair shone in the light from the huge lamps above her. A tiny drip of water ran from her hairline down her cheek. She was staring down at the stage as well. But her gun did not waver. It was still aimed at Robin.

As slowly, gently, nervously, Matt turned the disc. And time for the sand-people in their sand-city speeded up . . .

✞

The butt of Klein's gun slammed viciously into Venture's stomach. He doubled over, but he did not cry out. Klein's boot crashed into him, sending

Venture flying backwards. He landed between the banks of equipment in the central aisle of the computer suite. Sprawled on his back, he looked up at Klein's grinning skull-face.

'On your feet,' Klein said. 'I could shoot you now. But that wouldn't be half as much fun.'

Venture struggled to his feet. His face was contorted with pain. He swayed uncertainly, looking back at the brutal killer staring at him, taking in every aspect of the man: uniform, grenades, gun, attitude. Venture backed slowly away down the aisle.

'Got you scared, have we?' Klein gloated. 'On the run? Frightened for your life? Your little girl's life?' He advanced slowly on Venture's retreating figure. 'Because the way I see it, you'll soon both be dead.' He raised the gun.

But something in Venture's face made him hesitate. The pain was gone, dropped like a mask. Instead there was an expression of resigned determination.

Julius Venture moved like lightning. Not away from Klein and the gun. Straight at him.

The gun went off, bullets ripping wide and smacking into a set of computer storage units, tearing holes in the metal casings. Venture's weight drove Klein backwards. His arms were wrapped round Klein as he knocked him to the floor.

But Klein was twisting away, heaving the gun clear of Venture's grasp. He struggled free and knocked Venture back. Broke away and smacked the butt of the gun into Venture's face, sending him falling, skidding along the floor.

Klein got to his feet. Legs braced, taking his time, he aimed directly at Venture.

Venture didn't move.

'Thought you could get my gun, did you? Way I see it,' he said, breathless after the struggle, 'you're dead right now.'

By contrast, Venture's voice was calm and un-flustered. 'Maybe we see things differently.'

'You guys - amateurs. You think you're tough, but when you're really up against it you just go all to pieces.'

Venture was smiling, his lips moving slightly as if he was still talking under his breath.

It unsettled Klein. He paused, gun still raised. 'What are you doing? What are you saying?'

'I'm counting.' The lips continued to move.

'Counting? Why?' Klein jabbed the gun forward. 'Counting your last seconds? Get your hands up.'

Venture obligingly raised his hands. Still the lips moved silently.

'What's in your hand?' Klein demanded. 'What are you holding? Show me!'

Venture opened his hand and something fell out. Something small and metallic that made a tinny sound as it bounced on the floor.

'I wasn't after your gun,' Venture said.

✝

Time slowed down again. Harper and Katherine Feather were watching in awe as the tiny people went about their business.

'It's exquisite,' Harper said. 'Such detail. Such . . . control.'

'And see what it brought them,' Robin said.

The mound of sand at the back of the stage was moving, the top bulging. A sudden tremendous blast of sand and earth across the stage – over the sand-city. More sand was running down the side of the mound, crashing into the buildings below.

'The eruptions,' Harper breathed. 'So it's true.'

The water was rising in the narrow rivers. Washing out across the landscape, tearing away the bottoms of the buildings.

'Imagine that on real buildings,' Katherine said, smiling. 'Real people.'

☩

A tiny piece of metal bounced on the floor of the computer suite. A ring big enough for a man to push his finger through.

Klein stared at it and felt his whole body go suddenly cold. In front of him, Venture took a step to the side of the corridor, close to one of the large computer banks.

Klein barely saw him move. Still holding the gun, he looked down, already knowing what he would see.

Three grenades, hanging from his belt. One of them – the middle one – was missing its detonator pin.

And Venture was counting.

'Just about now, I think,' Venture said, and stepped behind the computer.

But his words were drowned out by the explosion that ripped through the room. It blew computers and equipment aside, shattering screens, tearing metal to shreds.

Through the smoke and the fire, Julius Venture walked calmly to the door. He paused to look back, checking that nothing remained intact. 'Thanks for your help,' he said. 'Amateurs,' he muttered, as he closed the broken remains of the door behind him. 'Think they're tough, but when they're really up against it they just go all to pieces.'

✟

'Ultimate control over the world,' Harper said, staring transfixed as the water surged across the stage and the sand crashed down. He was watching the tiny figures running for their imagined lives. 'That's what we shall have. That's what they were striving for. We can take events like these from the past and replay them at will – anywhere, anytime. Yes, imagine it!'

'You don't have to imagine it,' Matt told them. 'Because you're right – that's how the model works. Like your control over the elements. And like you said, what happened then can be replayed now.' He looked at Robin and found she was staring back at him.

'There are over 600 myths around the world that concern civilizations destroyed by a great flood,' Robin said. 'They were all inspired by this one event. The event being replayed here and now.' She continued to stare right at Matt, her eyes wide, face pale, looking scared but triumphant. 'Do it!' Robin shouted. 'Do it now.' She reached for the disc, turning it to a new position. Setting another location.

Harper took a step forward, as if realizing at last what was happening – what had happened. What was going to happen. Here and now. 'No!'

'Or what?' Matt turned the disc, changing the time to the present, just as Robin had set the location to the mountain above. Brought the end of Atlantis to them. Here and now. 'Goodbye, Robin,' he said.

## 21

The whole mountain trembled. The ground heaved beneath them, shaking the last of the sand model on the stage to pieces. Harper and Katherine were struggling to keep their balance. Chunks of rock crashed down from the roof of the cavern, and the lights toppled and fell, sending shadows lurching across the ground.

The river was a raging torrent, lapping over into the amphitheatre, washing across the stage area and sweeping away the last of the sand. The ground shuddered again, and the river seemed to rise up in a colossal wave, surging through the lower part of the ruins.

The water crashed down over Matt, drenching him, sweeping him away. He scrabbled for a hand-hold – found something, clung on.

It was Robin. She heaved him out of the water, pulling him up on to the lower tiers of the amphitheatre. They lay there, gasping for breath as the water rushed past.

'What have you done?' a voice hissed from behind them. Katherine Feather was still holding the gun. Her eyes were icy with fury.

Another surge of water. Matt and Robin ducked down, clinging to each other as the cold wave swept over them. It slammed into Katherine's legs and took them from under her. The gun went flying. Her cries were lost in the roar of the water.

For a few moments, as the water receded again, they could see the woman's ice-blonde hair matted to her head. Her features seemed to blur, as if they were being washed off by the force of the water that crashed over her. Her arms moved desperately as she tried to swim to the edge before the current took her into the tunnel. The whole cavern was shaking now. Dust and debris were falling like a blizzard. A huge section of the roof ripped away from the rest and crashed down. Into the roaring river. On top of Katherine. Sending her spinning away, into the tunnel, under the water. Out of sight.

Robin scrambled to her feet, pulling Matt up too. 'Where's Harper?' she yelled.

'Computers!' Matt shouted.

They ran through the confusion and falling rock, leapt over the puddles and the debris and the ruins. Towards the area where the computers and screens had been set up. The air was full of dust, like smoke. It curled and drifted. And it was *hot*.

Steam was coming from the raging river now. The puddles started to bubble and boil. Above them, the mountain was coming back to life. It rumbled and shifted. Glowing red was dripping through the cracks that opened in the walls and the roof. Bubbling up through the floor as the volcano awoke.

✟

People ran through the smoke while the pyramid shook around them. It was impossible to tell who was – or had been – on which side, who was wearing what uniform. They just ran, getting out as fast as they could. With Harper's computers wrecked, his control over Smith's attacking soldiers was broken. His own guards, less disciplined and outnumbered, were racing with their enemy for the exit.

Only one figure moved in the opposite direction,

knocking aside anyone who got in his way, kicking though the collapsed heaps of earth and stone and rubble. The corridors and stairways buckled and heaved around him, but Julius Venture seemed not to notice.

☩

Smoke was pouring from the top of the mountain and red rivers ran down its sides.

'We should get out of here,' the pilot told Mephistopheles Smith.

With an almighty crack, the side of the mountain split open and a torrent of orange and red poured out. The waterfall shifted, casting rainbow reflections of the eruption across the stepped pyramid now visible behind it as the angle of the cascade changed. The mountainside buckled and moved; the water sprayed sideways, slowed, then burst out of the rock again. But now it was no longer pouring with spectacular majesty into the lake below, but crashing down into the top of the pyramid, running down its sides, burrowing through the stonework . . .

'We wait,' Smith said. His dark glasses reflected the torrent of water and the anger of the fiery mountain. 'As long as possible. As long as it takes.'

Water was coming through the roof now – like someone had turned on sprinklers.

'I can stop it,' Harper muttered under his breath. Over and over: 'I can stop it. I can *still* stop it.'

He shouldered aside two of his guards as they ran past. The ground quaked and he staggered forward, into the office area to the side of the amphitheatre. The ground was at a crazy angle. Half the lights were out. But the screens were still working.

'I can stop it. I can change the model,' Harper said out loud, running for the keyboard.

'No, you can't,' someone told him calmly. 'Not any more.'

He spared Dr Stribling a glance. Then he was working furiously at the computer. 'I *can*. The program, the model – the whole of the compiled engine code – was copied down here.' He hit the Enter key and looked at the screen.

It showed a spinning, stylized 'H'. A window opened over it. An entry field and a prompt:

Enter password

'I stopped the copy and deleted the back-up,'

Matt's mother told him. 'Oh, and I changed your password too. That's good practice, you know.'

Harper was on his feet. 'You think you're so clever,' he snarled. 'You know nothing.' He lunged at her across the desk, sending keyboard and mouse flying.

Matt's dad dragged her out of the way. 'Time we were leaving,' he said. 'Come on.'

Harper's threats and curses were ringing in their ears, louder even than the exploding mountain, as they ran for the way out. Julius Venture was standing at the top of the amphitheatre, waving for them to hurry.

'Where's Matt?' Mrs Stribling gasped.

'And Robin?'

'They'll be here. Don't worry about them,' Venture said. 'You stopped the copy? Destroyed the code?'

They both nodded.

'Well done. Just in time too. The waterfall is pouring into the pyramid above us. I can hear it coming.'

'Harper's still down there, ranting and raving,' Dr Stribling said. He was staring into the thickening smoke. Coughing and breathless.

'Leave him,' Venture said. 'Just so long as you deleted the code. And destroyed his laptop.'

The laptop screen showed the spinning model of the amphitheatre and pyramid. It didn't hold the entire engine code, of course. Just a portion of it, just his first experimental program. Not enough to stop what was happening. But enough for Harper to take his revenge.

Walking through the smoke, Harper worked furiously. The ground was bubbling red around him and scalding water poured down. He didn't notice.

All his attention was on the laptop screen. He walked calmly and purposefully towards the two flickering, vague, outline figures struggling to get through the amphitheatre as it fell apart around them. A boy and a girl. Somewhere ahead of him in the choking smoke. Predictably, trying to escape.

And Harper was no longer alone. The bubbling pools swelled and coughed up molten rock in a fountain of fire. Sand and debris rolled together and formed into shapes. Lumpy, inhuman figures of sand and rock and fire and earth. Walking with Harper through the smoke and the rain that parted for them in the sudden, impossible breeze.

✝

The whole amphitheatre buckled and heaved around Matt and Robin as they raced through the hot fog. They had to be nearly at the entrance by now, Matt thought – had to be. But he could hardly see through the smoke. They leapt up another broken step, jumped over a boiling pool of mud, coughed and choked on the acrid air.

There was a roaring in their ears. The crack of the breaking rock, the rumble of the volcano, the crash of the water. Shapes loomed through the drifting smoke. Matt could make out dark figures, closing in. He gripped Robin's hand tight. She was looking round, aware of them too.

Harper appeared out of the thickening air. His hair was blowing in a gale that sent the smoke skidding away in billowing swirls. 'You think you are so clever,' he rasped.

Matt could hardly speak. His own throat was dry and raw. His feet were frozen despite the heat. A creature of glowing, molten rock was standing beside Harper. Its skin was blotched with dark crusts over the smouldering lava beneath. A steaming hand reached out for Matt and Robin.

Other figures appeared, encircling them both. Some earthy and dull. Some like sandpaper wrapped round a huge doll. Some glowing and smoking. All closing in.

And behind them, from the top of the steps, a running figure – lean and human, not crude lumps of elemental matter crushed into the rough shape of a man.

'The waterfall,' Venture shouted. 'Robin, Matt – the water!' Then he dived to the ground, disappearing in a flurry of smoke.

'Get down!' Robin screamed at Matt.

Smoking hands were reaching out for Matt. He could feel the heat from the stubby fingers. He dropped, straight down to the ground, lying beside Robin on the steaming stone floor.

Just before a wall of water crashed out of the gloom. Lights they could hardly see exploded as the water hit. The shadowy figures standing above Matt and Robin were swept away. The air itself seemed to be washed clean by the wave, smoke dispersing, the whole place lit by the eerie glow of molten rock. Steam hissed from the walls as splashes and droplets evaporated in an instant.

Then the water was gone. The wave had passed. Robin and Matt climbed slowly to their feet, splashing in the shallow waterfall that rolled down the steps into the lake now forming at the base of the amphitheatre.

'Where's Harper?' Robin asked.

Matt hugged her tight and they both stared at the scene below.

The water had crushed the elemental figures together and hurled them down the steps. They'd smashed into Harper, taking him with them. Weakened and broken by the water, the elementals were coming apart – rock and earth becoming mud, sand and dirt breaking to pieces.

In the middle of it, Harper was struggling, flailing. The water was rising as more swept down into the growing lake. He tried to clamber out, but he was mired in the mud. The lumpy misshapen figures were collapsing round him, over him. Dragging him down. Like quicksand.

His fingers grasped desperately for his laptop. But the water was pouring over it. He struggled to reach the keys, move the pointer. The screen hissed and went blank.

And now there was just his hand, scrabbling out of the viscous mud. The last of the creatures was sinking into the swamp, dissolving, melting . . .

Bubbles broke the surface, as if the mud itself was

boiling. But the volcano was sleeping again now. The water rippled gently, sand and dust bobbing on the tiny waves. Nothing else broke the surface.

☩

Mum and Dad were arguing. Of course. In the middle of a ruined ancient city underneath a smoking volcano with a spectacular waterfall crashing over the remains of a shattered pyramid, having just escaped death by less than the skin of their teeth, they were arguing about Matt. About which of them was more to blame for Matt being left to fend for himself over the school holidays.

'You're both as bad as each other,' Matt told them. 'You were both daft enough to take a job with a homicidal maniac who wanted to use ancient forbidden knowledge to rule the world. Deal with it.'

'You really shouldn't talk to your mother like that,' Dad told him.

'And your father is one of the cleverest people in his field. You should show him some respect,' Mum added.

'OK,' Matt said, 'so I guess it's *my* fault, then. Should have known. From now on, I'm going to be spending the holidays with Aunt Jane.'

'Jane,' Dad realized. 'I'd better call her. She'll be worried sick.'

'You never call her,' Mum told him. 'You always wait for her to call you.'

'That's not true.'

'Isn't it? When did you start calling her, then? I don't remember you ever calling her. *I* called her. Birthdays and Christmas it was *me* who called Jane.'

Matt left them to it.

Venture was speaking to Smith beside one of the huge helicopters. Robin was standing on her own, watching them. Her face was smeared with mud and her hair was wet and in a mess. But she still looked beautiful. Weird, but beautiful. Matt walked over to join her and she smiled.

It wasn't a twitch of the mouth. It wasn't a half-smile that might have been mocking him. It was a real, full-on smile. And Matt grinned back. He probably looked ridiculous, just as caked in mud and dirt, just as much of a mess. But he didn't care.

'I'm going to spend the rest of the holidays with you and Aunt Jane,' he said. 'I can help sort out the mess, after the fire. If it's OK?'

'That'll be good.'

She was still smiling, so Matt guessed she meant

it. 'You think it's finished?' he asked.

They looked back at the smouldering volcano and the ruined pyramid behind them. Black-clad figures were leading a dishevelled group of men in khaki uniforms through the ruins.

'I think so,' Robin said. 'The discs are lost for ever. The theatre is gone. And so are Harper, and Katherine Feather, and anyone else who really knew what happened.'

'And before,' Matt said slowly. 'When this all happened the first time – with Atlantis . . .'

'What about it?'

Matt hesitated. Julius Venture was walking over to join them.

'Well?' Robin prompted.

Matt shrugged. 'Nothing. I just wondered if it was the same last time. If someone deliberately destroyed a civilization.'

'And why would they do that?' she asked, head tilted to one side. Wet hair rippling in the light breeze.

It was her father who answered. 'To prevent anyone having the sort of power they were trying to create,' he said. 'Is that what you think, Matt?'

Matt shrugged. 'I don't know. All those lives for the freedom of everyone else. It would be quite a decision to have to take, wouldn't it?'

Venture blinked. 'I wouldn't know,' he said quietly. 'I wouldn't want to have to make that choice.'

'Matt's coming to stay,' Robin said.

Venture smiled. 'That's fine. Be nice to have you.' He reached out to shake Mat's hand. 'And thanks for your help. It's good that you're finally starting to think, to see things in perspective. Just . . .' He looked at Robin, then back at Matt. 'Be careful, all right?' Then he turned and walked back towards the helicopters.

'He meant you,' Matt told Robin.

'He did not,' she said.

'You may be a bit older than me,' Matt said, 'but you have a lot to learn.'

'Oh? Such as what?'

'Such as, don't get to like me too much, all right?'

She gave a snort of laughter. 'You wish.'

Matt didn't contradict her. He was watching Robin's father, again talking to Smith beside the helicopter. Watching the way that Smith patted the sweat from his forehead with his handkerchief. The way he had to remove his tinted glasses to do it. Just for a moment.

To reveal the startlingly blue eyes behind the darkness.